JAN TURK PETRIE

RUNNING BEHIND TIME

ALSO BY JAN TURK PETRIE

Until the Ice Cracks
Vol 1 of The Eldísvík Trilogy

No God for a Warrior
Vol 2 of The Eldísvík Trilogy

Within Each Other's Shadow
Vol 3 of The Eldísvík Trilogy

Too Many Heroes

Towards the Vanishing Point

The Truth in a Lie

Still Life with a Vengeance

'Play For Time' – Vol 2 in the Cotswold Time-slip Series

Contents

RUNNING BEHIND TIME

"The only reason for time is so that everything doesn't happen at once."

Albert Einstein

Chapter One

East Sussex, England

July 1982

Beth

The sky is darkening with unnatural speed; with it comes a silence she finds disquieting. Ominous. Gulls that had been reeling and squawking off the cliffs have mysteriously disappeared. Only moments ago, the soaring song of larks had accompanied them to the top of the headland; now the birds have all gone to ground.

Other people – perhaps twenty, maybe as many as twenty-five – have been drawn to this same commanding spot as if by enchantment or a shared instinct carried in some ancient race memory. On the way up, she'd caught snatches of excited conversation – a carnival spirit; now there's only whispering.

It's almost upon them. A collective hush descends on the small crowd. Faces turn upwards to wait for the spectacle about to take place.

To her left, the silvery streak on the surface of the sea dims and then goes out. Where there had been summer warmth the air is chilly; the fine hairs on her arms stand up in response.

'This is it,' Kyle says pulling on her arm until she sits down next to him. The dry grass feels rough against her bare legs. She can smell all the baked-hard sheep poo they're sitting amongst.

From his rucksack Kyle pulls out his binoculars and the piece of white card he'd rescued from the bin. He's already explained to her how this will work, how you only need to point one of the lenses at the eclipse and an image will be projected straight through the eyepiece onto the cardboard. The other lens is capped off – it isn't allowed to watch.

On the train down, he'd read a newspaper while she listened to the Planet Suite on her Walkman – not her usual choice of music but perfect to set the mood. She'd picked up the arts supplement he discarded and read a light-hearted feature describing some of the myths that had grown up as a way of explaining an eclipse. A traditional Norse tale put the blame on wolves eating the sun. In Ancient China it was dragons. Native Americans believed a bear had taken a great bite out of it. The Ancient Greeks took the whole thing more seriously; to them it was a sign the gods were angry and foretold coming disasters and destruction. It doesn't surprise her; now would be the perfect moment for someone in long robes to stand on top of one of these mounds, raise a wooden staff and spout some dire prophecy.

Kyle is staring down at the image on the card. Seen his way, the coming partial eclipse resembles a diagram in a textbook.

He's set the whole thing up in between them so they can watch together. She notices the small tomato stain in one corner from their takeaway pizza.

In her head she tells him, 'You might as well be watching it on the telly.' She's tempted to say it out loud but that would only spoil the moment for him.

'Remember, don't look at it directly.' This was ostensibly to her, but he'd raised his voice so that it would carry to any foolish person around them who might be about to do such a thing. 'Just one look and you could go blind,' he adds for good measure.

The darkness intensifies until it's impossible to make out the contours of the land or the line where it meets the sky. The colours of the day have all but drained away like they're in a black and white movie. Under her breath, Beth quotes from King Lear: *These late eclipses in the sun and moon portend no good to us.*

Some people are gazing skywards, wearing special glasses that look far too cheap to ward off the destructive powers of two heavenly bodies set on what, from this angle, appears to be a certain collision.

'Beth,' he says, interrupting her train of thought. 'I think we're approaching maximum. Look then, or you'll miss it.' His sharp elbow digs into her ribs to make his point.

To please him, she glances down at the facsimile he's created – the scaled down version of this momentous event he appears to be content with. His way is not hers; it never was.

Drawn back to the heavens but not quite trusting herself, she shuts her eyes and lets the moment take her. Such an extraordinary occurrence – it has to signify something.

By the gradual brightening of the shades of red inside her closed lids, she can tell the deepest darkness has passed. How strange this slow process of coming back to herself – to the promise of warmth on her skin. She opens her eyes, to watch the old world being reborn. Monochrome is being overlaid with colour. The spell broken, birds wake and remember their songs. A distant lamb cries out for its mother.

Kyle caps the other lens of the binoculars; roughly folding the piece of card in half, he stuffs both into his rucksack. Standing up, he says, 'We should head off, beat the crush at the station.'

Now that the everyday world has been restored, the colours seem so bright. Beth wants to linger here, to lie back and find shapes in clouds; follow the progress of the boat that's just a speck on the horizon as it moves across the newly sparkling sea.

For now, she complies, brushing the grass from her legs before she follows him down the hill towards the point where the narrow path splits and goes off in different directions.

Chapter Two

The Cotswolds

July 2020

Tom

Reaching the highest point, he's only mildly out of breath. Yet another blue-sky day with just the shadow of a stray cloud skidding eastwards across the bleached-out landscape. Shading his eyes with his hand, he scans through 180 degrees and spots a lone plane heading off towards America, leaving its feathering contrail behind.

Tom lifts both arms so the sweat underneath can dry a little. The breeze is laced with the smell of sun-bleached grass. If he could fly east north east from this spot at this exact altitude, he wouldn't hit landfall until he reached the Urals in around 2,300 miles. If only.

Alongside the trig point and mounted on its own stone plinth, the surrounding topography has been etched into a steel disc. He follows the radiating lines that tell him the precise distance to each point of interest on the horizon as the crow flies. Those bloody lucky crows.

A couple of tall, Lycra-clad men appear in his side vision. They've dismounted from their bikes and are breathing hard, hands on hips, as they wait for him to finish.

Under the pressure of their stares, he concedes the space and walks away.

He chooses a solitary spot further down the hill to take a well-earned breather, his arse awkwardly balanced on a boulder that forms part of a small outcrop. Sheep are littering the grassy plateau, the lambs already grazing, the ewes weighed down by heavy fleeces; no Antipodean shearers to do the job this year – or so he'd been informed by his mother's Sunday Times. Strands of wool are caught in the wire fencing along with a billowing plastic bag he ought to do something about but doesn't.

Taking the bottle from his rucksack, he swallows a few mouthfuls of sun-warmed water. As he's unwrapping an energy bar, a bright green grasshopper lands on his shirtsleeve and begins to saw away at the silence. Wind ruffling his hair, he bites into the bar, chews on sweet and syrupy oats and raisins that stick to his teeth.

The surrounding landscape was moulded by melting glaciers then rounded off over millennia to leave few sharp edges, no challenging peaks to scale. From here he has a grandstand view of the empty racecourse and the sprawling amoeba shape of Cheltenham. Off to one side is the unmistakable donut building – GCHQ – where right now men and women must be busy listening in to potential threats from around the world. Did they see this one coming, this virus, like countless microscopic landmines lying in wait to blow everyone's lives to pieces? Given a choice, he'd take his chances with the damned bug, but that option has officially been taken away.

He follows the glint of the meandering river to where it disappears in the heat haze shrouding a line of faded-denim hills. The view is a glorious invitation he can't take up. Squinting into the sun, he can just make out the Welsh mountains – now forbidden territory.

Tom hadn't heard the word *furloughed* until a few months ago – he would, at a guess, have thought it was something agricultural. Now it applies to him – defines him. With no work to leave home for, he'd dreaded being confined to his small flat in lockdown Bristol and fled back to his mother's place. 'So good to have you home again, Tom,' she'd said, squeezing him tighter than he felt comfortable with, pressing him into the smell of faded roses. Stepping back, he noticed how, unable to visit the hairdresser, her white roots were now showing.

The dog, Poppy, wagged her tail with enthusiasm on his arrival, beating the floor with it, while loose hairs flew off to form balls like tumbleweed in corners the hoover never delved into these days.

They were a pair, his mum and the dog, joints grown stiffer from arthritis, pale faced and hiding in the shade on hot days like this. The dog unable to summon up the energy to accompany him on the shortest of walks.

His old bedroom awaited, lured him in with newly laundered sheets, and birdsong through the open window with its view to the garden and the countryside beyond. A different kind of cage.

That first night she'd cooked him shepherd's pie, her face scarlet from the Aga's stored heat, the whole house reeking of onions afterwards. 'I've made it just how you like it,' she said. 'Lamb mince not beef.'

With no appetite, elbows out, he tackled the pile-up of a portion, didn't tell her his preference now ran more to Thai or Indonesian food.

Before this spring, the future seemed to stretch out in front of him with no limits. It pains him to recall the light bulb idea he'd pitched to his boss. 'I like it,' Andy had said, slapping his back. 'Let me think it over.'

All of that had been snatched away. The desire for off-grid adventure in far-flung locations was unlikely to be revived any time soon. *Unemployed* is likely to be the next label applied to him, forced to wait weeks for the cosmic sounding currency of *Universal Credit*. The universe gave no allowance for failure.

He's distracted by the blue and red kite riding the air above his head. The flapping tail is clapping and crackling to a rhythm of its own. Following the string back down to earth, he sees the small boy wrestling with it. A sturdy man rushes forward, grabs both strings to stop the thing tearing away. The bloke takes over the controls, enjoying this struggle for mastery, the challenge of steering the kite where he wants it to go.

The boy has become a spectator and soon begins to lose interest; head down, he lets go of the reins – leaves the head-strong kite to the man who is presumably his dad or stepdad. Deprived of the pleasure of flying the kite himself, the boy begins to kick at the grass, beheading a patch of daisies. The dad doesn't notice.

Tom stands up. For a moment, he's tempted to go over and say something – to intervene on the child's behalf. He tucks the water bottle back into its place and starts walking towards them. He would have to keep his distance, shout into the wind like an aggressor. Their two faces would snap round, the boy's curious, the man's expression hardening in the face of uninvited opposition. In reply, he'd say something like, 'What's it got to do with you?'

A good point.

Shouldering his backpack, Tom turns away. Not his problem. The walk home will take him three and a half, maybe four hours. Better be on his way. Besides, this is probably a lesson the boy needs to learn from an early age – what happens when you let other people take control of things.

Tom heads off at a pace towards the landmark of the three metal towers that bristle with transmitters and receivers. From there it's downhill most of the way. A plan is forming in his head; it might be a long shot but what's he got to lose?

Leaving the welcome shade of the wood, the heat of the sun is unabating as he follows the path that winds down into Stoatsfield. The roofs of a couple of outlying houses come into view and then a spreading rash of cottages clinging to the sides of the valley, the yellow stone glowing in the afternoon sun. Undeniably picturesque from this angle and to the casual visitor; his sense of confinement increases as he descends into the heart of the village. Nothing much is moving along the narrow main street as he walks towards his mother's place at the far end.

Tom drops his backpack on the bench, relieved to be free of its weight. Leaving his boots and sweaty socks in the porch, he pads barefoot into the kitchen. Despite the open windows, the low ceiling means the room is always stuffy. He welcomes the coolness of the worn flagstones under his feet.

His mum is sitting at the table shelling broad beans and, as usual, listening to Classic FM; harder of hearing, she turns it up much louder these days. Sensing his presence, she looks up. 'You left before I was up,' she says, her tone more an accusation than a simple observation.

'I needed some exercise.' He decides not to elaborate. 'Some fresh air.'

'Nice walk?'

'I hiked all the way up to the top of Cleeve Hill and back.' He checks the Fitbit on his wrist. 'Nineteen and a half miles in total, so I wouldn't exactly call it a *nice walk*. In this heat it was pretty gruelling, exhausting in fact.' He turns on the kitchen tap and waits for it to run cold before gulping water from the spout.

'Still, I expect you enjoyed it. I'm sure it blew away a few cobwebs.' She holds up a broad bean pod, her fingertips stained brown. 'Hugh from next door left these on the doorstep, which was very kind of him. The two of them are shielding.'

An unlikely image of the neighbours dressed in medieval armour pops into Tom's head. He splashes water on his face, wipes a handful along the back of his neck and lets it dribble down under his T-shirt. Opening the fridge, he's pleased to discover the remains of yesterday's quiche. He takes a bite from the largest slice and remembers to put it on a plate before he sits down opposite his mum.

'I wondered who it could be knocking on the door,' she says, her attention back on the task in hand. 'Poor old Hugh stood so far back, I had a job to hear what he was saying. I gather the garden's keeping him busy. Of course, he's diabetic and his wife, Marcia, has something – some unpleasant condition. Stomach trouble, I think. She did tell me once, but I can't remember now. Anyway, it seems broad beans don't agree with her these days.'

Tom smiles. 'Well they do have a reputation for being argumentative.' He's surprised when she laughs out loud. Doffing him on the head with an empty bean pod; she looks younger for a moment before the corners of her mouth turn down into those habitual creases. He rubs at his head, pretending the blow had hurt as he chews on the last few mouthfuls of quiche.

'All that exercise seems to have perked you up,' she says.

He frowns. 'When was I un-perked?'

Before she can answer, the music – he recognises it as Beethoven – builds to a crescendo that makes conversation impossible. He picks up a pod, splits it open, drops four beans into the half-full colander and saves the last one for himself.

His mother is waving one hand in time with the music. Before the joints in her fingers became so stiff, she was a talented pianist; in another life she might have been a professional.

He chews on the bean, has always preferred them raw like this. The music subsides and his mother says, 'I can see you've really caught the sun.' She continues to give him an appraising look, narrowing her eyes as if something about him offends her. 'Not sure I like you with a beard.' He rubs a protective hand over the stubble on his chin. 'Are you sure I can't cut your hair?' she says. 'It's got quite long – especially at the back.'

Tom leans away as if expecting her to brandish a pair of scissors and hack at it there and then. 'I like it this way. Steph reckons it suits me. She says it makes me look Byronic.'

'Does she now.' His mother scoffs. 'Byron was a degenerate. All that disgusting business with his sister.' She shivers. 'Hardly someone you should emulate.'

'Oh, I don't know, I quite fancy being a bit mad, bad and dangerous to know for a change.' He throws another bean into his mouth and drops the empty pod onto the pile of flaccid skins destined for the compost heap.

The chore finished, scraping his chair, he stands up. 'I'm just going to give Davy a ring,' he says above the renewed vigour of the music. Caught up in its passion, his mother gives no indication of having heard him.

Chapter Three

The only place he gets a decent signal is next to his bedroom window; if he moves half a metre in either direction, it goes. Davy always takes for ever to answer. It's hard to know whether he's genuinely busy or wants to give that impression.

While waiting, Tom stares down at the faint stain on the carpet from when he'd accidentally cut himself with a penknife he'd been hiding from his mum. The wound bled so much it required a trip to hospital and several stitches. Though it's faded, the scar is still there.

Come on, Davy. Tom runs his hand over the dent where he'd head-butted the wall after a drunken fall that had knocked him out and led to another Casualty visit. He could probably navigate the entire house by the chips and dents from his accident-prone adolescence. At the time, the doctors had suggested it was down to his inability to calculate the new parameters of his growing body. Looked at another way, he was already battling to escape.

He's about to hang up when Davy answers. 'Tom. How's it going?'

'Okay I suppose. I've been furloughed.' He stares at the

shelf in front of him; the tacky Young Scientist trophy he'd recently rescued from the bottom of the wardrobe.

His friend laughs. 'Lucky bugger. I wouldn't mind being paid to do sod all.'

'Yeah, I guess so.' He wishes he could pace the room. 'Anyway, how's things with you? Keeping busy?'

'Bit too quiet round here for my liking. London with hardly anything open and not much traffic – I mean, it's just wrong. Unnatural. Still, personally speaking, I can't complain.'

'Listen.' Tom clears his throat. 'I was wondering if you might know of any work going – anything you could possibly, you know, put my way?'

There's a long pause before Davy says, 'Maybe.' He goes silent again and, though he hasn't moved, Tom wonders if the signal's gone. He's about to speak when Davy says, 'It so happens I do know someone who might be hiring.'

'Great.' Tom raises a clenched fist. 'Tell me more.'

'It's difficult to, you know, describe exactly what's involved over the phone like.'

'Okay.' He's less certain now. 'So why don't I meet you somewhere?'

'Can you get yourself up here by lunchtime tomorrow? Say around half-twelve?'

'No problem.' Tom's beaming now. 'Where d'you want to meet?' Someone's talking in the background – an older man's voice.

'Listen,' Davy says. 'Gotta go. I'll send a drop pin.'

'Okay. Should I be carrying a folded newspaper?'

'You've lost me, mate.'

'Forget it, just a joke. See you tomorrow then.'

'Okay, cool.' The line goes dead.

Tom puts down his phone and picks up the science trophy he'd hidden with all the others after his mum had jokingly called them his *ego altar*. She'd hit a nerve with that one.

He picks up the little red Ferrari 250 GTO from the shelf below; his favourite car from his childhood collection. Most of them had been presents from Uncle Matt. After he outgrew toy cars, he'd hung onto them for sentimental reasons. Matt hadn't strictly speaking been a relative – just a *good friend* of his mum's. At least that's what she always claimed.

He checks the wheels by running it along the top of his chest of drawers. Manufactured in the early '60s, only 36 of the full-sized cars were ever made; one had sold for 70 million dollars in a private sale a couple of years back. He puts the little Ferrari back precisely where it belongs.

In his childhood fantasies, he'd dreamed of owning a real one, or failing that, a Porsche 911 or a Mercedes SL. What a joke. He'd learnt to drive in his mum's old Golf. What with the insurance and the other running costs, he still can't afford a car of his own.

The two of them are eating supper – opposite each other in their customary places. His mum says, 'Let me get this straight, you're planning to catch a train up to London tomorrow?'

'Yep, that's the general idea.'

'Despite all the risks involved?'

'Don't fuss, Mum.' Impaling a bean with his fork, he holds it up to inspect its skin; cooked, it's turned grey and wrinkly.

'I'll wear a face-covering on the train. It's compulsory anyway.'

She does that thing with her neck – like a turtle about to retract its head. 'Have you got a mask?'

'No, but I can tie a scarf or something round my face.'

'You'll look like an outlaw.'

Done with his food, Tom pushes his plate away. 'Doesn't matter what I look like, does it? No one's going to give a damn. Besides, the desperado look is part of the new norm.'

'Hmm,' she says. 'Well you wouldn't catch me on a train, or a bus for that matter, mask or no mask.' She puts down her knife to prod the air in front of him with her fork. (At least it's not the other way around.) 'What if you bring that wretched virus back here with you – have you thought of that?' Those three prongs come ever closer. There are tiny red veins in the whites of her eyes. 'Have you stopped to think about me?'

Not proud of his recent behaviour, he turns away from another argument, picks up his plate and water glass and goes over to put them in dishwasher. 'I'll probably be staying up in London for a while,' he says. 'If things work out.'

'What sort of *things*?' Her eyes are still fixed on him.

'Davy knows about a job that's going. I might apply.'

She sighs. 'You know, Tom, you have so many extraordinary abilities and yet you insist on wasting your time with one silly thing after another.'

'I'm sorry if I've failed to live up to your expectations.'

'You know that's not true.' She looks genuinely hurt. He's on the point of apologising when she adds, 'Just remember, it's an offence to work elsewhere when you've been furloughed.'

'Christ sake,' he mutters, not quite under his breath, turns his eyes up to the ribcage of dark beams overhead. 'I'm not about to break the law, Mum.'

'Glad to hear it.' She sounds anything but glad.

He turns on her. 'You might be happy enough pottering around here. Life hasn't changed much for the people in this village.' Frustration makes him thump the wood with his fist then, wincing, he does his best to hide the pain. 'I'm up to here with it. Bored sick just hanging around doing nothing day after bloody day.'

'Now there's a surprise.' She's not finished. 'You've been holed up here for months like a bear with a sore head. You know, Tom, you can't keep running away from things.'

'They locked us all down, in case you hadn't noticed.'

'Yes, well…'

'Yes well, what?'

Picking up her plate she says, 'I'll thank you not to take your anger out on me. I'm not the one still hopelessly in love with a lesbian.'

He scoffs. 'Glad to hear it, Mum. Not that I'd disapprove if you were.'

Stony-faced she says, 'Well, if you want to come back here, you'll have to self-isolate for ten days. You can use the downstairs loo, come and go through the back door.'

'Like a servant.' He shakes his head. 'You'd actually insist on that?'

'You can't expect to have the full run of this house after picking up goodness knows what in London. You know, when you're young, you imagine you're immortal, but when you get to my age, it's no joke–'

'Okay, okay,' he says, before she can elaborate. '*If* I come back here, I'll make myself scarce; you won't even know I'm here.'

'Good, that's settled then.' She brushes past him like he's already not there. It occurs to him she might not be as disappointed at him leaving as he'd imagined.

The crockery rattles as she loads pots and pans into the dishwasher. He says, 'I know I might have seemed a bit ungrateful–'

'A *bit*!' She knees the dishwasher door with vigour; it shuts with a thud.

'Look, Mum, it's not like I don't appreciate everything you've done for me over the last few months.'

She winds her neck in. 'As it happens, I need to collect my pills from the chemist tomorrow. Assuming you don't plan to leave here at the crack of dawn with your belongings hanging from a stick, I can give you a lift to the station.'

Normally rammed at this time of day, the station car park is two-thirds empty. She doesn't get out of the car but stays in the driver's seat with the engine running. 'Still time to change your mind,' she says.

Shaking his head, he gets out, shoulders his rucksack and walks round to give her a peck on the cheek. She kisses him back then her hand leaves the steering wheel to grip his chin. 'Just you be careful.'

'I will, Mum, don't worry.' He can still feel the impression of her fingers after she's let go. 'Thanks for the lift. I'll call as soon as I know what's what.'

'Then I won't hold my breath.' A joke of sorts perhaps, though he's not entirely certain of her meaning. Before he can ask, she puts the car in gear and drives away, staring straight ahead. He waves at the trail of dust the tyres are raising then pulls up his scarf as he walks through the archway into the station.

His breath soon moistens the fabric, which smells of the laundry stuff his mum uses – a fragrance that now permeates all his clothes. Too artificial for his liking; Steph always buys the non-scented eco products. Catching his reflection in a window, he has to admit his mum was right about one thing – he looks bloody ridiculous.

There's only one other person on the London bound platform – a smartly dressed, grey-haired woman wearing a proper surgical mask. Tom gives her a we're-all-in-this-together nod of acknowledgement, but the gesture isn't returned. Instead, she strides off to the other end of the platform, swinging her briefcase defensively.

The information board tells him the train is running eight minutes behind time.

A man in a black mask appears on the opposite platform. Hands in his pockets, he takes up a position directly under an advertising hoarding, his head in line with the wheels of a giant family car. *AT DEANS YOU'RE MILES BETTER OFF.* With a dark fringe obscuring his face, the man's head looks like a fifth wheel. Taken with the image, Tom gets out his phone but, before he can snap him, the man has moved on and the effect is lost.

Mid-morning and the temperature's rising, promising

another scorching day. Why is he covering his face when he hasn't even boarded the train yet? He pulls the scarf down, relieved to be able to breathe freely again.

On the opposite platform, he spots an ad for a firm of solicitors specialising in divorce. *DON'T BE LOCKED DOWN IN AN UNHAPPY MARRIAGE.* Like Christmas, lockdowns must be good for trade.

Apart from the three of them, the station is deserted. The waiting room and toilets are locked, no rail staff around. Tom hears the tracks humming well before his train appears. As it gets closer, he can see it's the old 125 model. Perhaps he shouldn't know the first ones were introduced in 1975. He'd thought they'd all been taken out of service a couple of years back. Obviously not. Brakes squealing, the train comes to a halt, belching burnt diesel.

After a moment of indecision, Tom pulls up the scarf, opens the door and steps up into dizzying heat. Damn it – the air-conditioning can't be working. No one's behind him, he slams the door. The sound echoes against the empty buildings.

People are already in the carriage – he counts four; two women sitting together at the far end and a couple of lone men some distance apart. On TV they'd shown footage of train seats taped up like a crime scene but there's nothing of that sort. No one speaks though they look up to eye him with suspicion. Everyone's luggage is sitting next to them, forming an additional barrier. He senses each person's lingering appraisal, though in truth, with their faces covered it's impossible to read anyone's expression. Dehumanised – the word floats into his head and lodges there.

Though the man he walks past has earbuds, his music is leaking into the carriage. Mindful of the new rules, Tom chooses a seat equidistant from himself and everyone else.

His T-shirt is already clinging to his back. The grimy window is sealed like all the others; the only fresh air is coming from the lowered top half of the exterior door – too far away to provide any cooling effect.

With a jolt they move off. A few minutes later they plunge into open countryside; the train accelerates past an endless stream of parched fields. Tom shuts his eyes and lets it all go by. Doesn't open them again until they crest a steep incline. He recognises a series of familiar landmarks on the horizon – compass points he's learnt to navigate by. As they begin the long descent, he feels a pang of regret that he's not out there in the sunshine instead of hurtling along in a hot tin can breathing air laced with the acrid stench of overheated brakes.

This is his first time on a train since his hasty escape from Bristol hours before the entire country went into lockdown. Popping up to London for the weekend had previously been a regular occurrence; today it's a journey into the unknown.

Why couldn't Davy discuss this job on the phone? His mum had voiced her suspicions and now his own are beginning to fester. He extracts his water bottle, lowers his mask and takes a long draw on it. Perhaps he should have considered this whole escapade a bit more. There's still time to get off at the next stop and catch a train back.

Instead of welcoming him with her arms open, if he goes back home now, his mum will treat him like a pariah for a fortnight.

In her day, she'd been a bit of a rebel, protesting against all kinds of things. He's seen photos of her on demonstrations holding various placards aloft. Strange then that she'd never once railed against having such fundamental freedoms curtailed. Instead, she claps for the NHS every Thursday evening, has stuck a rainbow picture in their front window that might have been drawn by a grandchild she doesn't have.

The train is already slowing down. They're coming into Upper Threshing – a tiny station which most intercity trains speed on through. Not today it seems. A long-dead landowner had insisted they build this station in exchange for permission to run the track through his land. Tempted, Tom's hand tightens on the strap of his rucksack. If he gets off here, how long would he have to wait for a train back?

The phone in his pocket pings. Davy's sent him a map with a drop-pin pointing to one of the gates into Hyde Park and not some dark alleyway in one of London's dodgier districts. After he's found out more, if he doesn't like the sound of this job, he can simply say no thanks. It's a sunny day, the two of them would just be having a chat while they walked around the Serpentine or whatever. He likes Hyde Park. In a normal year, they put striped deckchairs out in the shade, you can sit outside a café and have a snack, take a swim in one part of the lake. But this is not a normal year.

The brakes give a heartfelt squeal as they come to rest in the tiny station with its narrow footbridge. Should he bale out or not?

He stares at his reflection in the window, at his mum's multi-coloured scarf around his face – the only one she could spare, or so she said. Her way of getting the last laugh. So what? He can stuff the damned thing into his rucksack as soon as he's off the train.

Tom's hand relaxes its grip on the strap. It'll be great to have a face to face conversation with someone under the age of thirty. The caution urged on everyone recently must have made him more risk averse; robbed him of his usual appetite for adventure. Well, almost. He's never shied away from taking a gamble – why start now?

Staring at his own ghostly image, the corners of his eyes crease into an unseen smile. As the train pulls away, he leans back into his seat; whatever the outcome, he's determined to enjoy this trip.

Chapter Four

August 1982

Beth

She's glad to make it to the top of the stairs before the handles of the plastic bag break or the bottom falls out of it. 'Hiya, Beth,' Rachel calls out to her in a singsong way. 'Fancy a coffee?'

Beth carries her shopping through to the kitchen where the kettle is just coming up to the boil. On the worktop there are two mugs with instant coffee powder already in them.

Though she hates the taste of the economy brand they're making do with, Beth says, 'Thanks, I'd love one.'

Getting her breath back, she rubs at the red lines the handles have left across her fingers then unpacks her shopping – making sure to put her things on the designated shelf in the fridge. It looks suspiciously like she's missing a yogurt or two, but she decides not to make a big deal out of it.

Both windows are wide open to try to cool the place a bit. Sunlight is streaming in behind Rachel creating a halo around her shaggy blonde hair. She's changed into her new frilly-collared blouse. Pale blue like her eyes, it suits her.

Someone nearby is using what sounds like an electric drill. Above the noise, Beth shouts, 'So, who's the visitor?'

Kettle half cocked, her flatmate's lips hover somewhere between a grin and a pout. 'Promise you won't be angry with me.'

Beth stops what she's doing. 'How do you expect me to promise before I know what you're talking about?'

'Okay, well...' Rachel breaks off to concentrate on the boiling water she's pouring; then, milk bottle in hand, she says, 'I just want you to know I only have your best interests at heart.'

'You sound like a school prefect about to report someone. What have you done? Come on, Rach, you're really bloody scaring me.'

'Does this smell off to you?' Rachel thrusts the milk bottle under her nose.

She sniffs. 'Only a bit. I'm sure it'll be fine if you stir it in enough.' Beth frowns. 'You just did that on purpose – that thing with the milk. Come on, Rach, spit it out, whatever it is.'

'Okay, then you'd better follow me.' She hands a hot mug to Beth, then carries the other two into the sitting room where Kyle, of all people, is sitting on the sofa.

He stands up. 'Hi, Beth,' he says. 'Good to see you.' His face is strained, his skin pallid against his jet-black hair. The curtains behind him billow out, making her think of vampires and other blood-sucking things.

'Hi.' Normal manners suggest she should say the same back, but she stops herself because it's far from good to see him.

She turns to give Rach a long you-wait look. 'I was just

passing,' Kyle says. A lie; nobody *just passes* this part of Shepherd's Bush – their street is on the way to absolutely nowhere. 'I know your birthday's coming up soon,' he says, 'so I thought I'd drop off this mixed tape I made for you.' He's wrapped it up, tied it with a red ribbon like it's Valentine's Day.

He takes a few steps closer, holds it out for her to take. She notices the rings under his eyes. Four thirty in the afternoon and there's the unmistakeable smell of alcohol on his breath. Kyle never normally drinks due to some kind of adverse mood reaction; he calls it his kryptonite.

Rach looks at her as if to say, *the least you can do is take the poor man's gift from him.* 'Thanks,' Beth says obeying silent orders. 'That's really very, um, sweet of you.' Because it is, sort of.

'It's got all your favourite tracks on,' he says. 'Madness, The Specials.' A forced little smile. 'Roxy Music. Can't think what else. Oh yeah, some David Bowie and it starts with that Human League track you really love.' He shuts his eyes for several seconds before adding, 'Whole thing took me ages. I thought it would, you know, remind you of old times and that.'

'Great.' Her smile is short-lived. 'Well, I look forward to listening to it.'

'I was just going to leave it on the doorstep,' he says. 'But then Rachel asked me up for a coffee.' She remembers now – Dracula can't come in without an invitation.

'You know what.' Rach begins to retreat; she does this gesture with her thumb like she's hitchhiking. 'I think I'm going to take my coffee into the kitchen; got lots of things to be getting on with.' She makes a point of shutting the door behind her.

'So, Beth, how have you been?' Kyle sits down on the sofa, one hand extended to offer her the space next to him.

Instead she chooses the little rattan chair nearer the door. 'Fine,' she says, sipping her drink to buy time. It's impossible not to ask him back. 'And you; how have you been keeping?' She could be addressing a maiden aunt – not that she has a maiden aunt.

He looks straight at her. 'Not so fine.' His head droops along with his shoulders. 'It's been hell without you. I've hardly slept …' When his eyes start to water, she has to look away. It shocks her that the man in front of her could be the same one she'd known and loved. Well, not loved exactly, but something close to it – at least for a while. He'd always seemed so self-assured – she'd never once suspected this lesser version of him was lurking inside.

He says, 'I thought the two of us, we really clicked and then we…'

'Clacked?' Damn, she shouldn't have said that.

Beth stands up. Picking up her present, she says, 'If you don't mind, I won't open this until my birthday,' in case he imagines some scenario where the music begins to melt her heart. 'Thanks for going to so much trouble.' She takes a breath. 'I'm really sorry but I've got a lot of lines to learn for the play I'm in.'

'Ah yes, Rachel told me you've landed a leading role. Suppose I should congratulate you.'

Did she indeed. 'It's only a small theatre, but, you know, it's a start. My name will be on the poster and all that. It'll help with the CV.'

He stands up, a bit unsteady on his feet. 'She told me you're playing a tart.'

'Well, I wouldn't describe my character – Lexi – as a tart. She's more of a free-spirit; she's not constrained by what other people think of her.'

'Or the way she thoughtlessly hurts them.'

'If you want to put it like that.' She's at the door before him. Opens it quickly.

As she turns her head, he grabs her forearm. 'How would you like me to put it?' She tries to shrug him off, but his grip is too firm. 'Look what you're wearing.'

'It's a hot day, or hadn't you noticed?'

'Can't be too hard for you to act like a slut who leads people on and then just ...' His breath in her face is redolent of some dark spirit.

'Why did you really come here?' She rotates her arm, forcing him to lose his grip. 'Tell me, Kyle – did you expect me to fall into your arms and tell you what a terrible mistake I'd made? Well, I'm sorry, but I'm going to have to disappoint you.'

He raises his hand and then his gaze flicks past her. 'What the bloody hell's going on?' Rachel shouts.

'Kyle was about to hit me, weren't you, Kyle? You see, that's what weak men do when they can't bend a woman to their will.' When she stares him out, his hand drops back to his side. 'I'd say it was time for you to leave,' she tells him.

'Too bloody right,' Rach says, 'You need to fuck off right now.'

Kyle heads for the door. On the stairs he shouts something

incoherent though she catches the word *bitch*. If she had it to hand, she would have thrown his stupid mixed tape down after him.

Her knees weaken once she hears the street door slam. 'I'm so sorry,' Rachel says putting down the heavy ashtray Beth hadn't seen she was holding.

'I was only going to knee him in the balls,' Beth says. 'Good job you didn't brain him with that thing, you might have killed him.'

'He looked so dejected and lovelorn standing outside looking up at your window.' Rachel shakes her head. 'Can't believe I was daft enough to be taken in like that.'

'Don't beat yourself up; you're not the only one he fooled.'

'If you like, I can send a couple of my brothers round to teach him some manners?'

She laughs. 'You know, Rach, sounds to me like you've watched The Godfather far too many times.'

Chapter Five

Tom

Upper Threshing has already receded into a fold of the surrounding hills. Needing a piss, Tom makes sure his scarf is in place before he stands up. All four heads swivel to check what he might be up to. His rucksack is too bulky to take with him, so he leaves it on his seat remembering to extract his wallet and mobile; no one's likely to nick his clothes or water bottle. Seeing the suspicion in their eyes, he decides not to disturb the two women at the far end and instead heads in the opposite direction – the way of least resistance.

They're hurtling along, making up for lost time. Tom staggers past the bloke with the headphones who's already lost interest in him. The train sways as it corners at speed and the movement throws him against one of the many empty seats, forcing him to grip the grab-handles. The sign above the door tells him the toilet is vacant. Sensing his approach, the door opens.

For once, the toilet cubicle is spotless and only smells of bleach – one advantage of the nation's new obsession with hygiene. He's careful to sanitise his hands afterwards as per the laminated instructions above the basin.

Tom steps out into the cramped little vestibule and is about to pull up his scarf when the lights go out.

The darkness is total and unnerving. Oddly quiet, he could almost be floating in an immersion tank. Finding nothing to grab on to, he waits for his eyes to adjust but still can't see a damned thing. The train must be inside a tunnel and a long one at that; the overhead lights ought to have come on but must have stopped working along with the air con. Odd that he has no memory of this tunnel from previous journeys – they must have been re-routed.

His outstretched hands blindly locate a surface and he feels his way along a curved wall. It's a relief to hear the wheels against the track. And voices; quiet at first and then the volume builds to the sort of hum that emanates from many simultaneous conversations. He heads towards the sound, figuring someone must be watching a film on a laptop, although he can't make out the glow of a screen. Another step and he hears the swish of the carriage door opening.

'Bloody long tunnel this,' comes from close-by. A man's voice. Remembering his phone, he takes it out and with an upward swipe activates its torch function. The beam picks out a group of men and women standing right in front of him, blocking his way. He can smell body odour. Raising the phone higher illuminates more of the carriage. The place is packed out. No one appears to be wearing a mask; distancing rules utterly ignored, people of all ages are pressed up against each other, leaving no room for him to step inside even if he wanted to. What the fuck is going on?

When he backs away, the door closes, though he can still hear the din they're making. Like a switch being flicked, they emerge into daylight so bright it momentarily blinds him. Tom shuts his eyes and counts to ten and then some more, hoping that when he opens them everything will be back to normal – the new normal that is; not the old one. While he's counting, the hum of conversation continues unabated.

Reaching twenty, he gives up and opens his eyes. Nothing's changed. Five minutes ago, the carriage had four passengers, now it's so rammed it's impossible to thread his way through to retrieve his rucksack.

Shaken and shaking, he turns the opposite way. The door to the next carriage opens at his approach to reveal a luggage rack stuffed to capacity and standing room only. The people in there are pressed just as tightly together.

How did all these bloody people get on in the time it took him to take a piss? The train can't have stopped – he would have felt it slow down, heard the squeal of the brakes. There'd been no announcement, at least not one he'd been able to hear inside the toilet. He distinctly remembers being bounced around the whole time he was in there. No, they can't possibly have stopped.

Warm air is streaming in through the open half of the outside door. Tom gulps it in, hoping it will clear his head and help him make sense of what's happening. To keep his footing, he braces himself, his brain racing to construct a logical explanation. His gaze comes to rest on a small pentangle someone has scratched on the opposite wall.

Could he have blacked out while he was in the toilet? Had

he been totally out of it while the train stopped, and all these people had swarmed on and collectively decided to ignore the new regulations?

Perhaps he's hallucinating due to dehydration or something he'd eaten? Maybe all this is only happening in his febrile imagination.

The door to his right opens and a man about his age squeezes through. Thickset and tall, his curly hair cut short on top and long at the back in a classic mullet style that only accentuates his massive head. 'You waitin' for the bog, mate?' Never mind two metres, Curly is well inside his personal space.

'Um, no, I've just been.' Tom backs away. Under his breath he adds, 'Knock yourself out – I obviously did.'

The other man scowls. 'What did you just say to me?'

'A joke.' Tom holds his hands up. 'You know – this whole thing.'

'Yeah, know what you mean.' Relaxing his stance, Curly wipes the sweat from his forehead with a damp rag of a hand-kerchief. 'Make you pay through the bloody nose for a ticket, then they pack you in like cattle. In fact, I don't s'pose they'd be allowed to transport animals in these conditions. Bound to be against some EEC regulation or summat.' With a nod he shuts the cubicle door.

Tom's thoughts are running in too many directions while he does his best to ignore the sound effects emanating from inside. A few minutes later Curly comes out along with the stench of urine. The man doesn't head back into the carriage he came out of but digs into a back pocket to extract a crumpled pack of cigarettes. Tom's shocked when he taps one out and lights it with a Zippo retrieved from the other pocket. Pinching the cigarette between his thumb and finger, he takes a drag then, hunched over, lets the smoke pour out through his nostrils in the style of someone smoking in a film set in a prison yard.

Misinterpreting his expression, Curly offers up the pack. 'No thanks.' Tom shakes his head, restrains himself from wafting away the cloud of smoke though it's beginning to make his eyes water. The other man's black T-shirt is stretched to capacity. Against his expectations, there's not a single tattoo on his muscled arms or any visible part of him.

Between drags, he narrows his eyes on Tom. 'If you don't mind me sayin', you don't look too clever, mate... Me sister, she used to get terrible travel sickness 'till she got this special bracelet thing. Sounds a bit hippie-dippy, I know, but our Trace swears by it.' His nicotine-stained smile is not a pretty sight. 'You might wanna give it a go.' He takes another long drag. 'Bloody boilin' in here; don't s'pose that helps none.' Smoke flows over the man's upper lip to be sucked back up his nostrils for a double hit. 'Still, makes a change from all the bloody rain we've had lately.'

Tom turns his head away from the escaping smoke to be faced with another mystery. The weather reports have consistently shown scarlet areas above London and the South East – record temperatures and yet the countryside they're passing through is much greener than further west; the grass in the fields high and lush.

Movement draws Tom's attention back to Curly who's just dropped the butt and is grinding it into the floor. The carriage door opens. 'See ya, mate,' he says barging in as the door closes behind him.

The sun is directly on Tom's back. He should move but instead he shuts his eyes, hoping his mind will be soothed by the rocking motion and all this weird stuff will go away. Any time now logic will be back in charge of the universe.

Heart racing, a different thought worms its way into his mind – what if they'd crashed back there in the tunnel? With the carriage derailed, he could be lying unconscious, trapped in the wreckage, his concussed brain refusing to catch up. The packed carriages, even his conversation with Curly, might be something he's remembering from the past in his unconscious state – the last flickering of his dying mind.

He jumps when a hand touches his arm. 'You alright?' A woman comes into sharp focus. 'You don't look well – yer face has gone all sort of Gary Numan.' Late thirties, quite attractive; one bare shoulder emerging from an acid pink top. 'S'pect it's this heat,' she says. 'Us Brits just ent built for these temperatures.'

She slips the strap of a patchwork bag from her shoulder, roots around and brings out a half empty bottle. It hisses as she unscrews the top. 'Here you go,' she says, 'have a drink on me.'

Is she fucking joking? This has to be a wind-up. He backs into the corner by the door – much too close to where the outside world is speeding past.

'Don't look at me like that,' she says. 'It's just pop – won't kill ya, you know.' She wipes the top of the bottle with her sleeve. 'That better?'

When she waves the open bottle under his nose, he recognises the smell of orangeade from his childhood. She nudges him. 'Honestly, it's only Corona, darlin', I swear.' In an American gangster drawl, she adds, 'Every bubble's passed its fizzical.'

He says, 'Thanks but—'

'Ladies and gentlemen, Reading will be our next stop in approximately three minutes. Change here for Bath and Bristol Temple Meads…' This close to the speaker, the announcement is deafening. *'Birmingham New Street and all stops north. Once again, the next station is Reading.'*

Ears ringing, Tom wants her to take that damned bottle away. 'Thanks all the same but—'

'If you're leaving the train here, please make sure to take all your luggage with you. Once again, passengers are reminded to report any suspicious packages or any person acting suspiciously.' That last part makes him smile – it would be easier to report someone *not* acting suspiciously.

'That's better.' The woman plants one hand on her hip in a provocative stance. 'Anyone ever told you, you have a really nice smile?'

'Thanks.' He knows better than to return the compliment. The train's slowing down; factories and office buildings come into view.

She looks at her watch and tuts. 'Running behind time as usual. This is my stop,' she says. 'Your last chance, you know, if you want a drink; or anything else for that matter.' She gives him a stage wink.

'No, I'm good.' To illustrate his lack of interest, he gets out his phone. No new messages. They're approaching a major station, but he has no signal either – not even 3G.

Leaning over him she says, 'What you got there then?' She's taking the piss. Thankfully another deafening announcement puts paid to any further conversation.

Chapter Six

The train crawls into Reading. As it shudders to a halt, both internal doors open simultaneously. Trapped; he's now in everyone's way. Tom presses himself against the wall while emerging passengers bunch up ready to make a quick exit. 'Bye then.' Corona woman turns to wave as she steps down onto the platform. Out of politeness, he raises a hand, though in the general melee it's a pointless gesture.

White, black, Asian – most of the men in the queue have embraced the long hair of lockdown. The mullet also seems to be back with a vengeance. He pulls up his scarf while a seemingly endless line of unmasked passengers file past him. The thin material can't prevent the heady mix of perfume, sweat, stale tobacco and more sweat assaulting his nostrils. According to the scientists, covering his mouth and nose only serves to protect them from him and not the other way around; all the same he's pleased to have a layer of cloth between himself and whatever bugs they might be breathing out. Like he's invisible, everyone brushes against him. One or two coughing into their hands. They tread on his toes with only the occasional mumbled apology.

His memory of Reading station doesn't match the scruffiness of the platform. No more than five years ago, the whole building had undergone a major redesign and, once the construction screens were removed, a slick and shiny new-look station emerged. From what he can see, the previous air of decay is back. Gloomy and plastered with dog-eared posters, everywhere he looks there are discarded wrappers and cigarette butts lying where they fell.

Corona-woman has been swallowed up by the crowd heading for the exits. For some reason those passengers with suitcases are carrying them instead of wheeling them. Must be some sort of fitness trend.

Without respite, new people crowd onto the train and the whole process plays out in reverse. No face coverings; bunched up against each other – Reading folk have ripped up the new-norm rulebook. Confined to a sleepy village since March, he'd had no idea the government's edicts were being flouted on this sort of scale. No mention of it on the news. With his outlaw-style scarf covering his face, he's the oddity – the freak causing them to stare or avert their gaze as they file past him to squeeze themselves into whatever space they can find.

A portly guard is slamming doors along the length of the train. Whistle clamped between his teeth; he only needs to exhale to send the train on its way. Aside from everything else, Tom is worried about his rucksack. Someone will have moved it off the seat. He'd hate to lose his favourite jeans, the Cola Boyy T-shirt Steph gave him for his birthday, his blue jumper, his electric toothbrush – the list goes on. With its cracked screen, his iPad is unlikely to appeal to a thief. Damaged in a play-fight with Steph, he's sort of got used to everything he watches having a diagonal line across it.

The whistle sounds and a loud click tells him the guard has locked all the outside doors. With no more scheduled stops, he's sealed into this restricted space for the rest of the journey to Paddington.

The train picks up speed. *Taa-dum, ta-dum, ta-dum t'dum* – the sound builds in his ears like an incipient migraine. His thoughts keep returning to the blackout in the tunnel and how very peculiar things have been since. His mum once told him Victorian ladies were so concerned about the danger of dark tunnels, they'd hold pins in their mouths in case a man took advantage of the darkness and tried to steal a kiss.

They glide in on Platform One. Tom's the first one out the door, stepping well back as a human tide pours from the train. After months of very little noise, he's shocked by the volume of the echoing announcements, the cacophony created by hundreds of people striding off on their individual journeys. Trapped by the glass roof, diesel fumes catch in his throat. There's no evidence of social distancing anywhere. He'd seen a few tweets about how many Londoners are ignoring government guidelines, but never imagined non-compliance had reached this scale. Everyone's carrying on like an instant cure has been discovered. To rule out the possibility, he tries to check the newsfeed on his phone. Crazy – although he's in the heart of London, he still can't get a signal.

Hoping to retrieve his rucksack, Tom lurks outside the carriage until the last of the stragglers disembarks. Climbing back on board, he searches around where he'd been sitting but draws a blank. Undeterred, he works his way along the carriage and back again. Aside from the usual detritus, he finds nothing. Tom repeats the process, this time getting down onto his knees to peer under and around every seat. He examines every last metre of both overhead racks hoping to find his iPad or any other unwanted items abandoned there.

Not a thing. Frantic now, he extends his search to the carriages on either side then works his way along most of the empty train until he's forced to conclude that some thieving bastard must have stolen all his stuff.

The cleaning attendants are coming on board searching out all the discarded newspapers and food wrappers. Keeping his distance, Tom walks up to one of them – a middle-aged woman with a careworn face. 'I've looked everywhere but I can't find my rucksack,' he tells her. 'I think someone's stolen it.'

Her tired eyes could not care less. 'Try Lost Property,' she says, carrying on with her work. Another cleaner has appeared at the far end. To avoid being caught in a pincer movement, Tom jumps down from the train.

Apart from the clothes he's wearing, he's left with his wallet and phone. He's glad he left his laptop at his mum's. Tom recalls an ad on telly where some poor sod had been left naked after his stag-do with just a credit card. As the man runs, thanks to the card, underwear, a shirt and then a suit appears on his back; next he's driving a hire car – or he might be on a train. Armed with only that single card, he manages to arrive smartly suited at the church with seconds to spare before his bride makes her entrance.

Tom's hand goes to the wallet in his back pocket. Taking it out, he quickly checks the contents. It's all there including his debit and credit cards. Losing his rucksack is upsetting but not a complete disaster. If it doesn't turn up, he can claim on the personal insurance he'd taken out through work. He might even get a brand-new iPad out of it – a clear view might be better after all. Sometime in the future this disaster of a day will be just a story he'll tell in the pub. Assuming the pubs are open.

It's so hot – ridiculously so for England. At the start of his journey, he'd had a heavy pack to manoeuvre; now, with nothing to carry, he feels too light.

Coming into the main concourse he can smell fried food; his empty stomach growls. He's always been like that – one minute not particularly bothered about eating and the next ravenous. It's been a good four or five hours since breakfast; given everything that's happened, it seems much longer.

Led by gnawing hunger, he heads for the nearest sandwich kiosk. 'What can I get you?' The place is a furnace, but the round-faced vendor rubs his hands together like he's trying to warm them up. The selection of food on offer consists of crisps, peanuts, some dubious looking chocolate bars and a collection of sandwiches – white bread only – stacked one on top of the other on an open shelf. The chalked-up menu is a joke. The man waves his hand to scare away the flies. Despite reservations, Tom's stomach rumbles audibly at the sight of food – anything to fill the need. After all the street-food he'd sampled on his travels, he's convinced of his iron constitution. 'I'll have a cheese and tomato sarnie,' he says.

'There you go.' The man hands over an unwrapped sandwich sitting on a sheet of greaseproof paper; doesn't offer to toast it or anything. 'You want something to drink with that?'

'Yeah, a tall flat-white.'

The man smirks. 'You might well be son, but what d'you want to drink?'

Ignoring his feeble joke, Tom decides to repeat his order more slowly, 'I'd like a large flat–.'

'The estate agents round the flippin' corner.' The vendor chuckles; must fancy himself a comedian. 'You want tea, coffee, Pepsi, Lilt?'

Behind him someone clears their throat in the way people do to make someone hurry up. 'Tea then,' Tom says. 'I'll have a cuppa.'

'Black or white?'

'White, skinny –'

Wanting in on the act, the man behind him says, 'What's this then – Police Five?' People are chuckling; everyone's a joker today.

The vendor pours tea into a thin plastic cup. 'You want milk in it, son?'

'Yeah, low fat if you've got it.'

'It's the regular sort or nothing,' is said with pride.

'Fine.'

The man adds a slug of milk before he drops the whole thing into another plastic cup as a crude form of insulation. 'Careful son, it's hot. Sugar's on the side there. That'll be…'

A security announcement blocks his words. When Tom pulls a card from his wallet the vendor laughs. 'You got to be kidding me. Cash only.'

Tom takes a tenner from his wallet and hands it over. Holding it up to the light, the man laughs. 'What the hell's this – bloody Monopoly money?' He hands it straight back. 'You got a pound note in there? I can change a fiver, at a stretch.'

Tom searches his pockets. 'I've probably got a few pound coins. How much did you say again?'

'Pound coins?' Hand outstretched, the man rolls his eyes. 'Eighty-five pee.'

'Sorry, I misheard you. Say again?'

A voice from behind says, 'Eighty-five pee – you deaf or summat? Get a move on, lad, some of us have got a train to catch.'

Tom offers a handful of coins from his pocket in the way old people do when they get confused. He's certainly that.

Snatching the tea back from his would-be grasp, the vendor shakes his head. He looks past Tom to address the queue behind. 'He 'spects me to take his Mickey Mouse money like I was born yesterday.' All joviality leaves his face. 'Don't waste my time, son. Clear off.'

Taking his cue, the man behind dodges round to become the man in front.

Tom can only comply. What the fuck's wrong with his money? And how could a sandwich and a cup of tea cost less than a quid? Could this day get any weirder?

By the station entrance, a grey-haired man is holding out a folded newspaper, calling to entice all the people hurrying past him. Tom can't decipher the phrase he keeps repeating; like an unknown foreign language, the sounds all run together. The one word he can pick out is: *Thatcher*.

A terrible suspicion forms in his mind. Tom becomes a boulder in the stream of people rushing on past. Shoulder pads, upturned collars, big hair, stripy blonde highlights, most with a fag on the go; he's the only one dressed like he belongs in the twenty-first century. No way. This is just make-believe – they must be shooting a movie set in the eighties. Normally they film at night when no one's about. He looks around expecting to see lights and cameras, someone standing behind them with a clipboard about to shout *cut*, because, in his expensive trainers and Banksy Ratapult T-shirt, he must be spoiling their shot.

Tom rakes his hand through his hair several times. He'd read how they're not making any of the TV soaps at the moment due to the pandemic, so why the hell have they allowed a film crew to take over the whole of Paddington station in the middle of the day with no social distancing? It makes no sense.

He doesn't wear a watch and for some reason his stupid phone has stopped displaying the time. His Fitbit is inside his lost rucksack. Glancing up at the station clock, the hands have been set at 3:00 for the film, though it can't be more than 12:30. Better get a move on. If he has to hang around for too long, Davy's likely to bugger off.

Except, things are still not right here.

He runs over to the newsstand. For a bit-player, the grey-haired man is putting a lot into his performance. Auctioneer style, he's calling out something different though equally indecipherable. Tom grabs a copy of the Standard. As he turns away to read a headline about Princess Diana, the vendor grabs his forearm. 'Here, I ent bloody givin''em away, sonny Jim.'

'Seriously? Since when?'

The vendor scoffs. 'Since about 1820. Either you pay up or you give it back.' His thrust-out hand is stained with newsprint.

With no acceptable means of paying, Tom's forced to hand it back. Scanning the station from this new angle, there's still no sign of a film crew. He jogs up the slope into Praed Street. A black and shiny Mini Metro speeds past him. All the model cars he'd played with as a kid have come to life in front of his eyes. Red Cortina. Blue Fiesta – window down, the passenger's hand tapping out the beat of *Come on Eileen*. Another Cortina; a dirty white this time. *Clean me* scrawled in the grime. Horns honking, the white Cortina is cut up by a boxy Austin black-cab.

Breathless and sweating, Tom bends to rest his hands on his knees. The air is filthy with exhaust fumes. Unfamiliar smells, stranger adverts and an ever-advancing army of smokers. Blocking his view of the street, a red Routemaster bus pulls up in front of him to disgorge a stream of authentically dressed passengers. A bell rings twice before the bus moves off. He glimpses a uniformed conductor, his chest crossed with leather straps.

There's only one totally crazy explanation for all this – unless he's hallucinating or stark raving mad, he must have somehow travelled back in time. With growing proof wherever he looks, the reality becomes undeniable.

Admitting it sends a shockwave through his body. Tom's watched a lot of sci-fi. He's also familiar with quantum physics and the theoretical possibility of objects being in a state of superposition. All that stuff about time-portals and faults in the space-time continuum is hypothetically possible, but it's been only that, until now. As far as he can tell, he's not surrounded by a group of equally confused people, so how or why has this happened to him alone?

His plans for the day are lost; Christ, if he's right, Davy hasn't even been born yet. But then neither has he, for that matter.

Chapter Seven

Beth

A heaped spoonful and her coffee still tastes of nothing – the cheap supermarket brand fails to hit the spot. She hopes the caffeine hit will kick in soon.

Wandering into the bathroom, Beth catches a glimpse of herself in the mirror and recoils. She squints at her reflection, her head thumping with the sheer effort of remaining vertical. Rough; there's no other word for how she looks. Although a couple more come to mind: hollow-eyed, hungover, and that's just the Hs. Only her tan saves her from full-on bride-of-Dracula.

She grabs the aspirin bottle, knocks a couple back and washes them down with a mouthful of water; relieved to have the day off from rehearsals because, truth is, things aren't going too well. 'No – you're fucking *acting* again,' their director, Llewellyn – call me Lewi – keeps shouting along with 'cut' like he's directing a film and not a company of four. So far, he hasn't given her much of a chance to get into character. After only a few lines it's: 'Let's try that again shall we?' Always accompanied by a heavy sigh. Of course, he never says a word to Gary because Gary played first mate on the Onedin Line a few years back, which makes him a celebrity as far as Lewi is concerned.

The Herd Theatre might be only a large room above a pub in Shepherd's Bush but it's a start – or would be if Lewi was more supportive. Down in the bar after rehearsals last night, he'd lectured her about finding 'the authentic truth of her character'. Whisky-breath in her face and slurring his words: 'What I need from you, Beth, is acting that doesn't show. Do you follow?' Hand to his own breast, thank God, he told her to: 'Find the truth of Lexi within yourself'. Later, with one arm slumped around her neck and the *darling* count off-the-scale: 'I simply need you to *be* her, darling – do you think you can do that for me?'

Brushing her teeth, Beth decides that, for the next twenty-four hours, she'll do just that – she'll *be* Lexi. It might be a bit awkward as she's arranged to visit her Aunty Joan in Cheltenham. She'll have to break character for five minutes to explain. The old girl is usually up for a laugh; she won't mind playing along if it's just for a day.

'A' level Drama had introduced Beth to the theories of Stanislavski and Strasberg and the basic principles of Method Acting. 'There's no need to overdo things,' Mrs Logan used to warn them. 'I don't hold with starving yourself, taking drugs or any of that nonsense. For me it always began with choosing the right footwear.' A distant look on her face, she'd say: 'I always started by walking a mile in their shoes – quite literally. Of course, you need to choose the right pair for your character.'

Rooting around, Beth finds a pair of strappy sandals in the bottom of the wardrobe. They belong to Rach who is staying at her boyfriend's so she can't ask permission. Beth's pretty sure she won't mind her borrowing them. Trying them for size, they more or less fit, although they're a bit tight across the toes. She can harness the discomfort to keep herself focused.

Her own treasured Doc Martens would show Lexi's strength of character, her refusal to be bound by narrow gender stereotypes. Then again, chunky boots might be a bit predictable – bit of a cliché.

Barefoot, Beth puts that decision aside to consider the rest of her outfit. Lexi has rejected the norms of society and so, amongst other things, her outfits are a bit on the scanty side – fairly revealing it has to be said. Lewi is always banging on about subtlety so she shouldn't overdo it. A button or two left undone, heavier on the eye makeup – that sort of thing.

It's hot out there – Lexi would definitely dress for the weather. None of her skirts pass the first audition – too long or just too *nice*. Mmm.

Normally she only wears her cut-off denims when in the park or mooching around the flat because they're a bit short – she'd slipped with the scissors and had to cut more from the other leg to match. Lexi wouldn't bat an over-mascaraed eyelid about wearing them on a crowded bus.

She finds them at the bottom of the linen basket; they narrowly pass the sniff test. Turning this way and that she concludes they're covering the essentials. Bare legs not tights – she's got a good tan and she'd shaved them only yesterday.

What about her top half? Her T-shirts are anything but

sexy – they're mostly on the scuzzy side having been washed too often with other colours. Last week she'd bought a cheap lacy blouse in the market and still hasn't worn it because it's a bit see through in places. Lexi would definitely wear it without a bra but that's not going to happen. 'Leave it out,' she tells herself in the mirror. 'You won't catch me flashin' me tits around.'

Damnit, she's Eliza Doolittle's sister. Better tone it down – cockney but not totally common. 'What you lookin' at?' she asks herself.

Perfume? Maybe essential oils. Not patchouli – Lexi's no hippie. She would go for something sharp but not too floral. Orange base maybe. After more rooting around, Beth finds an old bottle of Aqua Manda in the bathroom cabinet. Perfect. Though it smells a bit like marmalade, she dabs it behind her ears and on her wrists hoping it won't attract wasps.

Drawing on eyeliner is difficult with an unsteady hand. Narrowing her eyes at her reflection, she hopes the effect is more Chrissie Hynde than undead.

Beth checks her watch. 'Here, you'd better get a move on, gal, or you'll miss the bleedin' bus.' Damnit, she's acting again. 'Relax into her' was another of Lewi's oft-repeated instructions.

Boots need socks, which would be a bit much in this heat. It'll have to be the sandals. She remembers to put some plasters in her handbag in case of blisters.

On her way through the flat, she picks up the postcard that's just arrived. Morocco this time. After almost a year of silence, in spidery writing, her mother talks about trekking with friends in the Atlas Mountains like some fucking gap year student. No apparent curiosity about how *her* life is going. Bloody typical. She was probably stoned at the time. Beth's tempted to rip the damned thing up. Instead, she puts it in her bag for Aunty Joan to mull over.

Wait. She'll need the right soundtrack. Beth's pretty sure that Lexi would, by lucky coincidence, share her musical tastes. The first one she picks up is the mixed-tape Kyle had made for her. She's in a rush and there's no point in it going to waste. After a brief moment of pity and regret, she loads it into her Walkman and tucks the machine into her handbag.

All set. Better get a move on. No time for breakfast; she grabs a banana.

The traffic is snarled up in roadworks. Already running late, her bus has been stuck in the same place for at least five minutes. Beth makes her way towards the open back, thankful for the fresher air. The conductor is standing in the aisle, blocking her exit. It might be better to say as little as possible while she's still getting under Lexi's skin. She taps him on the shoulder to get his attention above the mass chorus of pneumatic drills. Leaning into his ear she can smell the man's sweat. 'Can you let me off here, please?'

A big man with a seen-it-all expression on his pockmarked face, he says, 'Sorry, love, no can do.' He doesn't look at all sorry.

'Why not? We're goin' nowhere. It'll be quicker on foot.'

'Regulations.' He widens his shoulders. Already flushed, his face reddens to boiling point. 'Passengers are only allowed to alight at designated stops.'

'But I'll miss me flamin' train at this rate.'

He shrugs his lack of concern and turns to check another ticket. As he's sideways on, she seizes the opportunity to squeeze past him and leap off the back of the bus onto the pavement, almost colliding with a woman and her pushchair.

'Really sorry,' she says stepping into the road to avoid the crush of pedestrians.

'Oi!' the conductor shouts after her. The rest of what he's saying is lost in the general din that envelops her.

Several times she's forced into the gutter by the volume of people coming at her with their bulky suitcases and glowing cigarette ends.

Reaching the lights, she dashes across the road to the accompaniment of blaring horns and a chivalrous shout of, 'Silly bitch; you'll get yourself fuckin' killed like that.' She runs down the slope into the station. An echoing announcement tells her that her train will soon be departing from platform one. No time to buy a ticket, she'll have to do it on the train. By staying at the edges of the crowd, she's able to break into an awkward trot, her bags hitting her sides at every stride.

Once she's on the platform, it's safe to slow down. She strides past first-class, opens the next door along and jumps up onto the train.

The carriage isn't too crowded. With relief, Beth deposits her over-stuffed bag in the luggage rack and flops down into the empty seat below.

Once she's got her breath back, she fishes out her dog-eared script and turns to Act One, Scene One and the little ballpoint arrow pointing to her opening line. There's really no need to read it – she already knows the whole thing by heart.

Shutting her eyes, she tells herself: *You're Lexi and you don't take any shit from no one.* Then again, perhaps Lexi would say: *no bugger.*

Chapter Eight

Tom

The driving beat of *Tainted Love* is blaring out from a Mini Cooper stuck in the traffic; apart from the colour, it could be the one his Uncle Matt had restored. The song's familiar lyrics repeatedly urge Tom to *run away... get away* like it's some kind of message.

The people around him are going about their lives with no idea what's going to happen next. He could tell them about Thatcher's tearful resignation in 1990, or how in 1997 the nation's beloved Princess will be killed in a car crash in a Paris underpass. Think of the disasters he could warn people about. Chernobyl. Or 9/11 – the list is mindboggling and endless. But who would listen to some weirdo claiming to be from the future? The terrifying ramifications of his predicament hits him – in this world, this time frame, he's a penniless refuge. A nobody.

Too much; he's in danger of losing his shit. He takes some deep breaths before shouting out loud: 'Fucking focus!' A passing woman tuts at his language.

How could this have happened? Wishing away 2020, had he somehow willed this into being? Thinking about it could make his head explode if he let it. In any case, no point in speculating about any of that when the most important question is – how's he going to get back home again?

The only solution that comes to mind is to try to get back on that same train. It somehow brought him here, so there's a chance, however slim, it can take him back again.

It could have left already but what if it hasn't? They'd come in on Platform One so, if it *is* still there, that's where it will be.

Tom sprints back into the concourse, throwing himself left and right as he navigates through the mass of bodies. People of all shapes and sizes come at him from every direction almost as if deliberately trying to slow him down. Like the scrum half he used to be, he ducks and dives past each one, his sights set on the train that he can see waiting. Nearing Platform One, he slows to take stock. Yes – the train sitting there is an old 125 but then, damn it, they all are. Exhaust fumes are rising from it. He notices a red plate on the side of the engine bearing the name: *Gustav Holst.* This might not be the same train he came in on, but with no other choice, he has to take that chance.

The guard shouts, 'Stand clear,' one foot already on the carriage steps. Swerving past him, Tom grabs the handle of the next closed door, opens it and launches himself inside. Finding his footing, he slams the door shut as the train begins to move off.

He's landed in First Class. No matter; at least he's on the train. A dozen privileged heads pop up as they judder to a halt again.

Shit! Holding his breath, Tom tries not to panic. His ears are whooshing in time with his racing pulse. Beads of sweat roll down his back as the seconds tick by.

After a while, the train lurches and begins to glide away from the platform. Looking out of the window, Paddington starts to recede and, once they're clear of the station, Tom loudly exhales.

All eyes on him, he walks through the carriage towards the anonymity of lower-class travel. They're picking up speed. His heartrate had been slowing but it speeds up with the realisation that his ticket is on his phone and, in any case, no way will it be valid in the eyes of an eighties ticket collector. What happens if he's challenged? His cash is good for nothing. His mobile phone and wallet are his only possessions, and both are useless in this time frame. As things stand, he's destitute.

Fighting the urge to slump down into a seat – any seat would do – he leaves the carriage and works his way down the train hoping to find one that's crowded. The other carriages – still branded *second-class* not *standard* – aren't as busy as he'd hoped; the ticket collector will have no problem getting through. Whatever happens, staying onboard this train is his only hope.

Instinct tells him he needs to replicate the precise sequence of events that occurred earlier in the reverse order. Everything changed *after* they passed through the tunnel. Assuming he isn't crazy or in some kind of coma, that has to be where he passed through the time portal.

Tom's now fairly sure he's reached the same carriage he was in before and, thankfully, it's busy. He finds a seat with a good view of both doors and is close enough to the toilet for him to dodge into it while the tickets are being checked.

The carriage is sweltering and noisy in a different sort of way. Instead of talking on their phones, the people who aren't heads-down reading are chatting and laughing with their companions. Big hair is evident everywhere. The summer clothes they're all wearing seem so much more vibrant and stylish from his twenty-first century perspective.

Thirst and panic have parched his throat making it painful to swallow. What he wouldn't give for a sip of someone's drink. Not that he intends to ask. He almost wishes Corona woman would reappear.

Reading station should be their next stop – it's normally a half hour run out of London. If he's challenged about his ticket before then, they could throw him off the train there and he won't be on board when, or if, it goes back through that tunnel. His life – at least the one he wants back – depends on them not catching him before this train has left Reading station.

Outside is still a blur of urban decay. The carriage is super-heated from sitting in the greenhouse of Paddington. He uses his mother's scarf to mop the rivulets of sweat running into his eyes. It's the eighties – hell, he could roll the scarf up and tie it round his forehead as a bandana and not look out of place.

The train's picked up pace. They pass under a bridge with UP THE PROVOS scrawled across it. Aside from the usual obscenities, he notices the initials I R A sprayed on walls and gantries.

In the course of ten minutes a variety of swaying passengers walk past him balancing drinks and sandwiches – the lucky bastards. Every time either carriage door opens another waft of fried bacon permeates the air – it would make him drool if he had any moisture left in his mouth. He's finding it hard to sit still, his right foot keeps jiggling; he has to concentrate to make it stop.

The toilet sign shows it's free. Perhaps he should go in there and splash water on his face. Despite the warning notices about it not being drinking water, he'd be tempted to slurp a few handfuls just to alleviate the awful dryness in his throat.

Tom spots a pretty, dark-haired girl wearing headphones and it occurs to him he might not be the only time-traveller. When he follows the leads down, he can see she has a bulky cassette player sitting in her lap. This reminds him of his mum; she still uses her ancient Walkman to listen to taped music. Lump in his throat, he wonders if he'll ever see her again. In this time zone, his mum would be in her early twenties; younger than him. She could be sitting on this very train although that would seem an unlikely coincidence.

Tom can sense he's being watched. He catches the eye of a grey-haired woman and she quickly glances away as if she'd been studying him until that moment. Further along the carriage, a middle-aged man in a white shirt is glaring openly at him; not helped by the fact that he bears a strong resemblance to Liam Neeson in Taken.

Can people sense there's something off, something not right about him? Doing his best to adopt a nothing-to-see-here expression, Tom tries to shrink down into his seat. When he checks again, the Neeson lookalike is still staring at him, doesn't seem embarrassed to be caught out and meets his eye unblinking, as if to let him know he's been rumbled as an interloper. Tom gets that prickly feeling on the back of his neck; his palms, already sweaty, become more so.

He tries to stay calm. With no technology to distract them, it could be completely normal to stare at other passengers in this time. He takes stock of the other people in the carriage. The face of the man opposite Neeson is partly obscured by the newspaper he's holding. No head movement; he doesn't once turn the page. If it made any sense, he'd think he was under surveillance.

To avoid scrutiny – imaginary or otherwise – he's tempted to go and hide in the toilet but spending too long in there might create a queue, which would arouse more suspicion. Better to appear unconcerned and pretend an interest in the flat landscape they're travelling through. Leaning back in his seat, he tries to appear relaxed. Fields, houses, more fields, more houses; the ratio of the one to the other has changed a bit but otherwise suburbia looks the same as ever.

They break out into open countryside. Trees. A lake crowded with sailing boats. A few fair-weather clouds interrupt the endless blue of the sky. Cows are grazing; a cyclist negotiates a narrow bridge; someone up a ladder is fixing a roof – all glimpsed for a moment and then gone. As a child, he used to try to capture the very moment you're in the present. It's impossible. Some argue we live only in the past.

Fields give way to urban sprawl; they're entering a built-up zone. An announcement declares they'll shortly be arriving in Reading. The end door opens and a man in a peaked cap enters.

'Tickets please, ladies and gentlemen.' People are searching their pockets and handbags. The ticket man's progress along the first couple of rows is swift and efficient but, thankfully, there's something amiss with Walkman girl's ticket. A discussion follows. With the man distracted by this pretty customer, Tom makes his move.

Exiting the carriage, he darts into the nearest empty toilet cubicle and locks the door. A further announcement reminds passengers they're approaching the station and, right on cue, the train begins to slow. People are talking outside his door as they wait to get off. Tom tries the water dispenser. A dribble comes out and then nothing. Brakes squealing, the train judders as they come to a halt.

Closing the lid, he sits down to wait. And wait. Time drags on – or maybe only his perception of time. Does time get warped as you approach a portal? If so, this apparent delay could be a good sign.

A bored voice announces, *Ladies and gentlemen. On behalf of British Rail, I apologise for the delay; we're currently being held at a red signal. It's not clear what the problem is but we hope to be on our way again very shortly.*

Inside the tiny cubicle, the air is unpleasantly tainted and so close it feels like the oxygen's rationed. Without thinking, Tom checks his phone. No signal – but then how could there be when there's no network yet?

Someone tries the door handle and curses. Anything could be causing this hold-up – even the train crew don't know if it's serious or not. If they don't get underway soon, he might just melt in here. When they finally force open the door, he'll be welded to the seat like Rodin's Thinker.

The door handle flicks up and down again, but the lock holds against the weight of a would-be intruder. An unseen hand rattles it several times then gives up. The train lurches and then, miraculously, they're moving again. Tom raises a clenched fist in triumph.

What next? With someone trying the handle once again, he can't stay in here. He hesitates before unbolting. 'About bloody time.' As soon as he steps outside, a man pushes past him so close he's almost propelled back into the toilet.

The vestibule is empty. He scans the wall, seeking the reassurance of that tiny pentangle etched into the surface. It's there.

How long did it take from when the train left the tunnel to when it arrived in Reading? At a guess he'd say twenty minutes – possibly twenty-five. It happened only a few hours ago and yet his memory is unreliable. He's standing next to the outside door. The incoming air dries the sweat on his face as he scans the landscape in search of a landmark. This whole thing is massive gamble. The scenery offers no clues as to where or when he is except that it's unfamiliar. He's travelled along the M4 corridor many times and, though buildings come and go, the contours of the land don't change. The shape of the hills, the ponds and woodland they're passing – all of it is new to him.

The grey-haired woman he noticed earlier vacates the other toilet. She gives Tom a long look before she turns and walks back into the carriage. The impatient man emerges from the other cubicle adjusting his fly; he strides past Tom to disappear into the same carriage.

All these comings and goings would be farcical if the situation wasn't so serious. If the sequence of events isn't precisely replicated, it might not work. Assuming the tunnel is the portal, he should stay exactly where he is – where he was – though possibly just a fraction nearer the toilet door.

Taking a step towards it, he almost collides with Walkman girl. 'Sorry,' they both say at the same time.

'Great, it's free,' she says as the train lurches. Plunged into darkness, Tom feels someone grab his arm like he's been arrested. He can't be certain whether he hears a long echoing scream or whether he imagines it.

Chapter Nine

Blind, Tom could be floating for all he knows. The only thing that's real is the tightening pressure on his arm – a pain that keeps bringing him back into himself.

They emerge with shocking suddenness into the daylight. It's a relief to find he's still on the same train with the hot wind hitting his face as they hurtle through the sunlit English countryside.

Walkman girl is gripping onto him like life itself. 'I thought that was never going to end,' she says releasing him. They both stare at the fiery red band on his upper arm. Over her head, he searches for clues to what year they're in. 'I'm really sorry about grabbing hold of you like that.' She strokes his arm – a gesture that seems over-familiar. Then she clears her throat and says, 'That flamin' tunnel frightened me half to death, what with the lights goin' out an all that. I was beginnin' to wonder if I'd died.' Her laugh is way too loud. If she would shut up for a minute, he might be able to focus a bit better. 'I was half expectin' one of them skeletons to pop up – you know, like when you're on a ghost train.'

'It's okay. It's fine – no worries.' Tom holds up a hand in an attempt to stop her talking.

She tucks a strand of her long hair behind her ear then clears her throat. 'I don't usually accost–'

'Really, it's not a problem.'

His eyes dart to find the tiny pentangle and there it is in the exact same spot. He's light-headed, a bit off-balance. The train sways and the girl totters into him again, her oversized handbag clouting his knee. 'Whoops!' Giggling, she pushes herself off from his chest. 'This train seems determined to throw us together, don't it?' Her blue eyes look up at him expectantly. Head still woozy, Tom doesn't trust his own stability.

'Anyway,' she says, her hand poised on the handle of the toilet door. ''Scuse me for a sec, I really need the khazi.'

'Wait!' He remembers the sequence. 'Sorry, I didn't mean to yell at you like that. It's just I think I ought to use the toilet now.'

'Too bad – I'm burstin'.' She's inside the cubicle, claiming her territory. He can't exactly drag her out of there. 'Don't worry, I won't be long.' Her smile might be flirtatious but she's quick to turn the lock, shutting him out.

His head clearing, he wonders if the whole toilet thing is irrelevant. Logically, the tunnel has to be the portal; now he's passed through it again, one way or the other, his fate's been decided.

He takes a tentative step towards the carriage and the door opens. Inside there's only a handful of passengers; no newspaper man, no Leeson-alike scowling at him. All good signs.

Partway down the aisle, an unfamiliar dark-haired man looks up and, yes – he's wearing a face mask. Several seats behind him, a black woman with magenta hair turns her head.

Above her floral mask, her curious dark eyes examine him. He takes his phone from his pocket. As soon as he turns it on, the screen tells him it's 2:15 and he has 4G. Hands on his head, he almost drops to his knees, beaming like a lottery winner because all is right in the world. He has 4G again!

Though he's never been religious, he offers up thanks to the universe for delivering him back where he belongs. When he opens his eyes, the black woman is making strange gestures at him; it takes him a second or two to realise that she's miming – reminding him to pull up his scarf.

Ignoring her for the moment, he pumps the air. He can't stop repeating, 'It worked. It worked.'

Behind him there's a strangled cry. Tom swivels round to see Walkman girl has her hand clamped to her mouth and is staring in the direction of the two men in surgical masks advancing towards her.

Oh shit!

'You didn't half make me jump,' she tells them, hand on chest. 'Coming out of the loo and seeing the two of you dressed like that right in front of me, it really–'

'Excuse me,' the shorter one says. 'Could you step back a little please?'

'What's goin' on?' she says. 'Are you two really doctors? I mean, if you're off to a fancy-dress party or summat, you need to get hold of a couple of white coats as well.'

'Very funny,' the taller one says. 'Can you see me laughing?'

The shorter man nudges his friend. 'No one can see anyone laughing in these things.'

Fortunately, her cut-off jeans and cotton blouse don't mark

the girl out as a time-traveller. 'Seriously,' she says, adjusting her expression to match. "As somebody bin taken ill or somethin'?'

Tom pulls up his scarf before he intervenes. 'Please excuse my friend here.' He takes her arm and, as far as the space will allow, steers her off to one side. 'She's only just arrived.'

'Oh hello, it's you again.' The girl shakes herself free. 'Why've you got that silly scarf wrapped round your mouth?' A look of panic crosses her face. 'You're kidding me – I mean this ain't a robbery, is it?'

'Quite the comedian, your girlfriend,' the taller one says, brushing past them both. Grey hair, grey eyes – there's something familiar about him. 'She'll be laughing on the other side of her face if they catch her.'

'If who catches me?'

The short one shakes his head. 'Spot fine of a hundred quid if the guard sees you like that. Would soon wipe the smile off that pretty face.' He follows his friend into the next carriage.

'Bullshit!' she shouts after them. Then turning to Tom, 'What the hell's he talkin' about? What's goin' on here? Mean to say, them two didn't act like they was doctors, so why was they wearin' masks? Don't tell me the three of you are plannin' to hold up this train cos I have to say, you don't seem like the Ronnie Biggs type to me.' She's too close again. 'So why have you've got that silly scarf round yer face? You got toothache or summat?'

'It's just a precaution.'

Her frown deepens. 'There hasn't been some sort of poisonous gas leak has there?' She's slipping into a home-counties' accent. 'What's going on?' When he doesn't immediately answer, she clamps her hand to her mouth.

'Those are good questions,' Tom says, finding it hard to supress a smile at the idea that his mum's scarf would protect him from deadly gas. He tries to lead her into the next carriage, but she refuses to budge. Softening his voice, he asks, 'What's your name?'

'Beth,' she mumbles through her hand. 'Has something awful leaked out?'

'And I'm Tom,' he says 'Tom Brookes.' He waves his arms in front of her in what he hopes is a calming manner but might look more like a man treading water. He can't talk to her with most of his face covered so he pulls his scarf down. 'So, Beth, um, first of all, there's no need to worry about the air – not as such. I can assure you it's not poisonous. You know I really think it would be best if the two of us sit down somewhere while I try to explain what's happened – not that it's likely to make a lot of sense to begin with. In fact, if I were you, I wouldn't believe any part of what I'm about to tell you...'

Eyes wide, through her fingers she asks, 'Has somebody on this train got some sort of deadly disease or something?'

'Mmm.' Tom purses his lips. 'I suppose it's possible they might have; though, statistically speaking, it's unlikely. I mean to say, it's a–'

Beth gasps as a man emerges from the carriage masked up and holding a one-sided conversation using the type of glowing Bluetooth earpiece favoured by city wankers.

Once he's out of earshot, Beth taps the side of her head and whispers. 'Must have a few bats in his belfry.'

'Hi,' a woman's voice this time from behind. Tom spins round. 'I'm on the train,' she says into her mask. 'Should be there by five at the latest. Yeah, okay – see you then. Bye.' Turning off her phone, she disappears into the toilet.

Beth leans into him. 'This disease, this illness or whatever you mentioned – does it make people talk to themselves?'

Before he can answer, a red-faced, bald-headed guard appears, his forehead beaded with sweat. Clearly a man on a mission, Tom wonders if the two men they spoke to have just tipped him off.

He pulls up his scarf leaving the guard to focus on Beth. 'I have to inform you, madam, that there's now a statutory fine of one hundred pounds for failure to wear a face-covering on board a train–'

'You what?'

Tom holds up a hand in what he hopes is an authoritative manner. 'Yes, but the thing is, Beth here is actually exempt from that requirement.'

The guard looks unconvinced. 'And why would that be, sir, if you don't mind me asking?'

'Frankly, I do – *we* do mind you asking. I think you'll find it's discriminatory.'

The man's stance alters – chest a little deflated, he steps back as far as the space allows. Making good on his advantage, Tom says, 'If you must know, this young lady is exempt on mental health grounds. I'm sure there's no need for me to elaborate further.'

Beth frowns. 'I don't know what the hell's goin' on around here, but I can speak for meself, thank you very much.'

'I'm so sorry to distress you. A shame it was necessary to mention your mental health issues in public like this.' Tom gives her a long look then turns to the guard.

Hands on hips she says, 'Are you tryin' to make out I'm some sort of a loony?'

'As you see, this poor young woman is in a state of distress—'

'Who wouldn't be with him threatenin' to fine me a week's wages for no good bleedin' reason?' She's back in full East-Enders mode. 'If you ask me, I seem to be the only one around here who hasn't gone completely King Lear. There's people on this train talkin' to themselves and wonderin' around like they're fuckin' extras out of Angels.'

The guard is back on his high horse. 'I have to inform you, miss, that GWR do not tolerate the use of offensive language when addressing a member of staff. Furthermore, you yourself have admitted that you don't qualify as exempt from the need to wear a face covering. On that basis—'

'Wait. Listen,' Tom says resisting the urge to rest his hand on the man's shoulder. 'I'm sure you've had a long hot day, sir, and the last thing you need is having to deal with a couple of stroppy customers when there's a cold beer at home with your name on it.'

For a second the tip of the guard's tongue emerges; he doesn't quite lick his lips. Tom presses on. 'What if the two of us apologise for any offence caused and offer to get off at the next stop – which is?'

'Upper Threshing.' The guard looks at his watch. 'We'll be arriving in about four minutes. In fact, I need to make the announcement.'

'Okay – so you have a pressing task to get on with. My friend and I sincerely apologise and we promise we'll get off at the next stop without any fuss or bother.' He figures the girl can catch the return train once he's had a chance to explain her situation to her. 'This poor girl can't afford to pay a hefty fine like that.' He gives her a hard stare. 'Isn't that right Beth?'

'Not a chance,' she says. 'Think I'm made of bloody money?' He'd been bullshitting the guard but the way her accent keeps shifting suggests she might genuinely be suffering from some sort of multiple personality disorder.

The guard hasn't moved. 'The young lady's language may have been a little colourful just now,' Tom says, 'but she means no offence by it, do you?'

'Oh, right – pardon my French because that's what's really important here. What the–'

'Of course, she'd rather get off this train than pay a fine she can't afford.' Tom gives her another hard stare.

Faced with the guard's stony expression, she climbs down. 'Yeah – okay, it's like he said.' She jerks a thumb towards Tom. 'I was just feelin' distressed an' all that.'

The guard's nod is almost imperceptible. 'Don't either of you try to sneak back on board.' He points a finger at the girl. 'I'll be keeping my eye on you, missy, so no funny business.'

'Agreed,' Tom says.

'Yeah, okay.' Beth holds up both hands. 'Though I don't know what we're meant to do once we get to this Upper What's-its-face.'

The guard shrugs. 'Fortunately, that's not my problem.' With a satisfied smile, he walks away.

Chapter Ten

The guard's gone on his way but Beth continues to shake her head. 'Let me get this straight, I'm being booted off this train for no good reason. The whole thing with those stupid masks – it doesn't make any sense.' And now she's posh again. 'It's as if everyone is suddenly speaking a language I can't understand.' A catch in her throat. 'Feels like I've just fallen down the rabbit hole.'

Tom's about to compare it to entering The Matrix but then thinks better of it. Wrong era: wrong message.

She's understandably distressed. 'I'm supposed to be staying with my Aunty Joan tonight – she's expecting me. And I've never even heard of this stupid place I'm being forced to get off at.'

'Upper Threshing.' Tom does his best to sound upbeat. 'It's actually a rather pretty Cotswold village; all honeyed stone and that sort of thing. I've caught the train there a couple of times. The station's a little gem; one of Brunel's in actual fact.' Is he a fucking travel guide now?

'Great, so once you're done admiring the buildings and the landscape, what the hell am I going to do? How am I supposed to get to Cheltenham now?'

The guard's announcement prevents Tom from answering – that and the fact that he has no idea how he's going to break the news to her that her Aunty Joan is, in all probability, long dead.

His sigh is long and heartfelt. The girl wants answers but how to begin. 'I can actually explain all this.' He waves both arms in a pope-like gesture. 'At least, I'll do my best to account for what's happened – what's still happening. I promise I'll tell you everything I know once we're off this train.' He'll need to find somewhere private to break the news in case she freaks out.

The rhythm of the train alters as they begin to slow. When they enter another tunnel, Beth yelps. The lights stay on this time. She's making a strange noise in her throat that reminds him of a wounded squirrel his mother once tried to save. To calm her, Tom ventures an arm around her shoulders and, this time, she doesn't shrug him off. 'Everything will be fine,' he tells her with more conviction than is warranted. 'This tunnel's only a short one – we're coming out of it already. There's day-light at the end – see for yourself.' An apt metaphor, he hopes.

She relaxes against him. He says, 'I'm here for you,' a hackneyed phrase he's instantly ashamed of. He tries again. 'I'm here to help.' Now he's in customer services. How do you choose the right tone to break the news to someone that they've inadvertently travelled forward in time about forty years and, what's more, they've arrived in the middle of a global pandemic?

A skinny masked man pushes past them wheeling a large suitcase. Beth has nothing to say about him or his bad manners. Her earlier feistiness gone, she's subdued; possibly close to tears.

The skinny man clears his throat and turns his eyes on Tom in a way that suggests he's holding him fully responsible for the distressed state the girl's in.

Earlier, she'd said something about the two of them having been thrown together. Tom's reluctant to call it fate but what the hell does he know about anything anymore? The temperature must be thirty plus and she's shivering, which can't be a good sign. She's slim to the point of skinny; a lost teenager. He's the only one in the world with any understanding of the enormity of what she's about to face. Whatever happens, he has to help her.

The train comes to an abrupt stop and the physical jolt rouses the girl. 'What about my shopping bag? It's back there in the carriage.' Fresh alarm in her eyes, she turns ready to retrieve it.

'Never mind that now.' Tom steers her by the elbow with some force. 'We need to get off this train.'

'But–'

'It won't be there anymore; you've already lost it. Trust me, Beth, there's no chance of you getting it back now.'

With a head start, the skinny man and his suitcase are off and striding towards the exit. The pressure Tom's putting on her elbow means the girl has little choice but to jump down onto the platform with him right behind her. He checks both ends of the train, half expecting to see his imagined surveillance team disembarking along with them. No one else gets off.

Not daring to let go of the girl, he says, 'We need to step back behind the yellow line and let the train get on its way.'

'How do you know my stuff's not in there?'

'I just do. Listen, Beth – that guard is probably watching us right now.' With the train about to pull out, he leads her over to the nearest bench to watch it depart. Picking up speed, it rounds the bend and disappears, trailing its noise and a cloud of diesel fumes.

The sudden absence of sound and movement is unnerving. He pulls down his scarf so she can see his whole face. Aside from the country air, he can smell the fresh paint someone has used to pick out the flowers around the top of the green metal pillars holding up the canopy. He checks the announcement board in order to get some idea of when the train might arrive here on its return journey. It's completely blank.

Looking around, he sees nothing to alarm the unwitting time-traveller – no obvious giveaways they're in the twenty-first century. At any time during the last fifty odd years, the two of them could be sitting in this station exactly like they are now.

The enormity of what he's about to tell her weighs on him. The poor girl seems to be suffering from some sort of an identity disorder; the shock of all this might tip her over the edge. Perhaps he should put it off for a little bit – drip feed the information rather than come straight out with the whole thing.

He's been trying not to notice how shapely her bare legs are. Nicely tanned too. Instead, he concentrates on her face. She's really pretty – of course he'd noticed that in the carriage.

Although she's overdone the eye makeup, this close and in better light, he can't help admiring the contours of her cheeks, the band of freckles across the bridge of her nose.

'You said you'd explain, so tell me – what was all that business on the train?'

'A good question,' he admits.

'Yes, you said that before; several times in fact. You more or less manhandled me off that train on the promise that you would explain everything.'

'I did, didn't I.'

'So, come on, out with it. For a start, tell me why they were all wearing masks.'

'That must have been quite a shock. I imagine …' Bloody hell – he can't think where this sentence is heading; he can't even look her in the eyes anymore. Why does he feel guilty? None of this is his fault – at least he doesn't think it is.

When a buzzard's plaintive cry draws his attention, he looks up to see the bird circling over the station. She nudges him. 'Go on then.'

'Okay, um, the thing is, Beth.' He clears his throat. 'The thing is, there's this virus that's a bit like flu. In fact, on a microscopic level it's generally depicted as a round, greyish-green ball with red spikes – for illustrative purposes.'

She's tilting her head in the same way his mum does when he's struggling to get to the point. 'Anyway, the virus – well it's pretty nasty and, you know, it's really doing the rounds. So, the government's decided we all need to cover our faces – wear masks, scarves or whatever; just like people did in the 1918 flu pandemic – although obviously that killed around fifty million people worldwide.' Now she's looking scared; he's not exactly striking the right note here. 'Don't worry, this virus isn't as bad as that. In any event, we now have to wear a mask or some kind of face-covering when we're on trains or in crowded places to help prevent potentially infected people spreading it to others.'

'Really?' She narrows her eyes in suspicion. 'Then how come this is the first I've heard of any of this? There's been nothing in the newspapers or on the telly.' Her eyebrows come together in disbelief. 'Not one single person was wearing a mask when I got on the train in Paddington; then all of a sudden everyone was. Explain that.'

'You see, that's another –'

'Let me guess, *good question*.' She jumps when a swallow skims their heads to land on a nest built in the eves of the awning above them.

'Look at that,' Tom says, seizing the distraction. 'You can see the chicks in the nest peeking out. Look how their little yellow beaks are open ready to be fed. I can count four. No, maybe five. They jostling to be–'

'For God sake!' This time she grabs his shoulders and turns him around to face her. 'Don't go all Attenborough on me. I want to know more about this virus. Just how deadly is it?' She clutches at her face. 'I wasn't wearing a mask on the train; am I'm going to catch it?'

'That's highly unlikely,' he says, in what he hopes is a confident tone. 'For a start, everyone else had a mask on, so that would have protected you from getting the bug if they were carrying it – which is fairly unlikely.' Another thought. 'This may sound a bit odd,' he says, 'but how old are you?'

'What's that got to do with anything?'

'It's just that typically, when younger people catch this virus it's a really mild illness. Quite often they're asymptomatic. That means they have no symptoms; often they don't even know that they've got it.' He's now a public health announcement.

"Oh right. Well that's good,' she says. 'I'm going to be twenty in a couple of days.' When she smiles her face is transformed. 'That's actually why I'm going to see my aunty. My mum's taken herself off goodness knows where on a quest to discover her *real self.*' Beth gives the words air quotes. 'If she travels far enough, she's hoping to find a less shitty version of herself.' Tom smirks then straightens his face in case he's being insensitive. 'So, my Aunty Joan's all the family I've got really.'

'Right, well, like I explained, at your age, you'd probably be absolutely fine if you were to get this virus.' His confident grin begins to flag when it occurs to him that, biologically speaking, she must be nearer sixty than twenty. Her skin is smooth and unblemished – he scrutinises it for signs of impending wrinkles. Is she going to transform from a young beauty into an old bag before his eyes?

'What's wrong?' she asks. 'Why are you staring at me like that?'

'Like what?' He shuts his eyes, tries to dismiss the old and wrinkly version of her forming in his head. Following the same logic, hadn't he arrived in Paddington well before he was born? He hadn't immediately shrivelled up into an egg and been transported back into his mother's ovary. Or shrunk down to a sperm in some unknown bloke's testicles. To be accurate to the time, he should have been in both places at once. Back to the whole superposition idea.

Tom shakes himself. 'Right. So anyway…' The situation, his explanation, is getting away from him. He'd made a promise to tell her everything, but the next part is bound to upset her. Blow her mind as they used to say in the eighties – or was that the seventies?

A demonstration might be a more effective way of breaking the news. He looks up hoping the electronic arrivals and departure screen will come to his aid, but it's still blank. Inspiration strikes; he gets out his mobile phone. 'See this thing,' he says turning it on. 'Believe it or not this little device is a small telephone that doesn't need any wires. Using this, I can talk to anyone in the world right here, right now.' He jiggles it from side to side like a salesman. 'All I have to do is dial using these numbers on the screen here.' He can't recall anyone's number. 'That's not half of it,' he says. 'I can look up anything I want to know instantaneously just by typing a question into this little box up here.'

'And this is where Scotty beams you up to the Enterprise.'

She stands up, tucks her bulging handbag under her arm and says, 'Now I know you're just takin' the piss.'

Oh great – she's a cockney again. 'Wait a second,' he says before she can walk off – though goodness knows where to. Done with him, she takes no notice.

Chapter Eleven

Beth

She has no idea where she's heading – just away from him and all his nonsense. What an idiot she'd been to take a complete stranger at his word; to have allowed him and that ticket collector to bamboozle her into getting off the train here in the back of bloody beyond.

The little toe on her right foot is really hurting; Rach's sandal has rubbed it raw. She needs to put a plaster on it before it gets any worse. More importantly, she needs to call her aunty and explain she's going to be later than expected. She can't see a phone box but this is a train station; there's bound to be one around here as well as a timetable.

Drawing a blank, her best bet is to head for the main entrance, which, according to the finger post, is over the other side of the footbridge. If there's a bus stop handy, that might be an alternative way of getting to Cheltenham.

Damn, he's hurrying after her. 'Let me prove it to you.'

She speeds up. The footbridge steps are quite steep and it's difficult to hurry in her stupid shoes.

How had she let herself be taken in by him? On the train he seemed to be the only one on her side against that ticket man. Fancy demanding a hundred pound off someone just because they hadn't got a scarf tied round their face. If she's honest, she'd been a bit taken with Tom and those brooding good looks of his. For brooding, read weirdo. Why hadn't she noticed he was sky high on something? What sort of idiot would believe all his nonsense?

Like a dog on a scent, he's right behind her. Rachel calls men like him Klingons because they cling on to anyone stupid enough not to walk away in the first place. 'Starboard bow' was their code word for his type. She mutters it under her breath.

Apart from the two of them, there's not a soul around. As Lexi, she feels bolder, more certain of herself. Getting back into character, she turns her head and shouts, 'Bugger off, will ya?'

He keeps coming.

She stops. Lexi would stand her ground, confront him face-to-face instead of scurrying away. Turning all the way round, she tells him straight, 'Just piss off and leave me alone.'

'Wait. Please, I need you to listen to me just for a minute.' He tries to touch her but she snatches her arm away. 'Please, Beth, don't walk away.'

Ignoring him, she does just that, hating the way he sounds like a spurned lover. Like Kyle after she'd told him it was over. It was awful watching someone she'd once cared for reduced to begging. Where was his pride? His whining and pleading had demeaned them both.

Reaching the bridge, Beth glances back. He's only a yard

or two behind. 'Watch me,' he says, waving his stupid little gadget at her. 'I'll ring my mum right now. I'll demonstrate that –'

'Give it up, will ya?' she shouts over her shoulder, her accent wobbling under the strain. There's no one else around; she's beginning to feel afraid. When she breaks into a run, she hears his footsteps matching hers as they clatter down the steps.

Once they're on the other platform, he takes advantage of the extra space to overtake her. Walking backwards, he keeps pace with her as she heads towards the entrance. She carries on, does her best to show him she's not going to be intimidated.

When she emerges from the archway, he's already there blocking her way. She sidesteps him. There's no bloody time-table anywhere. Shading her eyes, she looks to her right and sees only fields and cows. To her left there are more fields and more cows. Of course, there's no waiting taxi, in fact there's still no one about.

Right behind, he starts calling her name. She's beginning to be really afraid of him and his dogged persistence. What else might he be capable of? 'Why can't you just go away and leave me alone?' It comes out as a wail.

'I'm sorry but I can't.' Tom holds up his hands like a criminal surrendering. 'I need to make sure you're alright. And if you let me make this one phone call, I promise you'll hear my mum answer it. Or possibly the answer machine – not that that matters for demonstration purposes.'

At least he's stepped back a little. 'Sorry,' he repeats like a stuck record. 'The last thing I want is to frighten you.'

Sounding braver than she feels, she says, 'I'm not frightened of you.'

'I'm glad to hear it because, believe it or not, I'm only trying to help. Please, I need to show you that things aren't quite what they appear to be. I'll ring my mum from this phone right now. How about that?'

Calling his bluff is probably the only way she's going to shake him off. 'Okay then – show me what your magical little device can do.' Instantly, she regrets putting it like that.

The thing lights up as soon as he touches it. He prods at it several times and then frowns and says, 'Oh bugger.'

She can't help but smirk. 'Let me guess – it's not working.'

Shaking his head, he says, 'It is, but I've lost the bloody signal again.' He waves the thing in the air, does a little dance around while holding it at arm's length as if summoning up a spirit or a bolt of lightning. 'Shit, I nearly had it then, but it's disappeared again.'

Up ahead a church spire is sticking up through the trees and, just before the trees, there's a red phone box. Halleluiah! Marching towards it, she's ready to swing her handbag at Tom if he gets in her way again. Without missing a step, she checks her purse and finds enough change to make the call. On either side of her the picture-perfect cottages are smothered in roses of various colours. She can smell their combined scent.

When she gets to the phone box, she pulls open the door to find there's no phone inside. Instead, there are books – loads of them, whole shelves full along with a handwritten notice: *Community Library – all these books are free for residents to borrow.*

Where the phone ought to be there's only a cash tin labelled *Honesty Box,* which wouldn't last five seconds down the Goldhawk Road.

Tom is standing behind her with his arms crossed and an I-told-you-so expression. 'In a lot of villages they've converted these old phone boxes into things like this because they're redundant; these days everyone carries a mobile phone like mine.'

'Yeah, course they do,' she mutters. A muddy Land Rover passes forcing Tom onto the pavement. Beth's tempted to flag it down but there's a large windblown dog occupying the passenger seat and a massive container taking up the space in the open back. Besides, the pinch-faced bloke behind the wheel doesn't look too friendly. No point in swapping one weirdo for another.

This one's not giving up. 'When I used the words *these days* just now, I wasn't talking about the nineteen-eighties or even the nineteen-nineties.'

Set back from the village green and its war memorial, there's a pub. 'Oh really,' she says hardly listening, playing for time as she strides towards what must pass as civilisation in these parts.

'Listen to me, Beth.' He's alongside her – out in the road while she's on the pavement. From his earnest tone it's clear he must really believe all the crap he's spouting. 'I don't know how to tell you this, so I'll just come right out and say it.' He jumps up onto the pavement in front of her. 'The truth is, you've time-travelled to the year 2020, which I know is a lot to take in all at once.'

She has to step out into the road to get round him. Against her lack of response, he raises his voice and, arms outstretched, pirouettes like a character in a musical about to burst into song. 'This is the year 2020,' he declares. 'I promise it's true. You left the eighties behind back there in that tunnel – the long dark one that is, not the shorter one we went through afterwards. So, the thing is, if you want to return to your own time – which I imagine you do – it's vital that you catch the next train back to London. I think, though I'm not entirely sure about this part, it only happens if you're standing in the same place on that same train. The one we were on was called the Gustav Holst, so you'll have to check that before you get on.'

'Like the composer?' She's almost there now, can read the sign. *The Green Man* – the same name as the pub in The Wicker Man. Not a particularly good omen.

He shouts after her, 'I'm not sure when the next London train is due but once I get a decent signal, I'll be able to check that for you.'

There's a beer garden off to one side, groups of normal-looking people sitting at wooden tables under sunshades. A masked man comes out of the pub entrance carrying a tray of drinks. So, all that stuff about the killer decease – at least that part must be true.

Beth rushes up to the barman. 'Is there a pay phone here I can use?'

He shakes his head, aiming to walk on past her. 'Sorry, can't help you, love. I'm a bit rushed...'

'Please.' She steps into his path. 'I really need to find out about the next train to Cheltenham.'

The man considers. His shaved head is shiny with sweat. Tattoos cover his bare forearms. He must be an ex-sailor. She's distracted by one of his earlobes because it has a half-inch hole in it with a metal rim around the edge that reminds her of the peg-holes you get on tents. The other earlobe bristles with metal pins.

She takes a step backwards.

The waiter puts down his tray. 'If it's that urgent,' he says fishing for something in the pocket of his shorts, 'I'll look it up for you.' She stares at the thing in his hand. Just like Tom's, it lights up at his touch. After prodding it a few times he says, 'Bad news I'm afraid. The schedule has been suspended due to what they're calling unforeseen circumstances – which covers a multitude of sins.'

He holds the thing up to let her read for herself. Just as he said, the words are printed there in front of her eyes.

Timetable suspended due to unforeseen circumstances

'Oh, sweet Jesus,' she says, sitting down at an empty table.

Tom says, 'Could be some sort of a signalling fault.'

'Or a jumper… Lockdown … not been easy,' the barman adds.

While the two of them carry on chatting, Beth's eyes dart to the line of parked cars she'd walked straight past and hadn't really noticed. None of them looks like any car she's ever seen in her life.

'They usually say… a fatality on the line.'

'Good point,' the barman says. 'In any case, I don't think your friend will be catching a train to Cheltenham any time soon. If you folks want to order … you know the drill; I'll need a mobile number and your email address.'

'Understood,' Tom says sitting down beside her. 'I know it's a lot to take in at once, Beth.'

The barman picks up the tray of drinks she'd been staring at. 'Menu's on the blackboard over by the entrance,' he says. 'Monkfish is off I'm afraid and we've only got one portion of the venison pie left.'

'I can't believe it,' Beth says shaking her head. 'No, I refuse to believe it. You're lying to me.'

'Sorry to disappoint you,' the barman says. 'We've got just about everything else.'

He clears his throat. 'Why don't I give you two a few minutes to, um, decide?'

She grabs the man's forearm to prevent him from leaving. 'What year is this?'

'Is this some kind of joke?'

'Please,' she says, digging her fingers in. 'Just answer.'

She sees him glance at Tom before he shrugs. '2020,' he says. 'And before you ask, Boris Johnson is the Prime Minister – God help us.' Walking away he adds, 'Hope I passed the test, doc.'

Chapter Twelve

Tom

Beth's eyes have gone worryingly blank; like a switch has just been thrown and she's gone off-line. At least the pub's umbrella is shading them both from the fierceness of the sun. 'Listen,' Tom says, 'why don't I get you a drink? I know I could certainly do with one.'

No reaction.

He'd almost gone past hunger and thirst but now, watching other people eating and drinking, his stomach groans to remind him of its pressing need. Someone has left a half-eaten burger and chips on the empty table opposite and he's sorely tempted to snaffle it – although such an act must be verboten during a pandemic. Besides, now his money is valid again, he can order anything he likes – a glutton's feast if he wants. Where to begin – it's a heady thought.

The barman is fully occupied. Tom's not sure of the prevailing etiquette – is he allowed inside the pub to order or must he wait until they come to him? He guesses it's the latter. Best be ready then. Turning to Beth, he asks, 'So, um, what's your poison?' He's fairly confident people used to say that in her day.

She doesn't answer. Her face has taken on the greenish tinge of the sunshade.

When he was a kid, most of his Uncle Matt's anecdotes involved the comedy cockney line: *of course I'd had a few sher-bets...* Beth's in a state of shock, which is understandable. If *he* had just discovered it was 2060 with no obvious way back, he'd need something pretty strong to calm his nerves. Should he get her a treble whisky? She might prefer vodka. Or gin – he knows the rhyming slang for that. 'This must have been a shock,' he tells her. 'I expect you could do with a Vera Lynn.'

At least that makes her frown – which has to be a good sign. 'Why don't I get you a large one?' When she doesn't answer, he reaches for her hand, finds her fingers clammy to the touch although she doesn't pull away. 'Let me get you something to drink to steady your nerves.' Her nerves. Mmm, given her odd behaviour – her two distinct voices and all that – she could easily be on some sort of medication. Perhaps she shouldn't drink alcohol. 'I'm sure they can rustle you up a nice cup of tea,' he tells her.

A middle-aged woman sporting a see-through visor is heading their way. Armed with a clipboard, she says, 'Welcome to the Green Man.' And then, 'First things first, you need to sign in – new government regulations I'm afraid.' Given the angle of her visor and the wide gap underneath, it's probably directing her breath straight down at them both. Tom's tempt-ed to point this out but, right now, it's the least of his worries.

Once he's supplied the required information, he orders a

jug of tap water and a triple gin and tonic for himself. With an air of disapproval, the woman pulls an order pad from her pocket. 'Would you like to see our gin menu, sir?'

Tom shakes his head. 'I really don't care – anything will do. And some ice – ice would be great.'

'And what about the young lady?' A good question.

Raising her eyes, Beth finally speaks. 'A glass of wine; red if you've got it.'

'Cote du Rhone? Merlot? Malbec? Or if you like Spanish wines, we've got a lovely full-bodied Rioja…'

Dropping her head onto her arms, Beth groans.

'That last one – Rioja – that'll do,' Tom tells her.

'Would the young lady like a 125 millilitres glass or 175 millilitres–?'

'Just make it a really big one,' Tom says. 'Better still, bring a bottle. Oh – and some food. We're not fussy – we'd be happy with whatever's quickest.'

The woman looks at her watch. 'We're near the end of service but the chef should be able to rustle up a couple of ploughman's.'

'Perfect. Oh – and some chips would be great. Two bowls – big portions.'

Once he's gulped down a glass and a half of iced water, Tom feels a lot better. Beth has only taken a few sips from the water he poured her and now she's resting her chin on both hands, staring up at the splats of the umbrella. 'In this heat, you need to stay hydrated,' he tells her.

His own thirst quenched, Tom pours a tiny amount of

tonic into his gin and knocks half of it back in one go. His throat burns with it.

Beth is still off with the fairies. He leans forward to get her attention. 'Are you okay?' When she doesn't respond, he hesitates over the water and then pushes the wineglass towards her instead. 'A drop of this will make you feel better.'

'You like to give advice, don't you?' He's surprised by her slow smile. 'It's okay anyway because none of this is real.' She smirks. 'I've dreamt you up, along with this pub.' Picking up her wine, she begins to wave it around. 'You and this ridiculously perfect village and that fudge-coloured church over there. And the war memorial on the village green. I mean, they'll be dancing round a bloody maypole next.' There's no humour in her laugh. 'This is bullshit; the future would never look like this.'

'Well, we are a bit out-in-the-sticks. In Cheltenham, you'd soon notice a few more, umm, anachronisms. Although, of course, they're not exactly that because –'

'Shush! You talk far too much. I should have made you the sexy, silent type.' She takes a long drink of wine then wipes her mouth with the back of her hand. 'Tastes great but then I imagined it would.' Another substantial gulp, then, twirling a finger in the air, 'Demetrius has this line that keeps going round in my brain.' Her voice mutates again, 'It seems to me that yet we dream, we sleep.' She tops up her glass. 'Can't remember the rest but I expect it'll come back to me in a minute.'

He's not sure this is a positive development. She takes another long slurp of wine. 'That's from A Midsummer Night's

Dream, by the way. Can't think why I needed to tell you that given you're just a sprite yourself.' The glass is now dangling from her floppy hand; he worries she might release it to prove there's no gravity in her dream world. 'I played Titania at school and I was pretty damned good – though I say it myself.' Home counties seems to be the default accent.

Of course, the barman would choose that precise moment to arrive with their chips. He says, 'Ploughman's on their way.'

'And wearing smocks I expect.' Beth giggles. 'Can't imagine why I've made *him* look like *that*.' She gestures towards the barman. 'I mean, just look at him – so bloody weird with all those ugly tattoos crawling up his arms like some skin deformity. And then there's that bizarre hole in his ear...'

Tom stands up and takes the two baskets of chips from the man. 'Thanks a lot.' Under his breath he mutters, 'Ignore my friend. All that business with the trains being cancelled – it's stressed her out.' Lowering his voice even further, 'She suffers from Tourette's.'

'No worries.' The barman gives them both an understanding nod. 'Friend of mine has it. Always gets worse when he's under pressure.'

As soon as he's gone, Tom sits down and knocks back the remains of his drink. He grabs a handful of skinny chips and, showing admirable restraint, posts them a few at a time into his mouth until the worst of his hunger abates.

Beth picks up a chip but instead of eating it she jabs it towards him. 'I'm just wondering what you're going to suggest next.' She bites the head off the chip.

It's a fair question. When he doesn't answer, she grabs a few more fries and chews on them without breaking eye contact. She leans in and his eyes automatically dart to her cleavage. He shuts them – can't let himself be distracted in that way. 'One thing at a time,' he tells her. 'For now, let's just eat.'

The visor woman is heading their way carrying two loaded plates any ploughman would be amazed by. Glad of the distraction, it doesn't stop Tom from wondering what the hell he should do next. He can't put Beth on the train back to London like he'd planned. The two of them are more or less stranded here and, while she's still insisting this is a dream, there's no point in him suggesting how she might get back to her own time.

'Here we are then,' Visor woman says.

'Wow,' Beth exclaims, 'this is a bit more than bread with cheese.'

Looking smug, the woman tells them, 'The Yarg there – the one with the nettle rind – comes from Cornwall, Our Cheddar actually is from Cheddar and the soft blue is made locally…'

His mum might be prepared to come and pick them up; that's if he can persuade her the girl is in trouble and could need somewhere to stay overnight. This has the advantage of being true. And with luck, the wine will have done its work and Beth will be more cooperative by the time his mum gets here.

'Oh, and our chef pickles the shallots himself in balsamic vinegar with a few aromatics. It's his own recipe.'

'Seems a lot of trouble to go to when you can just buy them from any supermarket,' Beth says, picking up her knife. 'Good job we don't really have to pay for any of this.'

'She's just kidding,' he says. Behind her plastic shield, the woman gives him a knowing wink. The barman must have warned her. He's far too sober to deal with all this; with luck the effect of his triple gin will kick in fairly soon.

Chapter Thirteen

He watches Beth absentmindedly squirt several sachets of tomato ketchup onto her empty plate. She starts to doodle in it with the end of a chip – spreading the red blobs of liquid out in various arrays that begin to resemble a series of blood-splatters. Not the most encouraging of developments. There again, at least she's calm.

She finally eats the chip by increments, guinea pig-style. Then she selects a sachet of mustard, squeezes a blob onto the plate and, using another cold chip, draws an interlinking pattern. Hmm. He's not sure if he should try to talk to her out of her current delusion or leave her be.

Having demolished his own ploughman's and the unwanted remains of hers, he feels able to tackle their next problem – getting out of here. Better take himself off into the car park so she can't interrupt, though not so far that he can't keep an eye on her.

She doesn't say anything when he gets up. From fifty metres and with her long hair obscuring her face, he can't tell if she's even registered his absence.

Shit – along with ones from his mum and Steph, there are

several text messages from Davy. The final one reads: *Sorry mate - the job's gone. Snooze you lose and all that.*

Damn it – that was quick.

His mum picks up on the third ring. 'Hi, it's me,' he says trying his best to sound upbeat. When she doesn't speak, 'Can you hear me?'

No answer. She's obviously determined to not make this easy. 'I'm back,' he tells her. 'Well almost back. I'm currently in Upper Threshing, of all places. Standing outside the Green Man pub.'

'Is that all you have to say when I've been worried sick. Your friend Davy phoned here when you didn't show up. I wondered if you'd been in an accident – I even rang a few London hospitals, though, with this pandemic on, it went straight to a machine. Where the hell have you been all this time?'

Frowning, he decides not to make an issue of her absurd overreaction. 'Listen,' he says, 'it's a long story. I won't go into detail right now but, the thing is, I'm sort of marooned out here in the middle of nowhere.'

'I see.' Her voice sounds a bit echoey.

'So, anyway, Mum.' He crosses his fingers. 'I was wondering if you wouldn't mind, I mean, if you might be prepared to come and pick me up.'

'Let me get this straight – you go off to London having arranged to meet your friend. But you don't show up for that and, what's more, I don't hear from you for more than a week and now you're telling me you've come back again and you want me to drive halfway across the county to pick you up, despite the possible risk that would pose to my health.'

'Hold on a minute.' He rubs at his forehead. 'What's all this about me being gone for more than a week?'

'You're not seriously disputing the fact that you left here the week before last?'

He's walking in circles, trying to get his head around this new piece of information. 'Why don't we put that to one side for now,' he tells her. 'The point is, I just caught the train back. Well, back this far. We unfortunately had a bit of an altercation with the ticket collector and had to get off at the station here.'

'You said *we*. Who's we?'

'Ah yes.' He takes a deep breath. 'I'm with this girl. Someone I quite literally bumped into on the train.' He looks over and Beth is still doing a Jackson Pollock with the condiments. 'And, the thing is, Mum, this poor girl, she's in quite a state and has no one else to turn to. The trains aren't running – they're up the creek for some reason – so she's completely stranded. She's only nineteen. I'm sure you wouldn't want me to abandon her in the middle of nowhere all alone. I was hoping you might agree to let her stay the night at ours if need be. Just tonight. Tomorrow morning, when the trains are running again, I can drive her to the station, and she can catch the train back to London – where she belongs.'

'Why is this girl in *quite a state*, as you put it?'

'It's a bit hard to explain over the phone.'

'Do your best.'

'She's had a big shock. And, um, she's a bit disorientated at the moment. Listen, we can open all the car windows. I'll keep the scarf you lent me on and maybe you can bring another one for Beth.'

'Why hasn't this Beth got her own face covering? She was on a train after all.'

The heat is beating down on his back. 'I don't know – I expect she dropped it. Or maybe it got caught by the breeze and flew out of the window or something. Anyway, we can both sleep well away from you. Not together, obviously. She can have my bed and I'll sleep om the sofa in the snug. I'll use my sleeping bag.'

'I gave that old thing to a charity shop years ago. You never used it and the mice had been at it.'

'Doesn't matter. It's so damned hot I won't need it.'

She's silent.

'I'm really sorry you were so worried, Mum,' he says. 'Things – well, they just happened. All of it was completely beyond my control but I'm so glad I've made it back. I know this is a big favour and I wouldn't be asking but, I'm at my wits' end and I really need your help. Please, Mum.'

There's a beat before she says, 'I'm standing in the checkout queue. In this heat, I'll need to get the frozen stuff back home before it all defrosts. After that, it'll probably take me at least half an hour along the back lanes. There are so many cyclists out and about these days. Anyway, at a guess, I'll probably be there just after four o'clock. Make sure you're outside the pub.'

'Will do. And thanks, Mum. I really appreciate –'

'While you're waiting, you could take this girl for a stroll along the riverbank there. Being in nature often helps to calm people down. As I recall, it's rather a pretty walk.'

'Good idea,' he says before she hangs up.

He sends Davy a quick message: *Really sorry for the no-show and everything, mate. Long story…*

'You again.' Beth rolls her eyes at him. 'I might have made you easy on the eye, but you've got way too much dialogue.'

He pulls out his debit card and, with a nod, waves it to get the attention of the visor woman. They're amongst the last to leave so she's quick with the bill. 'Hope you enjoyed your meal,' she says. He tries not to show how shocked he is by the grand total. 'As it's over the forty-five pounds limit, you'll need to enter your pin,' the woman tells him.

Beth scoffs. 'You're kidding me. Over forty-five pounds for fancy bread and cheese and a bottle of wine. That's the best joke yet.' She picks up the bottle which is still about a third full. 'At that price, I know what I'm having for afters.' She tucks it under her arm.

The woman makes no further comment while they complete the transaction. 'Enjoy the rest of your day,' she says retreating into the pub.

'Right.' Tom slaps his thigh for no good reason. 'I was thinking we might go for a quick stroll along the riverbank, if you're up for it.' He's swinging his arms like a man about to dive. 'I promise I'll keep my utterances to a minimum.'

Beth stands up. 'That's the whole problem with you,' she says, 'you're too damned wordy. No one uses words like *utterances* in normal conversation.' She leans forward on unsteady feet. He can smell the wine on her breath.

He could take issue with the fact that this is a normal conversation. Instead, he mimes a zip across his mouth, turns himself sideways and, with a slight bow, holds out a hand like a courtier to usher her in the direction the footpath sign.

'Much better,' she says, walking past him. She veers off to one side and then over-corrects herself with a giggle. Hmm, maybe getting the girl pissed before taking her for a walk by a river isn't such a clever combination.

Too late; she's setting quite a pace; he has to hurry to keep up. Before his mum picks them up, Beth needs to accept this is the twenty-first century. He hates charades at the best of times and this is most definitely not the best of times. She doesn't want him to speak but there's no way to mime the fact she's currently trapped in 2020 and has no chance of getting back to her own time unless she accepts his help.

He can hear the rush of water before the river itself comes into view. Channelled by low stone walls on either side, sunlight is bouncing off the surface. The water is flowing around a series of ancient stepping-stones leading to the other bank. Some mallards with their pale-yellow ducklings are making Vs in the water as they swim towards them hoping for crumbs. On the shadier side, a swan sails past unconcerned.

Bottle in hand, Beth hops from one stone to the next. 'This is fun. Like hopscotch.' He hardly dares to look as she wobbles on one foot, arms outstretched. The water's not very deep but it's enough to give her a shock if she falls in. Landing on that bottle would be far more serious. A final leap, she makes it to the other bank and he can breathe again. 'Come on, slow-coach, keep up,' she shouts across.

Once they're both on the same side, he follows her. The path is fringed by a line of weeping willows; it's a relief to enter their shade. An elderly dog walker stands well back to allow them to pass. Beth bends down ready to make a fuss of his wet, tail-wagging dog – some kind of poodle cross. 'Don't touch him,' the man yells. He yanks on the lead to bring the dog to heel.

'Why not?' She straightens up. 'Has it got fleas or something?'

'Covid is no laughing matter; not at my age.' The man forges a path through the long grass to escape them.

'Who's covid?' she says turning to him. He points to his closed mouth, holds up both hands and shrugs. 'You're allowed to answer my questions,' she tells him.

There's a bench under the willows facing the water. He leads her towards it, sits down and pats the seat next to him. She sits, unscrews her bottle and takes a swig before offering it to him. He shakes his head. Whilst she's distracted by the cuteness of a moorhen chick, he pours some of the wine onto the ground where it disappears into the cracks.

'Covid is the name of the disease I told you about – the one currently sweeping the globe killing thousands of people. It's called Covid 19 because it emerged at the end of 2019. Unlike more or less every citizen on this planet, you haven't heard of it because you've only just arrived here from the 1980s.'

'That's enough.'

Before she can move away, he grabs her hand and squeezes it. 'You can feel that,' he says. 'If I were to pinch you, it would hurt because you're awake – I guarantee it.'

'Go on then.' The willows have turned her face a shade of green. 'Pinch me as hard as you can.'

Chapter Fourteen

Beth

She hardly feels his pinch. 'Do it again,' she tells him, but he refuses to press any harder. And now the mark he made is fading. If she's imagining all this, would there be a mark? She can't decide and so she stares at the water flowing endlessly past them. On the opposite bank a fringe of green weed trails in the current.

She's always enjoyed the sound of running water. A hard thing to describe. Gurgling? Tinkling? It can lull you to sleep that sound – but then she's already asleep. She recalls that famous saying – some Greek philosopher, she's forgotten who – about how you can't step into the same river twice because the river wouldn't be the same and neither would the man. It's always about man, never woman. One small step for man hasn't proved much of a giant leap for womankind.

She's only half listening to the man currently sitting next to her. Tom. What was his last name? Did it begin with a B or a D? It's easier to let him have his say, though the cool promise of the water draws her attention away. She'd like to paddle in it, feel it flow around her ankles and feet – soothing the blister on her toe. If she were to step in and out of it and then do it again, wouldn't she still be her same self?

An interesting experiment. Okay, her balance is a bit unreliable at the moment; she'd be more than likely to fall arse over tit, as Lexi would say. She'd forgotten about *her* – about Lexi; about trying to be her for a day, which is too much effort. At least for now.

Bottle to her lips, she drains it of the last drops hoping to delay the point where her hangover will kick in. He – this Tom person – is saying something about how she'd grabbed his arm. And then something else about portholes – which they don't even have on trains so it's hard to work out where they come into things. He's especially proud of that silly device of his, keen to show her his vision of the *brave new world* she'd stumbled into on that train.

Upstream, some children are playing in the water – splashing each other and screaming in their excitement. The littlest one is on the bank alongside his mum, trying to throw breadcrumbs overarm to the flurry of ducks squabbling for it. She'd read somewhere that the collective noun is a badling of ducks – or did she just make that up?

'We're in the second decade of the twenty-first century,' Tom says, though it would be easier to believe she's gone *back* in time. With her eyes closed, the drone of his voice, the shrieks of children, the running water – it all begins to merge together.

Tom is shaking her arm, urging her to wake up now because his mother has apparently just sent him a message through the ether on his marvellous little device. 'She'll be here in ten minutes. Do you remember I told you she's going to give us a lift?'

'Is she taking us to Cheltenham?'

'Not right away,' he says.

She's not sure about all this. Besides, it's cool under the willows and she can't be bothered to move, never mind meet his mother. 'No need to pull that face,' he says. 'My mum's nice; you'll like her. The two of you will have a lot in common.' He laughs. 'After all, you're practically the same vintage.'

He won't shut up. 'You don't want to be stuck here for ever, do you, Beth?' It's a good question. 'Listen, Beth…' He's using her name too often, like salesmen do when they're trying to persuade you to buy something. It's a shock when he grabs hold of her shoulders, pins her so she can't look away. 'I can't leave you here by yourself. It wouldn't be safe.' And then, 'You need to come with me now.'

It's the path of least hassle though she trails behind hoping he might just forget about her. When he stops dead, she almost collides with him. 'Oh, and by the way, I think it might be better if you don't tell my mum where you're from.'

'What's wrong with Shepherd's Bush?'

'I mean the era – the eighties. Or the fact that you've just time-travelled here. She wouldn't understand.'

'She's not the only one.'

With the pub in sight, he begins to wave his arms above his head like he's signalling to an aircraft or a drowning man hoping to be rescued.

A middle-aged woman climbs out of a dusty car. Mostly grey-haired, she's wearing a pretty red and white shirt above tightish denim jeans. Not a very motherly outfit to conjure up.

The woman shields her eyes with her hand as they walk towards her. 'Hi, Mum,' Tom says. 'Thanks for doing this. You're a lifesaver.' When he steps forward to hug her, a raised hand forbids him to come any closer.

He steps back, then turns and says, 'This is Beth, by the way. The girl I told you about.'

'I guessed as much,' the woman says. 'Hello, Beth.' Her nod isn't especially welcoming.

Remembering her manners, Beth says, I'm Beth Sawyer. It's nice to meet you, Mrs… um.'

'Brookes – if we're being formal.' A smile softens her face for a moment. 'Why don't you call me Lana instead?'

'Oh – that's a really pretty name. Like Lana Turner.'

Tom clears his throat. 'Or like, um, Lana Del Rey – the singer.'

Beth frowns. 'Who?'

'You've heard of her; everybody of our age has. Good voice and all that but her songs are a bit gloomy and melodramatic. *Born to Die* is my favourite though, *Summertime Sadness* is pretty good. As you might guess, they're not exactly upbeat numbers and –'

'I think we get the picture, Tom,' his mum tells him. This

time she doesn't smile. He's really in the doghouse for some reason.

The word Golf is pinned on the back of the car as well as a VW badge. It doesn't look at all like the Golf Lewi has. Opening the driver's door, Lana leans across to fish amongst the junk in the passenger seat. She pulls out a tiny flower-patterned hammock and holds it out to Beth. 'This is for you.' She's stretching her arm so that she doesn't have to come any closer. 'You'll need to put this on in my car,' she says. 'Bit of luck that the WI in the village are selling these.'

It looks like a doll's sanitary towel; she's not sure exactly what to do with it.

'The loops are for your ears,' Tom whispers.

Lana says, 'Make sure you cover your nose as well as your mouth.'

Beth adjusts the mask as best she can. Her trapped breath is making her face hot; she can smell the wine on her breath. Would she dream all these details? Seems unlikely, but then all of this seems unlikely.

Lana turns to Tom. 'No rucksack? Let me guess, you lost it somewhere.'

'Not exactly,' he says. 'Misplaced is more accurate. It's a long story.'

'Yours usually are.' Lana sighs. 'Make sure you pull that scarf up. The two of you can sit in the back. And please don't close the windows.' Why would they do such a thing when it's so damned hot?

Lana has more to say. 'You've had me worried sick, Tom. I'd begun to think something dreadful must have happened to you. Why didn't you phone me? Or a simple text would have done.'

'I'm sorry,' he tells her. 'My phone wasn't working.'

'And yet, miraculously, it appears to be fully functional now.' She puts her own mask on, climbs into the driver's seat, slams the door and starts the engine. 'Of all the lame excuses.'

They get in the back. Dog hairs are clinging to the blanket draped over the back of the passenger seat. Beth can smell the absent mutt. Tom puts his seatbelt on and nudges her to do the same. The leather seat is sticking to her bare legs like Velcro. Tom leans across to whisper, 'Her bark's much worse than her bite.' Does he mean the dog or his mum?

They rattle along some very narrow lanes; the car juddering every time it hits one of the many potholes. A chewed rubber ball keeps rolling around in the footwell between her feet. It feels like she's been kidnapped. Raising her voice to be sure it carries to the front she says, 'I need to get to Cheltenham. My Aunty Joan is expecting me – she'll be worried if I don't show up soon.'

'Sorry, I can't hear what you're saying through that mask,' Lana yells back. She swerves around a cyclist, throwing Beth against Tom before she swings them back to avoid an oncoming car.

Beth keeps it simple. 'I said I need to get to Cheltenham.'

'But Tom says you're off back to London in the morning,' Lana yells back.

'No, I'm going to *Cheltenham*,' she tells her. 'If it's too far, you can drop me at a bus stop.' Along with her rising panic, Beth's head is beginning to ache. What the hell was she thinking getting into this car with these two complete strangers? They could be taking her almost anywhere.

'The bus shelters around here are for decorative purposes only,' Lana shouts back over her shoulder. 'A bus sometimes deigns to appear once or twice a week at the best of times; and, as we all know, these aren't the best of times.'

'Funny your name being Sawyer when mine's Tom,' he says. When she doesn't respond he adds, 'You know like in –'

'I get it,' she tells him. 'The Mark Twain character.'

'Exactly.' Lowering his voice, Tom says, 'There's no point in you going to Cheltenham, not now. Remember, I explained all that. I know it's a lot to take in – believe me, I understand.' He strokes the air in front of her like he's calming an invisible cat. 'For now, Mum is taking us both back to her house.'

Reaching a straight bit, Lana puts her foot down and Beth's head makes contract with the headrest. That cloying doggy smell, the sticky seats, the blare of car horns – it's all so real. Too real. She's not dreaming any of this. Beth shuts her eyes and prays this isn't how she's going to die.

And now she's beginning to feel nauseous; in fact, she realises she might be about to throw up. They're going too fast for her to jump out. She yells, 'I think I'm going to be sick.' She can taste the wine, the chips and tomato sauce… She starts to heave, rips the mask off to clamp a hand over her mouth instead. She could lean out through the open window, but it might all blow back in her face. The thought of that makes her heave again.

They've slowed down to walking pace to pass a horse and rider. Beth tries the door, but it won't open. 'Child locks,' Tom says. 'You look awful…Mum, you need to pull over right now.'

Lana yells back, 'Why – what's wrong?'

'Just do it,' he shouts. 'Stop the bloody car.'

Despite the heat, she's shivering – her teeth chattering cartoon-style. She's embarrassed by the smell rising from the red splashes on the grass verge; it's like looking down at a murder scene. Staring at the ground beneath her feet, she's mortified to see two pairs of feet are right behind her.

'I promise you she's not ill, as such,' Tom says, '… just had a bit too much to drink. My fault … I suppose. I thought a few glasses of wine would calm her down… I guess she overdid it a bit.'

'Getting the poor girl sloshed was hardly going to help.' A hand gives her shoulder a gentle squeeze. 'That's the worst over.' The hand belongs to an arm that belongs not to Tom but his mother.

It's a struggle to straighten up, to support herself again on wobbly legs. 'Better out than in, eh?' Hand under her arm, Lana helps to take her weight. 'That's it, dear. There's no rush. You'll feel better in a minute.'

'No, I won't,' Beth tells her, shaking her head though it makes the world spin. Tears cloud her vision and roll down her cheeks. 'I don't – I can't think…'

'Take a good deep breath,' Lana insists. 'And again.'

Beth does as she's told. 'Well done. Now, first things first, I don't imagine there can be anything left in your stomach, so let's get you back to the car, shall we?'

Like an invalid, she's led towards the open back door. 'Fasten the girl's seatbelt for her, Tom. There, that's better, isn't it?'

Lana starts the engine. 'I'm sure it would help if you could drive a bit slower,' Tom says. 'We were being thrown around all over the place back here.' Though his mother doesn't reply, she eases off on the accelerator. Beth's fingers find the mask on the seat beside her; she picks it up, fumbles to open the loops to fix it around her ears.

'I expect she'll feel better without a mask on,' Tom says aiming his words at the front seat. 'Besides, it's a bit late now. Bolting the stable door and all that.'

'I suppose she should have a few minutes to recover first.' In the rearview mirror, Lana's eyes crease up like they do when people smile.

'You need to re-hydrate.' Tom thrusts a plastic bottle at her. 'Only water this time.'

Thanking him, she swallows a few mouthfuls and, though it's tepid, it helps to cool her throat. 'Try not to gulp too much down at once,' Lana chips in. 'Better to be a bit careful to start with. Little and often is the best way until you're sure it will stay down.'

Overlooking the fact that mother and son are pretty damned free with their advice, she knows she should be grateful for their concern. 'Thanks for being so, um, understanding,' she says. It's hard to judge their mood when she's only able to see their eyes. 'Anyway, I'm feeling a bit better so I think I should put this mask back on.'

Tom's laugh is muffled by the fabric. 'You know, Mum, given where Beth has just come from, there's probably zero chance of her passing that damned virus on to you or anybody else for that matter.'

'Oh, and why's that?' In the mirror Lana's eyebrows knit together in the top half of what looks like an angry frown. 'Didn't you both just catch the train from Paddington of all places?'

'Yes, but the thing is, Beth's sort of been in isolation somewhere where they haven't had a single case of it.'

His mother scoffs. 'Unless the girl has just escaped from a closed order of nuns, I find that very hard to believe.'

'Funny you should say that,' he says. 'In actual fact, she's been living in a community which has no contact with our modern world; haven't you, Beth?'

'Yeah, I suppose I have,' she says, into her mask. Smelling her own foul breath is making her queasy again.

Over her shoulder Lana demands, 'Were you in some kind of commune, or a cult, dear?'

Tom answers for her. 'It was more a place where they don't have things like mobile phones and Netflix. They don't even have the internet.'

'You mean like the Amish?' Lana yells. 'Please don't take this the wrong way, dear, but I have to say the outfit you're wearing is a little at odds with the usual ideas about modesty of dress.'

She can speak for herself. 'Our clothes are similar to yours; the big difference is we don't have some of the stuff – all those gadget things you have. At least not yet, anyway.'

They're heading down a narrow winding road with a sheer drop on one side and she's anxious not to distract Lana from the task of staying on the road.

'I'm sure Beth would rather not talk about it anymore,'

Tom says. 'Whole thing's still too painful.' They hit a pothole and the car judders as Lana wrestles them away from the edge. Lana curses long and hard about the state of the roads but at least she slows down.

Beth's eyes run towards the wildflowers scattered along the grass verges, to the sheep and lambs grazing a meadow, the wood at the top of the hill beyond. Above it the sapphire sky has a little sprinkling of white clouds. For some people this must be a perfect day.

Welcome to Stoatsfield-Under-Ridge a roadside sign reads. *Please drive with care through our village.* Lana must find that hard. Looking around, the place bears a strong resemblance to Upper Threshing except these houses are more haphazard and mismatched and there are patches of land that haven't been neatly mown. They pass a row of parked cars, but she can't see anyone about.

Since all of them have stopped speaking, the atmosphere in the car feels a little strained. To break the silence, she asks, 'Is it always this quiet on a Sunday?'

Tom says, 'It's Saturday.' At the exact same time his mum says, 'It's Tuesday.'

Lana crashes down the gears. 'I have to say it comes to something when three people can't even agree on what day of the week it is.' The eyes in the rearview mirror have narrowed.

Tom checks his device and holds it up for Beth. It's a little calendar. 'Of course, I meant Tuesday,' he says. 'Silly me.' There's a red spot on the third Tuesday in July 2020. It seems it isn't August here. Then again why would a time tunnel stick to the rules about days and months when it can send you nearly forty years into the future without you even wanting to go there?

She spots a group of workmen in dayglow jackets and white helmets. Unlike the rest of the village, the handful of houses under construction seem to be made mostly of wood and glass. Their revolving cement mixer looks like any other cement mixer.

They pass a primary school with its gates chained and pad-locked; The Coach House Café is in darkness and We Pamper Your Pooch – which sounds vaguely rude – has a prominent *closed until further notice* sign in the window.

They pull in for a moment to let a lorry pass. The shop right next to them has its lights on and the front door propped wide open. An A-frame sign by the door reads: *Keep 2 metres apart at all times.* And below that: *Maximum of 3 allowed inside.* Not exactly a warm welcome.

They carry on along the main street. As the houses begin to thin out, Lana turns into a narrow entrance and parks up. 'Here we are then,' she says turning off the engine.

Her house – their house – is a proper house; a pretty white-painted cottage on the end of a row of three. It's the only one with a porch. The front garden is crammed with flowers. Sandals crunching on the gravel, Beth's careful to stay well back from his mum. Tom does the same. He pulls down his scarf. 'I imagine you want me and Beth to use the back door.'

Lana's shoulders droop. 'All things considered, I'd rather the two of you keep your distance.'

'It's okay,' Tom tells her. His smile is an olive branch. 'Better safe than sorry at your advanced old age.'

'Cheek.' Lana smiles back at him – a proper motherly smile that makes Beth envious. 'Give me a minute to open up,' Lana says. 'I'll make you both a pot of tea. Might even rustle up a few scones. If you two go into the snug, I'll leave the tray on the hall table.'

'Sounds great,' Tom says.

It's a relief to take off the mask. Lana turns to give her an assessing look. 'I don't suppose you feel up to eating anything just yet, dear.'

'I'm still feeling a bit sh– a bit rubbish,' she tells her. 'But thanks anyway.'

'Listen, Mum,' Tom says. 'It's possible we can find out a bit more about what's going on at the station – someone might be able to tell us when the trains are going to be up and running. Can I borrow your car for an hour or so to drive Beth over to Cheltenham?'

When Lana hesitates, he says, 'If you can find me some of that anti-viral stuff, I'll wipe over the steering wheel and the door handles when I've finished with it.'

'Well, I suppose that should be enough.' Rather than hand over the key, Lana drops it onto a ledge inside the porch. 'Make sure to check the fuel gauge. I don't want it back nearly empty.'

She steps inside the front door and then turns back to add, 'Tom, I really think you need to let this poor girl have a bit of a rest before you take her anywhere. Sounds to me like she's already been through enough for one day.'

Chapter Fifteen

Tom

What his mum likes to call *the snug* is a small lean-to building attached to the back of the cottage – some long-dead carpenter's workshop. Given the fluid nature of time over the last few hours, for all he knows the old boy could be about to pop up saw in hand to claim his territory back.

His mother was right about the state Beth's in. Clearly exhausted, she flops down on the sofa and shuts her eyes, looking more like some swooning Victorian lady than a time-traveller just arrived from the nineteen-eighties. Except for her bare legs, that is.

He paces the room, rakes a hand through his hair several times trying to figure out how to help her get back home. Hearing the rattle of the tea tray outside, he shouts through the door that he's planning to get some things from his bedroom. When his mum raises no objection, he waits to hear the kitchen door close before he bounds up the stairs.

His bedroom looks the same as always – the same as when he left it this morning; although, by his mother's account, he's been away for more than a week. It's strange to be back; this may not be the right moment to ponder the exact nature of the space-time continuum. He grabs his laptop, along with several large-scale OS maps and legs it down the stairs.

He's relieved to find Beth hasn't magically dematerialised since he left the room. She hasn't even moved, though, mouth slightly open, she's now quietly snoring.

The wi-fi in the village is notoriously unreliable so he's pleased when he gets a pretty decent signal. First thing he checks is the Great Western website. They're displaying the same uninformative information that the train service to Paddington via Reading is currently suspended. There's no indication of when the service will resume. If they drive over to Cheltenham, there is no immediate prospect of Beth being able to catch a train to London. For this to work, he's pretty certain she needs to catch the Gustav Holst and not some other 125. The regular Class 800 trains weren't introduced until 2017, so one of those would be out of the question. There's no way of discovering the identity of a specific train in advance – they don't give out that type of information on the website.

He fetches the tray his mum's left in the hall and pours himself a cup of stewed tea. There are scones, a double portion of butter and a ramekin of her homemade raspberry jam. No jampot or butter dish to potentially contaminate.

Beth's still out for the count. He decides not to wake her while he chews over the problem along with a couple of scones.

Following a different line of thought, he wipes his jam-sticky hands on his T-shirt and spreads out the maps on the rug to form a mosaic stretching from the Cotswolds via Swindon through to Berkshire and the county town of Reading. Starting at Upper Threshing, his finger traces the trainline through the adjoining maps searching for the exact location of the long tunnel they had passed through. It's not there. Starting at Reading, he does the same from the opposite direction and again draws a blank. As far as the cartographers are concerned, the tunnel they went through doesn't exist – at least not in 2018 when these maps were published.

If such a tunnel was in operation in the eighties, there's likely to be a reference to it – something that says *site of…* along with a broken line. On his hands and knees, Tom peers closely at the topography, tracing the route of the various disused railway tracks indicated. He can find nothing to suggest a tunnel of such length ever existed.

It's possible it only comes into being at the precise point in time you travel through it. It probably only opens at the approach of that particular train on that particular diversion from the normal route. In films, they usually depict a time-portal as a hole with an unstable halo of light around it. Or sometimes only a quivering haze in the landscape. He doubts that's based on any kind of science. If he forgets the train and tries to locate the portal on the ground, would the entrance stand out from its surroundings?

If the portal were permanent, wouldn't some shepherd, or a walker caught in fog, or a pair of hapless lovers looking for a bit of privacy, have stumbled into it and disappeared? There'd be a cluster of missing people – Gloucestershire's own version of the Bermuda Triangle. Surely then, he would have heard stories about it; in the same way you hear tales of puma-like black cats roaming the Cotswold hills; or crop-circles that appear overnight, made by aliens as a way of communicating with earthlings – although even true believers seem unable to understand the message. He's always been cynical about those things, but how can he scoff at such ideas now? With the exception of a few eccentrics and oddballs, no one's likely to believe what's just happened to him and Beth.

His mobile vibrates. Glancing at the screen, he sees the subject heading is: *Really sorry mate.* It's from Andy, his boss. He scans through the text. *Desperate times in the travel industry … no exception … plan to give up the lease on the premises when it ends in October… with a heavy heart… yadda ya.* He skips the rest and goes to the bottom line*: I strongly suggest you look for other work before the furlough scheme ends.* Apart from the matey subject line, there's no mention of him by name; Andy must have blind copied the same email to everyone in the office.

He takes a heavy breath. Though he'd long suspected it was coming, the confirmation is a blow to his stomach. A few more months of reduced salary and that will be it – he'll join the millions of unemployed. How the hell are you supposed to find work in the middle of a global pandemic and the huge recession in its wake? With less money coming in, he'll definitely have to give up his Bristol flat and all his hard-won independence and move back here for the foreseeable future. His mum's unlikely to relish that prospect any more than he does.

Lost in thought, he hears Beth stir and is reminded of his more immediate problem. She gives a long groan and then settles down again. Lying on her side now, she looks really peaceful – serene even. It's tempting to let her sleep because he'd rather not be the cause of her losing that carefree expression. But they might be facing a limited window of opportunity. She's more likely to get back to her own time if they act quickly – the tactic had worked for him, after all. If he drives her over to Cheltenham, she can be there waiting at the station as soon as the normal train service resumes – although normal service doesn't usually involve sending passengers forty years back in time. If the Holst train was the last to arrive there, it's likely to be the first to leave again.

He shakes her as gently as he can. She wakes with a start and a where-the-hell-am-I expression. 'It's okay, you're safe,' he tells her, giving her a reassuring look that might seem a bit creepy from her angle.

She sits bolt upright and then looks around her like a coma patient adjusting to the reality of being conscious. When her eyes come to rest on him, she gives a heartfelt groan. 'You.'

He's not thrilled to have this effect on an attractive woman waking up. 'I'm sorry,' he says. 'I humbly apologise for being real, but I am and, unfortunately for you, all this is too.' His gesture tries to encompass the world beyond the snug. 'In case your memory's a bit hazy, I'm Tom Brookes and you're currently in my mum Lana's house in *Stoatsfield-Under-Ridge* – the place where the size of your marrows is an acceptable topic of conversation, where takeaway deliveries are the stuff of dreams, where, even in normal times, the nearest pub empties out before nine o'clock at night; Neighbourhood Watch meetings are the most exciting thing on anyone's calendar and people count the number of empty beer bottles in your recycling box.'

He stops to draw breath. 'On the plus side – if you can call it that – the only noise at night is likely to come from the ducks squabbling on the village pond. Oh, and passing police cars are as rare as Santa's sodding sleigh.' He's pleased with the alliteration in that last phrase.

Shutting her eyes, Beth's lips continue to move; she appears to be counting. When she opens them again, he says, 'Yep, I'm still here. Can't get rid of me that easy.'

She swings her legs onto the floor and stands up. In such close proximity, her presence is disconcerting. 'There's tea in the pot,' he tells her, stepping back a little, 'though it's probably gone a bit tepid by now. And there's scones with raspberry jam. Although maybe jam might be a step too far given what happened on the way here. Still, everybody loves homemade scones, right? I mean, what's not to like about a scone?'

Her look tells him to shut the fuck up.

They're driving past grand Regency houses – relics of a time when London high society visited Cheltenham to take the waters, hoping to cure health problems brought on by their over-indulgence; the side of town most modern visitors stop to admire.

Traffic is light; with so many people working from home, there are none of the queues he'd expected at this time of day. In an eccentric piece of town planning, the railway station is at least a mile from the centre of town.

Beth hasn't said much. She might have agreed to come with

him, but her expression suggests she's in a sulk. Glancing at her turned-away face, Tom can't suppress his rising irritation. Ever since she woke up from her nap, she's been acting stroppy, like she's holding him responsible for her predicament.

Half a mile from the station she says, 'So, explain to me again how this plan of yours is supposed to work.' They're held at the lights and he takes a long breath before going through the whole thing again. This time she pays more attention. 'Right, so if I've got this straight, you're saying that I need to catch one particular train called the Gustav Holst.'

'Who was, in actual fact, born here in Cheltenham.' He can't think why he just said that.

'Yeah, I remember The Planets Suite. We did Holst in music. At school.' She straightens her shoulders. 'Anyway, you're saying it has to be the same train because otherwise this time-tunnel thingy won't open up and I'll just arrive in London now and not in the proper London.'

'London now *is* the proper London,' he tells her as they pull away. 'It's just not *your* London.'

'Even if you're right and it works, how do you know I won't end up in some other time; like, I don't know, back in the seventies? I've watched Doctor Who – that Tardis has a mind of its own. What if I arrive in some hideous future time, where Martians have invaded; or supposing there's been a nuclear war and everyone's dead?'

When he doesn't answer, she yells, 'Stop the car right now.'

Tom's had enough. 'Fine by me,' he tells her. He turns into the nearest side street and, spraying grit, pulls up alongside the kerb.

Beth's hand is poised on the door handle, but she doesn't get out. He says, 'Before you flounce off into the sunset, think about how you're going to buy a ticket with no valid money. If the whole thing doesn't work, are you happy for me to abandon you when you have nowhere to live, no job, no friends or family and no understanding of the technology necessary in order to function in the twenty-first century?'

'You could be wrong, Mr Know-it-all. My friends – all the people I know here and in London – they could still be alive for all you know.'

'True; but think about it for a second – even if you manage to track them down, you can hardly swan back into their lives looking exactly like you did forty years ago.'

She says, 'Thirty-eight years, actually.' And then, 'I suppose it would freak them out.' After that she goes silent on him.

He begins to regret his outburst; from her forlorn expression, he can see his words must have really hit home. 'Listen, Beth,' his tone is kinder now. 'I don't pretend to have all the answers; I only know that when I caught the same train back again, I ended up here in my own time. Well, admittedly I seem to have lost about ten days but it's not like they were ten days that might have changed the course of my life.'

As soon as the words are out of his mouth, Tom wonders if that's the case – could those lost days have been crucial? Might the loss of them change his whole future in some way? Given how similar each day has been since lockdown, it seems unlikely, but the possibility begins to niggle at him. In his teens he'd read his mum's copy of Ten Days that Shook the World; a lot can change even in one day never mind ten.

'Okay.' Beth rubs at her eyes smudging her mascara to such an extent she's beginning to look ghoulish; he has to fight the urge to suggest wiping some of it off. 'I really don't mean to sound ungrateful,' she says. 'It may not seem like it, but I do appreciate you're only trying to help. You reminded me of this person I've been trying to get away from, but you're not really like him at all.' She gives him an apologetic smile. 'You're much nicer.' She settles back into her seat. 'Before we go to the station, would you do something for me first? It won't take long.'

That smile has disarmed him completely. 'Name it,' he says.

'Will you drive me over to my auntie's house? It's not very far from here and I know the way. The thing is, I need to go there and knock on her door just to be certain...' She doesn't finish the sentence – doesn't need to.

Chapter Sixteen

Beth

They've entered a warren of backstreets – a stark contrast in scale to the grand houses of the posher bits. She knows this part of the town and there's no denying a lot has changed since her last visit. For a start, most of the front gardens have been sacrificed to create parking. Painted in a variety of ice cream colours, the houses themselves seem pretty much as before except they've been smartened up. She spots the chapel's belltower sticking up above all the other roofs. Her aunty can be found there most Sundays although, according to Lana, today isn't Sunday after all.

'You need to turn left here,' she tells him. 'And now left again by that telegraph pole at the end.' Without a word he follows her instructions. They pass the road sign she always looks for: *St Wilfred's Terrace.* This place was her childhood sanctuary – somewhere to escape to when things got bad with her mother. Seeing the name of the road in black and white reassures her like she's come home. Out of step with the grid of streets surrounding it, St Wilfred's Terrace curves around to accommodate a small park. As always, kids are playing on the swings and kicking balls around. The smell of barbecued meat is in the air. Grin on her face, she turns to Tom. 'We're almost there. Aunty Joan's house is right at the end.'

Families are out and about enjoying the sunshine; Tom creeps along, hugging the gutter, showing a lot more concern for pedestrian safety than his mother.

The houses come to an abrupt end. Where Joan's semi used to stand there's now a horrible gap. Beth clamps a hand over her mouth. Along with her auntie's house, the Cliffords' house next-door has gone. On the other side, the Townsends' house and the Fitzgeralds' place with the overgrown front garden that caused the neighbours to tut-tut – both of them have disappeared. All four have been razed to the ground. Occupying the land where their houses used to sit, there's only tarmac and lines of parked cars.

Having run out of road, Tom pulls up. 'Did we pass it?'

'It's gone,' she tells him. 'They've fucking demolished it.'

'Oh,' he says. 'I'm really sorry.'

Against all the evidence, she'd wanted to prove him wrong – had convinced herself that the house would be right here the same as always. And when she knocked on the front door, her Aunty Joan would pad along in her fluffy slippers to answer it and everything would be unchanged; and the two of them would have a good laugh at Tom's ridiculous time-travel theories.

'I didn't imagine … I thought, you know, even if she wasn't here…'

Extracting a small pack of tissues from the glove compartment, he hands them to her.

'I thought at least the neighbours…' When she dabs her eyes, black streaks come away. She must look a fright. Shoulders back, she blows her nose. 'Worst case, I sort of assumed somebody would be able to tell me, you know, what happened to her. But it's hopeless…They've gone – everything's gone.'

'Must be a horrible shock. I'd feel the same if Mum's house had disappeared.' His arm comes to rest on her shoulder. 'Must be a lot to take in.'

'I can't believe they would tear down those houses just to make some stupid bloody car park.'

'Maybe they were substandard,' he says. 'Perhaps, being on the end, there were structural problems – subsidence or something. They could have rehomed them somewhere much better. As for your aunty – like you said before, she'd be pretty old, but she could still be alive for all you or I know.'

'What do I know, eh?' She throws up her hands. 'I know nothing. The ground's fallen away, everything I thought I knew before – it's all gone.'

When she can speak again, she says, 'They might not have been perfect, but they weren't just houses, you know, they were people's *homes*. They raised their families in them; buried their dead from them. I'm certain of one thing – Joan would never have left here without putting up a fight.'

'You know, Beth,' he says, 'there are lots of ways to track people down these days. Databases – literally thousands, even millions, of records you can search instantly with one of these.'

When he holds up his precious device, she's tempted to snatch it and throw the thing out of the window. 'That stupid little thing is your answer to everything. I expect you think it's a bloody miracle we ever managed without them.'

'Well, yes, I do think that.'

She shrugs off his comfort. He removes his arm. 'Listen,' he says. 'I don't suppose any of what I said just now made sense to you, but the point I was making is that I can help you find out what happened to your aunty.'

She doesn't reply – has no words. He squeezes her hand and says, 'The thing is, Beth, if we can get you back to your own time, there'd be no need for any of that; your aunty will still be right here along with her house – you'll be able to visit her just as you were planning to.'

She says, 'I suppose your theory could be right,' although she's not convinced. If the laws that govern the universe can be broken in an instant, nothing holds. If an ordinary passenger train can transport a person nearly forty years into the future, how can anyone be sure of anything?

Without a word, Tom turns the car round and, though he doesn't say as much, she can see they're following the signs to the railway station. She needs to think all this through, but the journey there takes no time.

They pull into the car park. As soon as Tom's manoeuvred into a space, she jumps out, thankful to have some room to pace out some of her grief and frustration. The sun has lost its fierceness and the air feels fresher – not that it's any consolation. All the cars around her look so strange because this isn't her time –by rights she shouldn't be here. It's all a mistake. If the trains are running again, she's just going to chance it and hope for the best.

Impatient to get on with it for better or worse, she leaves Tom feeding coins into a machine and strides off towards the station. 'Remember you need to wear your mask,' he shouts after her.

A line of spaced-out and masked-up passengers are waiting on the nearest platform. (They look spaced-out in every sense.) A lit sign draws her attention upwards. The words tell her that the next train will arrive in approximately six minutes. Unfortunately, it's heading off to Penzance via Bristol. Below this, there's something about a *landslip*. She has to wait for the message to come around again before she can piece it together:

The service to Paddington is currently suspended due to a landslip.

Tom arrives at her side and she points to the sign. 'Shit and bugger it,' he says. 'Well I suppose that's made the decision for us – at least for the time being.'

Together they try to find out more information from a pot-bellied man sitting behind a screen. Tom asks him when the landslip is likely to be cleared. The man cups a hand round his ear. 'Can't hear you. You'll have to speak up.'

Tom has to shout. 'I said, when is the landslip going to be cleared?'

Leaning back in his chair, he answers in a local accent, 'Your guess is as good as mine.' The smirk on his face suggests the problem has got nothing to do with him.

'That's not strictly true, is it?' Tom leans into the screen. 'I mean, presumably you're employed by the train company to give out information to the travelling public – or in this case the non-travelling public. In that capacity, and with more channels of communication available to you, you must be better placed than we are to give an estimate of how long it's likely to take to clear the line and reinstate the service to London. I mean, are we talking hours? Days? Weeks?'

The man leans forward in his chair, his smirk widening. 'Like I already told you, *sir*, I can't answer that question at the moment.' After an unhurried pause, he adds, 'They might put on a replacement bus service to Reading in the morning.' He holds up empty hands.

Red in the face, Tom scoffs. 'But that's no bloody use to us.'

'I suggest you curb your language, young man. Mean to say, if the two of you are in that much of a flamin' hurry to get to London, why don't you try the coach station instead?'

She grabs Tom's arm to pull him away, but he's clearly not finished. 'It's hard to know what value you add to this service when you seem to delight in not giving out any information. Have you even bothered to ask anyone? Surely the line engineers must have some idea about timescale.'

'Come away.' Beth is tempted to add the immortal line, *he's not worth it* because he really isn't. 'Please Tom, let's just go.'

The man stands up, though he's careful to remain behind his invisible barrier. 'Your girlfriend has a darn sight more sense than you.'

'She's not my girlfriend,' Tom tells him. 'Not that it's any of your business.'

'Well, now there's a surprise.' Without any subtlety, the man eyes her up and down. 'Pretty girl like her, she could do a lot better.'

Tom's fists are curled tight. She pulls harder on his arm, causing him to take a grudging step backwards. 'Come on let's go,' she says. 'None of this is helping the situation.'

'You tell him, sweetheart,' the man crows. As they walk away, Beth turns to flick the V sign at the smug bastard.

Still arm in arm, they emerge into the sunshine. It occurs to her that anybody watching would think they're a couple instead of virtual strangers. Tom touches her hand and asks, 'Where next?'

She lets go, quickly disentangles herself.

'I'm sorry,' he says. 'I realise I shouldn't have lost my temper back there. Put it down to frustration.' He rakes his hair back leaving random cowlicks sticking up. 'It's just so bloody infuriating not being able to *do* anything.'

'It's not really your problem,' she tells him.

Tom raises her chin until she's looking into his eyes. He has extraordinary eyes – they're the colour of dark chocolate. 'Why don't we head back to mine,' he says. 'For the time being. You happy with that?' When she wavers, he adds, 'Unless you can think of a better idea.'

Defeated, she nods her agreement. He opens the car door for her, and she slumps down into the passenger seat.

'Don't worry, I'm sure, between the two of us, we'll find a solution,' he says climbing in beside her. 'There's got to be a way to get you back home again.' His words carry less conviction than before. 'Seatbelt,' he reminds her, starting the engine.

A buzzing noise draws her attention to a trapped bee. Pulling out an OS map, Tom uses the edge to guide the bee towards freedom. 'Come on, little fella – you shouldn't be in here.' When that doesn't work, he opens the doors; the through-draft ought to carry the bee outside but instead, attracted to light, it continues to bumble against the sunroof.

Like her, the poor thing's trapped in the wrong place. There's a sudden whirring noise and the glass roof panel slides back by itself. Clever. Like a lunar module taking off, the bee rises up and disappears. She's tempted to applaud. Bloody hell – things must be pretty bad if she's identifying with an insect.

They stop for petrol – the pungent smell of it leaks into the car, turning her empty stomach.

After that the two of them say very little. The roads narrow around them, twigs from the overgrown hedgerows scratch at the sides of the car like fingernails. Aunty Joan didn't drive so Beth is used to viewing the countryside surrounding Cheltenham from a safe distance – not up close like this.

The lane winds up to a vantage point. On a normal day, she would admire the view it offers – all those sun-baked fields leading down to the shining river and the hazy graph-line of hills beyond. Today the sheer scale of it unnerves her. They're in the middle of fucking nowhere – which just about sums up her situation.

A memory surfaces of her aunty jiggling around to a Dusty Springfield song on the radio; the lyrics are all about being stuck in the middle of nowhere. It's a catchy tune; the chorus repeats in her head. It's a comfort of sorts to remember how safe, how loved, she'd felt back then.

After a while, she finds herself humming the tune under her breath.

Misreading her mood, Tom turns to smile at her. He also has a nice smile. 'My mum's a really good cook,' he tells her. 'You're bound to feel better after a proper meal.'

As if it were that bloody simple.

Chapter Seventeen

Tom

To placate his mum, he stops off to put a few gallons in the tank. 'What next?' he'd asked her back at the station and she'd shrunk from his touch like it was kryptonite. It might be a good question, but he ought to have kept his mouth shut.

Watching the digits on the pump roll by far too quickly, he wonders if he's missed something vital. Best guess, the Holst train is parked up in a siding ready to depart for London as soon as the landslip is cleared. From a distance, any 125 looks the same as the next; without binoculars it would be impossible to get close enough to read engine names. The blockage and resulting disruption must be newsworthy; there'll be something about it on the local TV news. With luck, one of their plodding reporters might have interviewed somebody in authority able to predict how long the clear up will take.

Fifteen pounds worth is more than enough. Despite the plastic glove, his hands stink of spilt petrol as he hangs up the nozzle.

The longer the delay, the less confident he is that the time portal will open again. How will Beth cope if she's trapped here permanently? Once the trains are running again, he can't simply wave her off and hope for the best.

At the cashier's booth, the machine spits his card out. This month's bills will have hit his account and yet surely he can't be down to his last few quid. He keys in his number again and this time the transaction is accepted without a hitch.

When he gets back to the car, Beth is staring straight ahead – she doesn't seem to have moved; she doesn't appear to register him getting back in the car.

'Right then, let's go,' he says. It's an effort trying to sound upbeat for her sake. In truth, he feels exhausted and so dog-tired it's as much as he can do to concentrate on the road. All he really wants is to get home, put his feet up on the sofa and watch something mindless on the box. With the sitting room currently off-limits to them both, that's not going to happen.

They're less than halfway back and he's really struggling to keep his mind on driving and nothing else. Beth is making an odd sound which takes him a while to identify. Shit, she's gone from a near catatonic state to humming a perky little tune under her breath. On the train, he'd suspected she might have some sort of multiple personality disorder; her current predicament would be enough to tip the sanest person over the edge. In any case, it looks like Chirpy Beth is back in charge.

Her face is turned away, but he notices she's moving her head in time to a beat only she can hear. Hoping to snap her out of it, he asks, 'What's that song you're humming?'

'Oh,' she says, 'Was that out loud?'

He nods. 'Yep.'

'It's a Dusty Springfield number. She was big when I was little – if that makes sense? Although I don't suppose you've even heard of Dusty.'

'You're right – I haven't. So, what's the name of the song?'

'It's called *In the Middle of Nowhere*.' She smiles. 'Seems appropriate, don't you think?'

'Can't argue with that.'

On impulse, he pulls into the next layby, plugs his phone into the USB port and searches for it. Beth is wide-eyed when the intro plays through the car's speakers. 'I don't believe it. Wow! And you did it so quickly. Can you find any tune you want on that thing?'

'Pretty much.'

The mood in the car lightens, along with the music. They're humming in unison as he waits for a van to pass before he pulls out. The lyrics are repetitive and not very sophisticated – a needy woman demanding to know where she stands with her lover – but the singer has a gutsy blues voice that carries the whole thing along. The song is brilliantly of its time – classic Swinging Sixties. It occurs to him that, if Beth is about to be twenty, she's a child of the sixties – born in 1962 to be precise. Only four years after his mum. What a headfuck! His brain's doing summersaults again.

Beth's in full voice now – singing along lost in happier memories. Her dark hair is billowing around her face like she's in an ad for something cool and desirable. He'd buy whatever it is. When the chorus comes around again, he waves his free arm in the air and joins in with the *hey-hey-heys* of the background singers. Their arms swaying in unison; steering one-handed, he's laughing out loud because it's so good to see her happy and he doesn't want the journey to end.

Arriving back at the cottage, their mood sobers. He lets them in through the back door. His mother's been baking and he narrows the smell down to some sort of fruit – possibly strawberries or raspberries.

Beth trails behind him into the snug. In an attempt to stave off a complete mood-change, he shows her his mum's impressive record collection, which occupies the whole of one wall. With some pride he says, 'Mum's into all kinds of music – classical, big band, pop, soul, R&B – you name it.'

'Really? Not what you expect at her age,' is said without irony. Ignoring the CDs, Beth runs loving hands over the alphabetised vinyl racks. 'I've got this one at home,' she says, pulling out a single with a geeky-looking bloke on the cover. 'This was one of the first records I ever bought.' Head on one side, she adds, 'Tell me you've heard of Elvis Costello?'

'Yeah – I've heard of him but...' he shrugs.

Her face is alight with excitement. 'You have to listen to this. I dare you not to like it.'

Tom's not sure what emotion he's experiencing. 'I'm just going to the loo,' he tells her – the coward's way out.

Passing the kitchen door, he hears his mum talking to someone – her voice unusually raised. The gaps in the conversation tell him she's on the phone. He can't make out much but it's clear that she's getting angry about something. 'Don't tell me to be reasonable, I'm not the one who...' He misses the last part of the sentence. 'No, I won't calm down. You can't expect me to sort out your mess.'

Who can she be talking to like that? She probably didn't hear them arrive and assumes she's alone in the house. Intrigued, Tom puts his ear to the gap in the door. 'That's enough!' He recognises the sound of the phone being slammed down.

It's unusual for her to get so riled. Could she be in a relationship he knows nothing about? She refuses to talk about his father; he's often wondered if he was conceived through IVF so she could avoid the messy business of relationships. He's been living in Bristol until the last few months, she could have been conducting an affair for months – years even. It's hard to think of her in that way – sexually active. If she's in a relationship, he's fairly sure it's with a man. Could be a woman. She's been alone for a long time so whatever makes her happy. Although, given what he'd just overheard, she isn't happy at the moment. Has he got in the way – stopped their developing romance in its tracks? Could that be why the two of them were arguing?

He's getting ahead of himself – she could just as easily have been angry with that shifty bloke who did a crap job sorting out the gutters a while back.

He tiptoes down the hallway to the toilet. Better to leave it a bit before announcing they're back. If he's in her way, bringing Beth here will have only made things worse. He'd told her it would be for one night, max. What if she ends up having to stay longer?

In the toilet, he picks up an old copy of Private Eye dating from before the pandemic – a time when political skulduggery and alleged corruption were the main preoccupation of most journalists.

When he finally emerges, he hears music. 'We're back,' he shouts. There's no reply. The music is really loud and coming from the snug. Hurrying, he opens the door. 'I think you'd better turn that...'

His mum is in the room and standing far too close to Beth. Not put off by the noise, the dog is sitting at Beth's feet, her tail beating the floor for attention.

Looking from one to the other he asks, 'What's going on?'

'No need to stand there with your mouth open,' his mum tells him.

'But I thought ... I mean, you were worried about us giving you the virus. You said we had to keep our distance.'

'Well, I realised I was being a bit over-cautious. As you said yourself, Beth here was more or less in isolation until she caught the train. And you wore a mask – well, my scarf at any rate.' Her smile seems just a touch lopsided and Tom wonders if she's had a stroke, though she's not slurring her words and seems to be moving around okay. Perhaps the bitter row she's just had with her lover has made her fatalistic – or given her some sort of death wish.

He takes a step back from them both. When no one speaks, the lyrics of the song fill the room; like the singer, Tom's not sure how much more of this he can take.

Chapter Eighteen

Dogs barking, snapping at his heels. Heart racing, Tom wakes panting in fear. The room comes into focus. No one is chasing him; no guards with searchlights. Hot and sweating, his sheets are in furrows underneath him. The light in the room is fluctuating as the swaying curtains let in the sunlight and then block it again.

All that barking is coming from outside. It mutates to a yapping yowl. Poppy sounds frantic about something. Her snarls subside into more high-pitched yapping. Tom can't recall the last time the old girl made as much fuss.

Is she in trouble? Leaning out of the window, he's relieved to see her sitting on the path below and not caught in some hideous trap. She's staring at the back door, hoping it will open. When he calls her name, she doesn't look up but continues to concentrate on the door. He calls her again, but she doesn't respond.

He checks his phone – it's only a quarter past six. His mum's an early riser especially at this time of year when it gets light at some crazy hour. She must have let the dog out, so why hasn't she let her back in?

When Poppy stops barking, he thinks he can hear people talking. He picks out a male voice and then a second one which he's pretty sure is his mum. She has a habit of talking to the radio – arguing aloud if she disagrees with what's being said.

Though he can't be certain, both voices sound live. It's impossible to hear what they're saying. It can't be any of the neighbours because they're all keeping their distance these days. It's six-fifteen in the morning and some man is down there talking to her. Tom wrinkles his nose up at the thought that her gentleman caller might have snuck in during the night.

It's possible. Exhausted by the events of the day, he'd gone to bed very early. Beth too; his mum had shown her to the spare room, given her a couple of clean towels, even offered to lend her a change of clothes since she had no luggage. Perhaps she'd been making sure Mr Lover-Boy could steal in through the back door once the coast was clear. If he's down there now, why shut Poppy outside? Could be allergic to dogs or something.

Should he throw on some clothes, go down and say hello, shake the man's hand to show he's mature enough to cope with this new situation and they don't need to sneak around like a couple of adolescents?

Weighing it up, he decides to leave them in peace. Although peace isn't the right word; whatever had briefly mollified Poppy hasn't lasted – she's now baying like a dog half her age and twice her size.

When she starts whining pathetically, he toys with the idea of letting her in and coaxing her up to his room, so neither of them has to confront the lovers. As far as he can tell it's gone quiet down there. He can't hear much above the dog's racket. What if they've stopped talking because they're snogging? Or worse. Closing his eyes, he tries to unthink that last thought. Too hot and wide awake for sleep, he stares up at the shifting light on the ceiling.

Like an ache only temporarily forgotten, a thought resurfaces to crowd out his other concern – what the hell is he going to do about Beth? The Network Rail spokesman they'd interviewed on Points West said it *could* take several days to clear the line. Hoping for better news, Tom checks the train company's website but the only new information concerns the replacement bus service. For the time being, there's nothing more he can do.

A door slams downstairs. Was it taken by the wind or had someone just stormed out? Tom rushes to the window, hoping to catch a glimpse of the departing visitor. The dog is still on sentry duty at the back door so whoever it was must have gone out the front.

Naked except for his boxers, he sprints onto the landing. Through the window at the end he gets a glimpse of a tall, rather overdressed, man climbing into a dark blue car – some big SUV; possibly a Range Rover. The lilac tree in the front garden blocks his view as the car pulls away. Its engine has the distinctive wooffling sound of an older V8.

'It's very noisy around here.' Rubbing at her eyes, Beth is standing right behind him. She's wearing an outsized checked shirt of his mother's. On her it's even bigger.

'Oh, hi.' Aware of his near-naked state, he retreats towards his bedroom. To cover his embarrassment, he asks, 'Did you sleep okay?'

'Sort of. I had all these really weird dreams.' Her laugh is more of a snort. 'Though not half as weird as waking up in a strange bed, in a strange village, nearly forty years in the future.' Without all that makeup she's even prettier. 'Does your dog always make that much noise?'

'Um, no, she never does – well when I say never, obviously she was making a hell of a commotion just then but that's really unusual. Out of character as it were.' The bedroom door is his shield. 'I should probably get dressed...'

'Have you got the time?'

'About half-six.'

She smiles. 'That wasn't meant, you know, as a come-on line.'

'It's still pretty early,' he says, stating the bloody obvious.

'Really early.' She yawns. When she stretches her arms wide, the movement reveals her pale blue panties. He's quick to look away – hopes she didn't notice how his eyes had strayed. 'Do you and your mum normally get up at the crack of dawn?'

'Um – no. Well, Mum often does. I certainly don't if I can help it.'

'Well, seeing's I'm fully awake now, is it okay if I take a shower? Should I ask your mum?'

'No, it's fine. She won't mind – you go ahead.' Damn, he's really hungry. He'll have to use the one downstairs – the tiny cubicle his mum had put in so they can hose down the dog when she's rolled in something hideous.

She turns around to ask, 'Could I borrow a T-shirt?'

'Sure,' he tells her, though he's not sure how many are clean. 'I'll leave one outside your door.'

Dressed and showered, hunger leads Tom into the kitchen. His mother's sitting at the table eating her usual bowl of muesli with fresh fruit and yogurt. For once the radio is silent. 'You're up early,' she says between mouthfuls.

'The dog woke me up with all that howling and barking.' He looks for a reaction – a tell, as poker players call it – but she continues to chew, doesn't miss a beat. Better be more direct. The dog is snoozing under the table – exhausted by all the energy put into her recent protest. 'Why was Poppy making such a fuss earlier?'

Cool as can be, his mum takes a sip from her coffee before answering. 'Probably to do with her age. She's getting a bit puggled – as they say round these here parts.'

'Do they? That's a new one on me.'

'It means going a bit gaga – not quite right in the head. Although I think in other parts of the country it means drunk.'

'Who's drunk?' Beth says coming into the room. His Y-OU O-NLY L-IVE O-NCE T-shirt looks way better on her. She's pulled her hair up into a high ponytail; it really suits her.

'Hopefully no one at this hour.' His mum stands up, though her bowl is half full. 'Can I get you something to eat, dear?'

'Finish your breakfast, Mum,' he says, 'I can sort Beth out.'

Beth gives him quite a look. She follows him over to the fridge. 'I don't need sorting out.' Keeping it low so his mum can't hear, she adds, 'I'm grateful for your help but I know what I need to do and I'm pretty sure I can manage by myself.'

'I was only talking about breakfast,' he says. This morning there's a light in her eyes that wasn't there yesterday.

'I've been thinking,' she whispers. 'I will need a bit of money for my ticket. I won't be able to pay you back but, assuming it works, I could put the money in a bank account for you. Over 38 years it ought to build up quite a bit of interest.'

'That's quite a thought,' he says. It really is.

'In any case, you don't need to worry about repaying me,' he tells her. 'As for the rest, you know I'm more than happy to help – when the time comes.'

Louder for his mum's benefit, he says, 'How about some eggs? We've got a few rashers of bacon left and I think there's some mushrooms in here somewhere.'

'On the top shelf,' his mum calls out.

Beth wrinkles her nose. 'I'm really not much of a breakfast person.'

'How about some cereal then?' He points to the boxes on the shelf.

'Honestly, a piece of toast will do.'

'Brown bread okay? I can always nip to the shop if you fancy some sinful white. They sometimes have a few croissants.'

'I happen to like brown bread,' she tells him. 'Maybe with some Marmite – that's if you still have Marmite.'

'Of course,' he says. His mother is watching them – *study-ing* them in fact. Meeting his eye, her smile is an afterthought. 'There's some coffee in the cafetiere,' she says shifting her gaze back to her cereal bowl. 'Should still be hot.'

'Take a seat,' he tells Beth pulling out a chair. He puts a mug and the cafetiere in front of her. 'Brown toast with Marmite coming up.' He turns to his mum. 'Your visitor was round here very early.'

'What visitor?'

'The tall man I saw earlier.' The dog is quietly snoring. 'I assume that's why you shut the dog out.'

'Oh him.' His mum gets up, goes over to put her empty bowl in the dishwasher. 'He's a builder. He just called to price up some work I'm thinking of having done.'

'Really? What sort of work?'

'I decided it might be a good idea to have the front porch properly enclosed – to stop all the wind and rain blowing in. Mr Howard is going to quote for the job.'

'You've never mentioned it before.' The toast is done; he finds a plate for it. 'Why did you risk letting this Mr Howard inside the house? Couldn't he have priced the job from outside?'

'He needed to take some internal measurements. You know, to satisfy the planning people. The front door was wide open all the time he was here. I kept my distance.'

'Did you really?'

His mum opens her mouth to say something and then changes her mind. She picks up the Marmite, takes it over to the table and plonks it down. When he comes across with the toast, they brush against up each other. She says, 'You smell a bit odd today, darling.'

She only ever calls him darling when she's being sarcastic. 'Must be that shower gel,' he says. 'From the downstairs loo.'

She doubles up, cackles like a hen laying a very large egg, clutches her stomach as if she's about to wet herself. 'That's for the dog,' she manages to say. 'Stops her getting fleas.' Tears in her eyes, she straightens up. 'There'll be no flies on you from now on.'

Beth splutters into her coffee.

He may be the butt of the joke right now, but he's on to her and this Mr Howard with his fancy blue Range Rover; Stoatsfield's not the sort of place you can keep a secret for long.

Chapter Nineteen

Beth

Tom lifts one of the domed lids on the range cooker to toast four pieces of bread in a wire cage shaped like a tennis racket. Seems pretty bizarre for 2020. That enormous Aga – the name is written in big letters on the front in case you might miss it – must keep this kitchen cosy in the winter; at this time of year it's making the room uncomfortably stuffy. To circulate a through draft, all the windows are open and the door is propped wide with an old flat iron.

It's quite a sizeable room but feels smaller because of all the low beams. Lana can pass underneath them; Tom's forced to duck in some places. He does it automatically. Pottery, packets, cartons, photographs, candles, books and other random objects crowd the open shelves. Beth can't work out any obvious system for what goes where.

While they eat, mother and son discuss things she's not part of. She wonders what Rach must be thinking, whether right now she's back at the flat eating breakfast at their tiny table. It's a jolt to think the life she was leading will have happened – did happen – decades ago. Rach won't be young and lively anymore. Did she marry Terry? She could be a grandmother by now. Will she – does she – sometimes tell people how an old flatmate mysteriously left all her stuff behind and disappeared?

She's staring at the label on the Marmite jar which, for some reason, boasts that its lower in salt. Why would they do that – change such a winning formula? The toast is burnt around the edges and she has to swill it down with more tepid coffee.

Her gaze falls on Tom; she follows the careful movements of his hands, the prominent veins in his forearms. She pictures his tanned, tightly muscled chest now hidden by his T-shirt. He really ought to be overweight given how much butter and jam he's slathering on the last of four big slices of toast.

As soon as they finish eating, they don't sit around chatting but jump up to clear the table. Beth tries to help but only gets in the way and so she retreats to the cushioned window-seat on the far side of the room. Outside, the cloudless sky suggests they're in for another *scorcher* as the headline writers say. Do people still read newspapers?

They're loading crockery into a dishwasher, their well-rehearsed movements synchronised so they avoid getting in each other's way. Beth says, 'It must be really handy having one of those.'

Lana screws up her eyes. 'I'm sorry?' she says in a way that makes it clear she's not apologising but perplexed.

'Your dishwasher,' Beth says. 'My aunty dreams of having one of those.'

'Seems a modest wish.' That sharp tone is back in Lana's voice. She goes over to wipe the wooden tabletop. In the next breath it's, 'Tom, why don't you show Beth around the village?' She might as well have said, *Why don't you two bugger off out.*

'Yes, why don't I. I'm sure the many delights of Stoatsfield will astound her.' He slaps his thigh. 'Come on, old girl, a gentle stroll around the village will do you good.' Before Beth can protest, she sees him unhooking a leather lead. After a lot of sighing and what sounds like proper grumbling, the dog gets to her feet.

'Can you pick up a loaf,' Lana says. 'Oh, and you'll need one of these.' She pulls out a drawer and hands Tom a black mask covered in outsized red ladybirds.

He's not keen to accept it. 'You're not serious.'

Lana shrugs. 'I'm sure you'll find it's a bit more practical than my scarf.'

'And there wasn't a more appropriate option available?'

'It was the only one the WI had left.' After giving it to him, his mum holds out both hands to demonstrate her innocence. 'Beggars can't be choosers.' Lana doesn't quite conceal a smile before she adds, 'In case you haven't heard, they're now compulsory in shops.'

Tom stuffs the thing into his pocket. At the front door, he shouts, 'Won't be long.'

'Take your time,' his mother calls back.

As they leave, the church clock strikes the hour; each low dong echoes around the village like a summons to bring out the dead. No wonder she couldn't sleep. The place looks pretty enough – all that buttery stone glowing in the morning sun. It's as deserted as before; their progress along the pavement is hampered only by Poppy's reluctance to walk.

A man with a walking stick emerges from one of the cottages. As soon as he spots them, he crosses to the other side of the road.

'Everybody seems really terrified of this illness,' she says. 'You said it wasn't that serious, but they act like it's bubonic plague.'

'It's not as bad as that. But if you're old, or ill in any way, it can be a killer.' They pass a couple of shops with the shutters pulled down and closed signs on the door.

'I just thought of something that will cheer you up,' he says. 'You won't know it but these days, provided they have access to the right drugs, most people with HIV can now live well into old age.'

She's at a loss. 'HIV – what's that?'

When Tom stops walking, the dog immediately sits down. 'What, you haven't heard of HIV? AIDS doesn't ring any bells?'

She shakes her head. 'I don't think so.'

'I suppose it must have started a bit later than I thought. Anyway, HIV was a killer disease in the eighties and nineties. Freddie Mercury, Rock Hudson, Liberace and a load of other famous people died from it. Of course, lots of non-famous people died as well.'

'That's really awful.' Beth wants a moment to mourn the passing of one of her all-time music heroes. 'Poor Freddie.'

'I'm sorry.' Tom puts a hand on her shoulder, hesitates, and then pulls her into an awkward embrace. 'So stupid of me; I didn't think.' It feels good to be hugged. For a moment, she relaxes against his chest. Unfortunately, he does smell a bit strange.

She hears a tiny ping like Tinker Bell's just appeared. Tom breaks away to check his device. Whatever it is, it makes him smile. Seeing her expression, he says, 'Just a message from my friend Steph.'

'Oh,' she says.

He pulls on the lead to encourage Poppy to stand up. The dog starts to amble along behind him. Beth is left with no choice but to follow.

Tom says, 'Just so you know, to catch HIV, or AIDS, you usually have to have unprotected sex with someone who's already got it. Although some unfortunate people got it from blood transfusions. When you get back, you should probably warn all your friends, you know, suggest they use condoms because it could save your life.' He clears his throat. 'I mean, their lives – people's lives.'

They've reached the village grocery store. The dog laps at a bowl of water that's been left out for that purpose and settles herself in the shade.

'You said *when* not *if*,' she says. 'You think there's still a chance I can make it home?'

Tom squeezes her hand. 'I'm sure we'll figure out a way between us.' He stands back a little, rubs at his mouth like someone about to tell a lie. 'You know, I've been thinking about what you said earlier – how money invested in the eighties in the right way would be worth a lot more now. Think of every time someone says they could have made a fortune if only they had a crystal ball; or how, with hindsight, they would have bet on a horse or bought shares in some company when they were cheap. I reckon, if we play our cards right, there might be a way both of us could make a bit of money out of this time travel business.'

She looks down at the words printed on the front of her T-shirt – which is his T-shirt. You only get one life and hers isn't here. 'I just want to go home,' she tells him.

'Yes, of course. But – just hear me out – what if you and I could also make a small fortune at the same time. We could end up being rich. Just imagine.'

She frowns. 'How would that work, exactly?'

He's staring past her at a woman with a pram who seems to be heading for the shop. 'We should talk about this some-where more private,' he says as the woman gets closer. 'Just think about it – that's all I'm saying.'

His expression alters too quickly, like a bad actor. 'D'you mind holding Poppy while I pop in for that loaf?'

The dog's lying on her side, eyes firmly closed. Beth says, 'I don't think there's any danger of her making a break for it.' Nevertheless, he hands over the lead and heads into the shop. NO MASK – NO SERVICE the sign on the door reads. As she's forgotten the one Lana lent her, she can't follow him. How long has Tom been hatching this money-making idea? Is that the only reason he's helping her – so he can make some money out of it?

Her mood darkens at the thought that she's been taken in – duped by him. Metaphorically, Tom's been wearing a mask all along. He wants to go somewhere private to discuss his idea, but she's determined to have it out with him right here and right now.

Damn it, he only went in for a loaf but he's taking his time. The door is propped open and she can see he's holding the bread under his arm like a rugby ball but he's still chatting away to the two women behind the counter. Seems in no hurry.

Both women are wearing matching stripy green tabards with clear plastic screens covering their faces; from a distance it looks as if their heads aren't fully attached to their shoulders. Tom is keeping them entertained and laughing. Despite being middle-aged or more, they're red in the face and obviously succumbing to his charm – what they can see of his handsome face. When daylight flashes on their plastic shields, the women look like a double act on telly, not real people at all.

Chapter Twenty

Tom

The women in the shop greet him with their usual enthusiasm; the two of them have always been good sports. A few years back they would have slipped him some sweets while his mum's back was turned.

Tom lingers over his choice of bread; waits for them to serve the woman with the baby before he goes up to the counter.

'Good to see you,' the older one, Kirsty, says. 'Thought you might have gone back to Bristol without saying goodbye – didn't we, Mar?'

'Can't say's I'd blame the boy if he did,' Marion says. 'Not when it's as dead as a ruddy door nail round here.'

'It's a dodo,' Kirsty tells her. 'As dead as a dodo – which is extinct after all.'

Hands on her substantial hips, Marion counters with, 'And some say as dead as mutton. I could just as easily have said as dead as Elvis, God rest his soul. Or as dead as Dracula; it don't make no odds which way up.'

'It's okay,' Tom says. 'I get the picture.' He pays for the loaf and a copy of the Financial Times – a publication he'd never imaged he'd find himself buying.

Twinkle in her eye, Kirsty says, 'Nice mask you got there.'

'Just ignore her,' Marion tells him.

He starts to turn away and then thinks better of it. 'My mum is hoping to get a bit of building work done. She's asked Mr Howard for a quote. Obviously, I wouldn't want her to get ripped off, so I was wondering if either of you ladies know if he's any good or not.'

Kirsty's frown adds to the many wrinkles on her forehead. 'Can't say I know of any builder by that name – not round here. What about you, Mar?'

'I think there's a Bob Howe down Charlton Kings way – or it might be nearer Andoversford. He does quite a bit of dry-stone walling round these parts. Got a waiting list as long as your arm, I shouldn't wonder.'

'I'm pretty sure she said Howard,' Tom tells them. 'What does this Howe bloke look like?'

'Far as I can remember he's a bit of a short arse; bald on top with one of them thin grey ponytails hanging down his back.' She turns to Kirsty, 'The sort that makes you want to take a scissors to it.'

Tom smiles. 'Okay – well thanks anyway.'

Kirsty leans forward, all eyes. 'I can see there's a pretty young girl out there waiting for you, Tom Brookes.' She nods towards Beth. 'Don't suppose you should keep her waiting too long, eh?'

'She's just a friend,' he tells them.

'Talking of which.' Marion pauses for effect. 'P'raps I shouldn't say this, but I think your mum should know about the talk. Elsie Kirby opposite you, was in here earlier. Old dear's one of them curtain twitchers – can't help herself; one of them that's fond of making two and two add up to seven or eight. Anyway, Elsie told us how your mum had just had an early mornin' visitor. Some tall, distinguished looking chap with a big fancy car.'

Tom says, 'That must have been Mr Howard – the one I was talking about.'

Marion chortles. 'Well now, according to Elsie, he's some actor she's seen on the telly. Quite excited about it she was.'

Tom chuckles. 'Dare I ask which one?'

'Elsie couldn't quite remember his name; she reckoned it would come to her eventually,' Kirsty says. 'She thought he had one of them funny Irish names.'

'Course, lots of actors have second homes round here – more's the pity,' Marion says. 'We think she was probably meaning that chap out of that film where the WI women strip off and Helen Mirren says they need to get considerably bigger buns to hide their you-know-whats. Didn't I roar at that?'

'Same bloke that was in the final Harry Potter films,' Kirsty says. 'Not that I would have watched any of 'em if it hadn't been for the grandkids.'

Tom shakes his head. 'So, let me get this straight, the neighbour opposite us is convinced my mum is having some kind of dalliance with a famous actor.' He laughs out loud.

'That's about the long and short of it,' Kirsty says.

Stepping back into the brightness of the day, Tom takes off his mask, relieved to breathe in fresher air. He smiles at Beth. 'Sorry, that took longer than I thought it would.'

Poppy's still flaked out in the shade, hasn't moved a jot as far as he can tell. A tractor and trailer passes them, leaving the stench of fresh manure in its wake. When he can be heard above the tractor's racket, he says, 'Thanks for looking after the dog.'

'As you can see, it was as much as I could do to restrain her.'

He smiles at Beth, hoping she'll reciprocate but she doesn't. For the first time in a long while, he's excited about the future – the many opportunities open to a person with a bit of money behind them. And not just his future; he hopes to persuade Beth that by making the right investments at the right time it would be like winning the lottery for both of them.

The lottery. What if you knew exactly which numbers were going to come up? Did they have the National Lottery back in 1982?

First things first, Poppy really does look half dead. The energy she put into all that barking she did earlier has really exhausted her. In his most encouraging voice he says, 'Come on, Top of the Pops – let's go.' When she doesn't respond, he strokes her head. 'Come on – shake a leg, old girl.' The dog's eyes open. As if she's caught Beth's mood, she regards him with something close to suspicion. It might have been kinder to have left her at home. He would pick her up and carry her back like when she was a puppy if she wasn't so bloody heavy.

Down on his knees, he tucks his hands under her collar and pulls until she lifts her nose up; as soon as he lets go, she gives a heavy sigh and lays her head back down.

'Poor things don't like this heat.' Kirsty is standing in the shop doorway. 'Why don't we try a couple of these?'

He moves aside while she holds out a dog treat, comes closer to waft it under the dog's nose like smelling salts. It does the trick; miraculously, Poppy is up on her feet, tail wagging as she waits for another one to come her way.

'Thanks,' he says. 'You're a lifesaver, Kirsty.'

'Here – keep the bag. Reckon you'll need 'em all to get her back home.' She turns to Beth, 'Hello there, lovely. Can't say's I've seen you round here before.'

Beth reddens under her scrutiny. 'I'm just staying for a couple of days.'

'Down from London, are you?'

Beth nods.

'Well, don't worry, we locals don't bite – least ways not often.' Kirsty laughs long and hard at her own joke. In return, Beth gives her the briefest of smiles. 'My name's Kirsty by the way – Kirsty Lennox. And you are…?'

'Beth.'

'Well, it's very nice to meet you, missy. Don't know where Tom's been hiding you up till now. Afraid of competition I 'spect. I'd shake yer hand but we ent allowed to do that these days, are we?' After a throaty chuckle she asks, 'You stayin' at his mum's place then?'

'She is,' he says, holding another treat just out of the dog's reach. 'Thanks for your help. I'd better get her back home while she's still on her feet.'

The woman doesn't budge. 'So young Beth here likes a drink then, does she?'

He smiles. 'I was talking about the dog, as you well know.'

'Be a poor world if we couldn't have a laugh once in a while, eh?' Kirsty folds her arms, heaving her bosom a little higher. 'Specially when it's nothin' but bad news soon as you turn on the telly or open a ruddy newspaper.'

'It was nice to meet you,' Beth tells her before striding off like she's on a mission.

'I'd better go,' he tells Kirsty.

'Feisty one you got there,' she shouts after him. 'Best you keep her on a tight lead – an' I ent talkin' about the dog this time.'

Beth is waiting by the open front gate. The ponytail makes her look even younger – like she's a schoolgirl who's forgotten her key. As he gets closer, he can see she's playing with the latch, lifting it up and then letting it fall.

He lets the dog off the lead, and she waddles past Beth and on up the path seeking the shade of the back garden. Without looking up Beth says, 'I'm not sure I can do this, keep this up for very much longer.'

'Keep what up?'

'This act. Being here with you, pretending that everything is normal, that I'm normal and not some freak from the past who doesn't belong.'

'You may be here because of a freakish accident, but you're not a freak.'

'Look at me,' she demands. 'Do I look to you like I was born in 1961?'

'No, of course not. But –'

'That old woman back there, Kirsty, was probably born not long before me. I get that you want to make money out of this – out of *my* situation.'

'That's not my only concern. I thought perhaps we could both benefit–'

Her raised hand stops him. 'Okay fine,' she says. 'We'll play it your way. I'll do what you ask as long as you help me get back home before… before my brain explodes.'

'Deal,' he says holding out his hand.

She shakes her head. 'We ent allowed to shake hands these days.' She has Kirsty's accent down perfectly.

In the kitchen there's a note propped against the teapot: Gone for a walk with Sylvie – thought we'd stretch our legs before it gets too hot.

Sylvie is a stocky woman with a no-nonsense hairstyle and a fondness for gin and bridge. Her rescue greyhound is never on a lead but always trots two paces behind her like one of Pullman's daemons. Theirs is a recent and unlikely friendship – he wonders what his mother and Sylvie find to talk about.

He fills a glass with water and offers it to Beth, then fills one for himself. While she's staring out of the window, he sits at the table. Flicking through the FT, he circles a few possible investments. He'll have to check how long these companies have been trading.

The car keys are hanging up in the usual place. 'Listen,' he says to Beth. 'I'm just popping out for an hour or so to buy a few things. You going to be alright here by yourself?'

'As alright as I can be.'

'You could play some music, read a book or whatever.' He fiddles with the keys – keen to be off before his mum returns. 'Make yourself some tea if you're thirsty. Mum swears by camomile if you're, umm, feeling stressed. There's usually a few rather too healthy biscuits in the tin – the one with the flying swans on the front.'

'I know how to occupy myself.' A grin of sorts. 'When you're an actress you spend a lot of time *resting*.' She puts air quotes round the word.

'I didn't know you were – are – an actress,' he says. 'Will I have seen you in anything?'

'What, some old black and white movie, you mean?'

'Not what I was suggesting.' He smiles. 'Listen, I ought to get going. Won't be long. With luck, I'll be back before my mum.'

Beth gives him a half-hearted thumbs-up and then turns away.

A quick Google search tells Tom precisely what he needs but is less than helpful about where he's likely to find it at such short notice. Non-essential shops should all be open again in the main towns – though the message doesn't appear to have reached Stoatsfield yet.

A wall of heat hits Tom when he unlocks the driver's door. He turns the key so he can open the sunroof and windows and then waits for the interior to cool down to a bearable temperature.

His phone pings with a new message from Davy: *Guessing your mysterious disappearance involves a woman!!* Tom sends back a couple of thumbs-up emojis.

By reputation, Stroud is the go-to place if you're after anything that's out of the ordinary or downright weird. Whilst more picture-perfect Cotswolds towns attract tourists and middle-aged Barbour wearers with loud voices, Stroud and its independent shops appeals to less conventional, arty types. Evangelical about buying local produce, his mum had dragged him along to Stroud's farmer's market a couple of times when she was stocking up and needed a bag-carrier. He'd enjoyed it all – there was a buzz about the place that reminded him of the street market near his flat in Bristol.

Tom parks up near the church and goes in search of a cash machine. Most shops might now insist on card payments, but it doesn't hurt to flash a bit of cash when you're bargaining. He's careful to check behind him as the machine disgorges his maximum daily allowance.

Occupying quite a steep slope, the town's more practical shops congregate down at the bottom; for the more esoteric or unusual, you generally needed to venture further up the hill.

Starting at the top, he works his way down. A yawning woman in a vintage clothing shop directs him to a narrow side street he would otherwise have missed. Doing his bit to keep her in business, he buys what's described as a *gentleman's vintage paisley silk scarf* to replace the ladybird mask.

The sign above the shop she recommended reads: *Bygones be Bygones* – which seems more a declaration of peace than an enticement to buy. Its front window is taken up by dusty old radios and classic toys – the sort children have never been allowed to play with.

He pulls up the scarf before opening the door. A bell tinkles. It takes him a moment to spot an old man bent over a wooden bench and in the process of repairing an old-fashioned circuit board with multi-coloured resistors that look like tiny sweets. The man doesn't acknowledge his presence in any way but simply continues with his work.

Tom makes a show of pottering around, reading the shocking price labels on fifties television sets and wind-up gramophones – *Working order not guaranteed*. His scarf does little to mask the reek of damp.

Barely turning his head, in a gravelly voice the man says. 'You lookin' for somethin' in particular, son?' The subtext suggests he's irritated to have someone other than himself poking around in his shop.

As Tom approaches, he notices the man's fingers look too arthritic for the fiddly soldering job he's attempting. 'I'm after some old banknotes,' Tom says. 'Have you got any in stock?'

'Depends.' Not quite under his breath, the man curses an errant blob of flux. 'If you're after anything pre-war – old white fivers an' that sort of thing – you're out of luck.'

'I'm actually interested in more modern notes – ones that would have been in circulation in the early eighties.'

The man puts down his tools to peer at him through glasses that make his eyes look too big for his face. 'What you after, exactly?' he asks, like they're about to do a drug deal.

Getting out his phone, Tom scrolls down. 'Okay – so specifically, I'm interested in the predominately brown fifty-pound notes first issued in 1981 – has to be without the 1988 security thread. Predominantly green one-pound notes, also first issued in 1981 – again without the security thread; and brown ten-pound notes first issued in 1975 – without the window security thread introduced in 1987.'

'Hmm.' Narrowing his eyes, the old man pulls down a Perspex visor.

'Oh, and if you've got any of those big fifty pence coins that would be great,' Tom says. 'I'm only interested in the pre-1982 ones with *new pence* not *fifty pence* on the back.'

The man straightens up and begins to wipe the grime from his hands with an already filthy cloth. 'Old money's gettin' pretty hard to find these days. Nothin' comes cheap.' When he takes off his glasses, his eyes shrink into suspicious lines.

'Understood.' Tom gets out his wad of banknotes. 'I'll be paying in cash.'

The right switch flicked, the old man's eyes light up. He puts a hand under his visor to scratch at his sparse grey beard. 'Well now, as it happens, you might be in luck.'

He totters over to the outside door and locks it, turning the sign around to *Closed*. 'Can't be too careful these days.' Head bent, he shuffles back to the counter area and pulls back a curtain to reveal the doorway to a steep wooden staircase. Hand gripping the rail, he says, 'Wait here.'

It's all gone quiet above. Tom checks his phone – the old bloke's been gone more than ten minutes. It's possible he's forgotten what he was looking for and is taking a nap up there. He weighs his options. If he walks out, it means leaving the shop unlocked; if some opportunist were to rush in and rob the till, he'd be responsible.

Before he can decide what to do, Tom hears creaking on the stairs and, after a minute or two, the old man reappears in the doorway breathing heavily from his exertions. Getting his breath back, he heaves a shallow cardboard box onto the counter. 'Here we are, then.'

Before opening the flaps, the man raises one hairy eyebrow at him. 'Let's be clear, son, this lot may not be legal tender, but that doesn't mean they come cheap. These days, even worn old notes have what we call a *rarity* value.'

'I'm not after anything collectable or in mint condition,' Tom tells him. 'I'm just looking for ordinary used currency. I'll be more than happy to pay a fair price but not an extortionate one.'

When the old man chuckles, it mists up his visor. 'One man's extortionate is another man's highly reasonable – it's all in the eye of the beholder.' He puts his glasses on before opening up the box. 'Right then, let's see what we've got in here, shall we?'

Chapter Twenty-One

Beth

From the window she watches the car pull away, glad he's gone, thankful to have some time alone. Rachel's sandals are pinching her toes; it's such a relief to take them off and pad along the cold floor in her bare feet. Chances are she'll never get to play Lexi in any case. In the welcome cool of the snug, she drops into the nearest chair, drops the act, drops her head down onto her folded arms. She would weep if she had the energy.

The thick tick of the hallway grandfather clock fills the otherwise silent house like a repeated declaration that there is no future, no past, only this moment; then this one; and this one … Every second the present tense reasserts itself over and over. There ought to be no way to interfere with such certainty.

As a child she used to do that thing of expanding her address until she got to the universe and there was nothing else beyond. At this precise moment in time she's sitting in Pathways Cottage, in Stoatsfield-Under-Ridge, in Gloucestershire, in England, in Europe, in the world, in the year 2020.

Everything that was about to happen in August 1982 – the time she was happily living in only yesterday – has already occurred. The same is true for the year 1983 and all the years between then and now. Events will have been written down in the history books and can apparently now be read from a device small enough to fit into the palm of one hand.

Until Tom planted the seed, it would never have occurred to her to use such foreknowledge in order to get rich. He wants to exploit this opportunity to make money; as if that was the only reason, the only point of her going through this awful ordeal.

If she were to walk into any library – the one in Cheltenham for example – and locate the relevant history section, she could look up almost anything that's happened over the last thirty and more years. If that is true – and it's undeniable – how is it possible she can ever regain a future that's still to be lived; still to be decided?

Besides the relentless baritone tick of the clock, another noise intrudes. She tries to ignore the whimpering and scratching at the back door, until the dog's cries become so pitiful it's impossible and she gets up to let her in.

Delighted with this victory, Poppy follows her into the snug. The doggy smell that soon fills the small room is neither pleasant nor unpleasant – it's both. Beth sits down. Instead of curling up on the floor, the dog comes over to nudge her knee with a snout that's flecked grey with age. The dog's insistent, won't let her be until she lifts her head again.

Those two red-rimmed eyes look straight into hers. 'What do you want?' Beth asks out loud. In a world that no longer obeys logic, she half expects the dog to answer her in perfect English. Poppy nudges her with her snout and then emits a world-weary sigh. 'You and me both,' Beth tells her.

As soon as she stops stroking her ears, the dog loses interest, lowers herself down onto the flagstones and arranges her limbs for another nap.

In daylight, the room looks a lot scruffier than it seemed last night. It's orderly – everything most definitely has a place, but a layer of dust sits along the bookshelves and other less frequently used surfaces. Beth's gaze comes to rest on a framed black and white photograph of a much younger Lana standing in a busy city street. An arty pose, the wind is blowing her long hair away from her smiling face and revealing the round contours of her pregnant belly. Tom's never mentioned his dad and the man clearly doesn't live here with them. Was his dad the person who took the picture? Lana could be a widow or a divorcee.

She hears the front door open and at the same time the dog gets up and trots out into the hallway wagging her tail. 'Hello, sweetheart,' Lana says greeting the dog with more enthusiasm than she'd shown for her son.

'Hi.' Beth hadn't intended to startle her.

Lana clutches her chest. 'I saw the car was gone and didn't expect anyone to be in.' Recovering her equilibrium, she says, 'Tom's left you behind then.'

'He said he'd be back soon – he's popped out to buy a few things.' To bridge the awkwardness between them, she asks, 'Did you have a nice walk?'

'Yes, it was very pleasant. I find it helps to clear the head and soothes the troubled soul.' Lana goes to say something else but instead she bends down to remove her heavy walking boots and stows them under the bench in the porch. Her hair is less controlled, her cheeks enlivened by the exercise or something else. The pair of shorts she's wearing stop just short of her knees. Beth becomes aware of how much shorter her own are. Do they look a bit slutty to twenty-first century eyes?

The smile Lana gives her seems genuine enough as she walks past her into the kitchen. 'I'm going to make a pot of tea – would you like some?' Grumpy Lana seems to have left the building – but for how long?

'Why not?' Beth says.

'Why not indeed.' Lana opens all the kitchen windows, which she must have closed when she went out. 'Strange isn't it how a warm drink can be just the thing on a hot day.' She picks up the newspaper Tom's left on the table. 'I see some- one's been studying share prices.' She shows her the page. He's drawn circles on it here and there. 'Is this yours, dear?'

'Tom bought it at the shop when he went in for the bread.'

'I've never seen him read the Financial Times before. Recently he's avoided all newspapers – he's says they only ever carry bad news.'

'Your cooker really does belt out the heat,' Beth says.

'Yes – it's tempting to turn it off in the summer but that would only leave us with the microwave.'

'Must be handy having a microwave oven, I should imag- ine.'

Lana hands her the tin with swans on. 'Why don't you take this out into the garden. I'll bring the rest when the tea's brewed. Oh, and could you prop the backdoor open, there's a dear – it'll help get some air in here.'

Beth does as she's told. It's a long garden with a central lawn surrounded by flowerbeds and a separate veg patch down the end. The grass tickles her bare feet. To one side of the lawn there's an elderly fruit tree with a wooden table along with a collection of mismatched chairs positioned to take advantage of its shade. Beth chooses one of two upright chairs someone has inexpertly painted light blue. Above her head there are dozens of small, sharp-looking apples – tiny missiles waiting to strike.

The chink of crockery heralds Lana's appearance. Poppy trots at her heels. 'I can manage; sit yourself down,' Lana says placing a laden tray on the table. 'Here we are then.' Instead of mugs, she's brought out a set of delicate cups and saucers.

After pouring the tea, she sits down opposite Beth in the only other upright chair. It seems neither of them plans to fully relax.

'This is nice with just the two of us,' Lana says, stirring in milk. 'Gives us a chance to get to know each other a little better.' She holds the open tin out for her to choose one of the dull-looking biscuits inside.

'Not for me, thanks.' Beth puts down her cup and presses a hand to her stomach. 'Still full from breakfast.'

Lana tilts her head, peers at her with unblinking eyes. 'If you don't mind me saying, you seem a little unhappy. I assume yesterday's visit to your aunty in Cheltenham didn't go well?'

'No – she wasn't there in the end.' A few yards away, a hopping blackbird stops to dig a worm out of the lawn.

'That must have been disappointing after you'd gone all that way.' Lana rests her untouched biscuit on the edge of her saucer. 'I hear the trains to London still aren't running.'

'Tom looked it up. There's been some sort of landslip; they've got to clear it.'

'Tell me, dear, how do you feel now about the community you were living in – the place you left behind? Leaving must have been quite a wrench.'

'Yes, it was. It is.'

'Sounds like you already regret leaving.'

'I do, very much.' Beth's voice catches. 'I really want to go back. In fact, I wish to God I'd never left there in the first place. But for now I seem to be stuck here. Not that I'm not really grateful to you and Tom for letting me – a complete estranger – into your home like this.'

Lana bats away her gratitude. 'Think nothing of it – we can't have you sleeping on a park bench, can we?' She sips at her tea, then puts her cup down to say, 'You've got quite a blister there.'

'Yes – I borrowed my friend's shoes. Silly really.' Beth stares down at her feet, at the criss-cross tan lines that have appeared on them. 'She'll be wondering where they've got to – where I've got to, come to that.'

'Then between us we'll have to make sure you catch the first train back – once they're running again, of course.' Lana doesn't quite disguise a look of satisfaction at the prospect.

'There you are.' Tom is standing just inside the back door. From his confident smile, she guesses he's feeling pleased with himself. Poppy's tail begins to beat but she doesn't budge from her spot in the deepest shade. 'Taking tea in the garden – how very civilised,' he says. 'A couple of long skirts and a parasol apiece and you could be in a Monet painting.'

'What a fanciful notion.' Lana touches the side of the pot and then peers inside. 'Plenty left and still warm if you want to fetch yourself a cup.'

'Yeah sure. Be with you in a sec.' He disappears. A few minutes later, Beth catches a glimpse of him at an upstairs window; he'd been looking down on them.

It's late – too late for her to concentrate any longer. Outside the window, dusk has deepened into the sort of blackness that never occurs in London. The two of them are sitting side by side on Tom's bed, staring down at what he calls his *laptop*, which is the name for a computer small enough to sit on someone's lap. Tom is keen to go over everything again like a primary school teacher attempting to coach a particularly slow-to-learn pupil.

She's learnt that the phone he's so wedded to is known as a *mobile* in the UK but a *cell phone* or *cell* in America and a *handy* in Germany. It's hard to see why they couldn't agree on one word.

Being between times is exhausting. Her physical energy sapped by the heat; today each hour has stretched long into the next. Their walk in the woods had been a pleasant enough interlude before Tom disappeared into his room, leaving her stretched out on the guest bed flicking through a novel she had no interest in.

During their evening meal, his mum had opened a bottle

of wine and everything had seemed quite jolly until, on her second glass, Lana began to quiz her. Under the older woman's curious gaze, Beth had felt obliged to reveal a few details about her childhood – how they'd moved from county to county, circling the capital about thirty miles out like an aeroplane unable to land. Lana had wanted to know more about her mother; she was grateful when Tom joked that the lamb chops they were eating had endured less of a grilling. Put in her place, his mum did her best to laugh along. Tom's wink had made them co-conspirators.

Beth rubs her eyes; it's been more than enough for one day but he's not finished. 'I won't remember half of this,' she tells him. 'Why don't you give me a list of simple instructions *on paper.*'

'Look, I'm new to this sort of thing too.' He sweeps his hair away from his face though it soon flops back to where it was before. 'As for strategy, as I said, I don't think we should invest in the really obvious big brands. Seems to me, we need to target a group of small emerging companies where we can get in on the ground floor.'

'Like burglars.'

'We haven't got a lot in the way of seed money, so we will need to invest when their shares are still relatively cheap and then hold our nerve until the time comes to sell big.'

'Only *I* will be the one holding my nerve and waiting,' she reminds him. 'For you, the pay-off will be instant.' She snaps her fingers in his face to demonstrate.

He goes back to raking his hair; a man trying to square a circle. Finally, he says, 'Then why don't we increase our pot of money to start with. There's a film you won't have seen yet called Back to the Future. Well – three films in total, though the first one's way better than the sequels –'

'Tom, I'm quite tired and –'

'In Part Two, the antagonist – the baddie.'

She digs him in the ribs. 'You think I don't know what an antagonist is?'

'Sorry – that was patronising.' He looks genuinely remorseful.

She yawns. 'What's your point?'

'My point is, this complete slimeball gets hold of a sports almanac from the future and then, back in his own time, he gets mega-rich by betting on the winners. You and me – we can do more or less the same thing. We only need to place some carefully chosen bets at really good odds. We'll split the winnings 50:50 – half goes into your back pocket and you can invest the other half in the shares I will have earmarked for you.'

'I don't agree with gambling,' she tells him. 'It's a mug's game.'

'But don't you see,' he says, 'we can't possibly lose.'

He types a question into the laptop and a list appears on the screen. 'Here we are. Let's start with some of the big horse races of the year.' He hits a few more keys. 'Sadly, it'll be too late in the season for some, but you can spread your bets into the whole '83 season. Okay, so here we have the result of the St Leger held on the 11th of September. Which obviously wasn't a significant date in those days.'

'What's so significant about September the eleventh?'

Tom rubs at his beard like she's noticed he does when he's mulling something over. Then he says, 'I think it might be better for you not to know about some things that are going to happen.'

He carries on writing down the name of the winning horse. Before she can argue, he says, 'Right, let's try greyhounds for a change. The 25th of September is fine. And here, through the magic of the internet, we have the winner the Catford gold collar.'

He turns to her beaming. It takes a moment for the edges of his mouth to drop. 'I had a friend at uni who was pretty good at picking winners. He put on all these accumulator bets – that's where the money from one race gets carried over to the next and so on. When he started making serious money, he had to spread his bets around, even got his flatmates to put some on for him. Of course, you won't be able to bet online, so as soon as you start winning too often for chance, if you use the same betting shop, they're likely to get suspicious and stop taking your bets. You'll need to mix things up – choose different betting shops, different types of events. You might even need to lose once in a while.' Smile back in place, he says, 'Aside from that, nothing can possibly go wrong.'

'Except, how do you know I won't just take the money and run?'

That grin is less certain now. 'I don't,' he says. 'I'll just have to put my trust in you, won't I?' The light from the glowing screen is illuminating his face, turning his tanned skin pale blue.

'Only kidding.' She tousles his hair just to watch him

wrestle it back into shape, then laughs when he does exactly that. She says, 'Have you thought of getting an Alice-band to keep your fringe in place?'

'No, but these days lots of men wear them – 'specially when they're playing sport. Buns too – man-buns are a big thing. Well, not in Stoatsfield obviously; but I'm one of very few people under thirty around here. Your arrival must have upped the tally by about 25%.'

'Except, I'm not my real age. Not here, not now.'

'I have to say you don't look bad for an old lady.' He chuckles. 'In fact, you really put the sex into sexagenarian.'

She picks up one of his pillows and belts him over the head with it. 'Don't give me any more instructions,' she tells him. 'I've had more than enough for one day.' When he closes his laptop, they're plunged into total darkness. She shivers – remembering that tunnel.

Her eyes begin to adjust; there's enough ambient light to make her way over to the window. Leaning on the sill, she stares out at the thin arc of the moon; it's good to think of the planets still up there just the same as always. In the cosmos, forty years is less than a blink of an eye; time it doesn't even register.

'I can see the evening star,' she tells him.

He comes to stand behind her. 'Yes, that's actually Venus. Though it's a planet, it's often called the wandering star. One of five…'

'Five what?'

'Doesn't matter. I'm sure you've had more than enough of my nerdy stuff for one night.'

'But the stars are interesting,' she says.

'Unlike most of the stuff I rabbit on about.' When he laughs, she feels his hot breath on her neck. 'In that case,' he says, 'would you care to see my telescope? It's not that big or particularly powerful but it does the job.'

She sniggers. 'That sounded like something Dick Emery might say.'

Into her ear he says, 'Dick who?'

Chapter Twenty-Two

Tom

He sets up the telescope then turns off the bedside lamp to improve their night vision. In front of him, Beth's head and shoulders are silhouetted against the open window. The warm breeze is ruffling her hair; it carries with it the sweetness of the honeysuckle clinging to the wall outside.

He covers her hand with his, ostensibly to direct the barrel of the telescope to the right angle. 'Okay, you should be able to spot Saturn directly in front of you.'

'Wow!' she says. 'There it is. I can see the rings around the middle.' She's close enough for him to smell her scent – not the artificial kind but the pleasant indefinable aroma rising from her warm skin. She leans back a fraction until she's more or less in his arms. It's hard to resist the temptation to brush that ponytail aside and kiss her bare neck. He could be Dracula about to take a first delicious bite.

'Tell me about the wandering stars,' she says.

He clears his throat. 'They were the five identified by the Ancient Greeks; they could see that they were moving in relation to the other stars. In actual fact, they were looking at the planets Mars, Venus, Saturn, Jupiter and, um, Mercury. Did you know, the word planet comes from the Greek word for wanderer?'

'I did not know that.' She giggles. 'You really are a mine of information.'

'Or a pit,' he says.

The two of them fall silent as she stares at the planets. In the stillness, there is only this moment: the two of them alone looking up at that vast and overwhelming array of stars. He says, 'On a night like this it's easy to see why the Greeks built their myths around the planets; how they imagined them to be gods.'

She says, 'In the Planet Suite, Saturn is the bringer of old age.' He feels the smallest of shivers run through her. 'I really hated the first part of that tune; you can really picture all these old people slowly dragging themselves towards death.'

Not the note he was hoping for; in an effort to salvage the mood, Tom says, 'Why don't we move on to Jupiter.'

'Yes. My favourite – the bringer of joy.' She starts to hum a familiar part of the melody as he adjusts the barrel of the scope.

'Okay,' he says, 'you should be able to see it right there in front of you. It's the big, bright one – you can't miss it.'

'Yeah, I've got it. Amazing.'

'It is amazing. You wouldn't know just by looking at it that Jupiter's surface isn't solid – it's actually a gas giant. Can you see the cloud belts? It's also got four little moons that shuttle around it. Then there's that giant red spot just south of its equator, which is actually a massive cyclonic storm that's been raging possibly since the mid sixteen-hundreds here on earth. That storm is actually bigger than the Earth.'

'Doesn't sound like a very joyful place,' she says. 'That big red spot looks a bit like Jupiter is looking down at us with its one angry eye.'

'I never would have thought of it like that.'

Moving her head away from the eyepiece, Beth steps to one side leaving the telescope in his hands. The moment – their moment – is lost before it began.

'You know what,' she says, 'I think I've probably had enough stargazing for one night.'

'I can't tempt you to check out the other three wanderers?' A dreadful line.

'When I was growing up, there was a song about being born under a wandering star. I don't suppose you've heard of Lee Marvin – he had this deep gravelly voice…'

'Before my time.' He'd said it without thinking.

'You know what, all things considered, I think this day has been strange enough already.' She's starts stumbling around, forcing him to turn on the main light. The sudden glare hurts his eyes.

At the open door she lingers with one hand on the frame. 'Thanks. Oh, and like I said earlier, if you write down my instructions, I'll do my best to follow them. At least, that's if I get the chance.'

'I'm sure we'll get you back home soon enough.'

'I hope you're right; no offense but I'd hate to be stuck here, forever out of place.' With a sigh she turns away. 'Let's see what tomorrow brings.'

'Sleep well,' he says though she's already gone.

Tom wakes with a start. Outside his window the birds are in full chorus. Bloody noisy. Morning then – early. Staring at the ceiling, he tries to retrieve the last remnants of his dream. He'd been back in Paddington – in the station. Not now; not the eighties either. Earlier. Yes – there'd been steam trains; they'd hissed at him like snakes.

A sense of urgency overcomes him. He grabs his mobile, checks the time, then the trains. The website informs him that the scheduled services to London are due to resume at 11.58 today. Shit – it's too soon. He rubs at his eyes. He hasn't finished compiling that list of shares for Beth.

It may be stupid o'clock but he's fully awake. In case he bumps into Beth, he pulls on his jeans before he goes off to the bathroom.

Washing his hands, another problem occurs to him – how can she leave him his share of the money? Beth's bra and pants are hanging on the heated towel rail. They look dry. He thinks about putting them outside her door, but then thinks better of it – it might seem pervy that he'd handled them.

Back in his bedroom, Tom opens up his laptop and enters lots of variations into the search bar. He can't find much in-formation about the UK banking regulations back in the early eighties. Logic suggests the same basic principles must apply today. It seems it's easy enough to open a savings account for your children or grandchildren. That leaves only two problems:

he's no relation of Beth's and in 1982 he's not due to born for another ten years.

Refining his search terms, he discovers you aren't allowed to open an account in someone else's name if they're not physically present at the time.

Fuck!

After ten minutes, he's no nearer to finding a solution and decides to grab a shower while the bathroom's free.

It's seven o'clock – late enough. Hair still wet, he pulls on a fresh T-shirt and, after checking his mum's not about, knocks on the guest room door.

Beth pokes her head around the frame. From what he can see she's wearing the same baggy shirt as before – the one his mum lent her. Even bleary-eyed from sleep she looks lovely. 'I've got some good news,' he tells her. 'The London train will be running again soon. First one leaves a couple of minutes before twelve today.' He checks his phone. 'In a little under five hours.'

'Oh right. Then this is it – for better or worse.'

'Well – we'll have to make certain you catch the same train. And it will still need to be diverted via that tunnel.'

She nods several times. 'It's not exactly a racing certainty then.'

'Also, I may have hit a couple of snags with our money-making plan.' He checks again; there's no sign of his mother.

'*Your* money-making plan, you mean.' She tucks a stray strand of hair behind her ear.

'Okay, well, I don't think we ought to discuss it out here

181

on the landing.' Without a word, she opens the door wider and moves aside. Tom does his best to avoid looking at the crumpled bed and all it suggests to his imagination.

He glances over his shoulder to be certain the door is closed, then says, 'The problem is, I don't think you'll be allowed to open any sort of savings account in my name – not without me being there at the time.'

'Oh right.' She sits down on the bed, her tanned legs a stark contrast to the white sheets. He's tempted to sit down beside her but decides he ought to stay where he is, keep his distance.

'I suppose I could always come and find you later on,' she says. 'Once you've been born that is.'

'I thought of that.' He rubs at his forehead. 'It seems to me it would have to be after today and not any time before now. If you'd come to see me in the past bearing a massive cheque, I'm pretty certain I would remember.' He smiles, inside he shrinks at the idea of an encounter with an elderly version of her.

'Yes, but what if I get hit by a bus, or die of some horrible disease before then – before now?'

'For both our sakes, let's keep our fingers crossed that doesn't happen.'

'Yes well, obviously, I'm not particularly happy with that idea either, but it's possible all the same. You could look me up on that laptop of yours to see if I'm still alive in 2020.'

Shocked, he can only say, 'That's an appalling idea, Beth. Besides, as things stand right now, you'd be a missing person.'

'There's an obvious alternative.' She gets up and walks over to the window. 'You could catch the train with me. Once we're safely back in '82, we go into the first bank we find and open a joint account together. We both sign the forms, put a few quid in to officially open it and that's that.' She holds up both hands. 'I carry on paying money into the account and you'll have access to it in the future.'

He's thrown by her phrase: *safely back.* She comes over to stand in front of him. 'Then we say our goodbyes, you catch the Gustav Holst back to the here and now, and then you more or less sit back and count your money.'

'There's a risk I could get stuck. What if the train doesn't reappear, or the tunnel doesn't open for some reason?'

She closes the gap between them. Reaching up to brush his damp fringe away from his eyes, she says, 'High stakes, big win.'

Tom finds his mum out in the garden kneeling on a sponge pad like a penitent. A wave of affection tightens his chest as he watches her pluck slugs from a row of lettuces they've been busy munching despite the beer traps he'd helped her sink into the soil. 'A terrible waste of good beer,' he'd joked at the time.

'Look at all the damage they've done.' She holds up the ruined stump of lettuce. 'Where do they keep coming from?' she asks the cosmos. Finally, she looks at him. 'You've trimmed your beard, Tom. It looks much better like that.'

There are flowers and busy insects everywhere – a garden of Eden he's about to turn his back on. 'Is it okay if I borrow the car again?' He rotates the keys dangling from his finger.

'Where are you off to this time?'

'Cheltenham. The trains are running again so I thought I'd take Beth to the station – see her safely onto the London train.'

'Good idea.' She takes longer to get to her feet than she used to; he would offer a hand but knows she'd only bat it away.

'What time does Beth have to be there?' Backlit by the morning sun, her hair is a wiry halo – a seed-head. When he was little, he liked to stroke her long dark hair, marvelling at how soft it felt between his fingers. How can he contemplate leaving like this without warning her there's a chance she might not ever see him again? Was this how his father left? Did the man wake up one morning and, like the coward he obviously was, casually leave his pregnant girlfriend to cope alone?

'Her train's due in just before twelve.' Tom clears his throat. 'Think I should get her there by quarter to – just to be on the safe side.' If only he could rewind all those petty arguments – things he'd said to her in the last few months that he hadn't really meant. At least he can leave today on a more positive note.

'She seems a nice girl,' his mum says. 'Very pretty too.' He can't read her expression when she asks, 'Not tempted to go with her, are you?'

Tom has to look away, focus on the dog who's sprawled out in her usual place under the apple tree.

It's a struggle to meet her eye. 'Well?' A deep V creases the skin on her forehead.

'What if I am?'

'Listen, Tom, I've got nothing against Beth, but she's not right for you, and I think you already know that.'

'How can you possibly tell who's right for me and who

isn't?' He should rein it in but can't stop himself. 'I'm a grown man, in case you've failed to notice. I can make my own choices. You know, I bet you and that old bat Sylvie discuss me on your walks. I can picture the two of you peering into the fucking tealeaves, or some stupid crap like that, and deciding on my future.'

'Now you're being totally ridiculous. There's no reasoning with you, not when you get like this.'

'And what about that bloke who was sniffing around here yesterday morning?' he spits. 'Builder my bloody arse. When were you planning to come clean about him? Did you think I'd swallow all that rubbish about him filling in your porch?' He snorts. 'Can't say I've ever heard it called that before.'

'I don't have to explain myself or my actions to you.' She takes off her gardening gloves. 'What I said about Beth was for your sake and for hers. Yes, you can borrow my car; and yes, you are entitled to make your own decisions – I'm just warning you not to do anything stupid and risk ruining your life.'

'Ruining what life? I'm about to lose my job and I certainly don't hold out any hope of finding another one for a while – not in the worst recession in living memory. I can't even afford to keep my flat on. If I don't do something, I'll be stuck here, in this village for the living dead for who knows how long.' Hands hanging limp, he takes a couple of zombie-style steps to illustrate his point.

Unamused, his mum shakes her head at him. 'I've said all I'm going to say. Every action has consequences; if you decide to catch that train, Sylvie will have to give me a lift over to pick up the car.' Her sigh is long and dramatic. 'I just hope you're not planning to do something stupid you might live to regret.'

Poppy appears at her heels, trots into the kitchen behind his mum as if to illustrate whose side of the argument she's supporting.

Chapter Twenty-Three

Beth

Looking pleased with himself, Tom shows her a thick roll of banknotes and a bag of fifty pence pieces. He springs the elastic band and spreads all the money out on the bedcover for her to inspect. 'Does it all look authentic to you, Beth? I mean, they should do – they're not fakes; at least as far as I can tell they're not; but you're the expert here.'

Without counting every note, she guesses it's around £250 – more than two weeks wages for most people. She examines some of the notes, turns over a couple of coins and then nods. 'It all looks okay to me.' The money gives off a stale odour from having been out of circulation for so long. There are two fifty-pound notes in almost mint condition. They look about right, but she can't be absolutely certain they're the real thing because she can't remember the last time someone flashed a fifty in front of her.

Reassured, Tom rolls the notes back up and secures them with the band. He hoists a small backpack onto the bed and stows the roll inside an inner pocket, which he then zips up.

He puts the fifty pence pieces back into the coin bag and puts them in another pocket.

She can see he's also stuffed some clean clothes in the bottom of the backpack. Tom notices her noticing. 'Thought I'd put a change of boxers and clean T-shirt in,' he says, 'just in case, you know…' He doesn't finish the sentence. Neither of them knows if any part of this plan is going to work.

'You need to put this somewhere safe,' he says handing her a printed sheet of paper. 'I've listed all of the shares you should buy into. In this column, it shows the optimum time to buy them and, in that one there, when I reckon you should sell.'

'Oh,' she says, 'so is that why you've written BUY and SELL in big letters at the top?'

'Sorry,' he says. 'It's just I wasn't sure how familiar you might be with spreadsheets.'

'No, you're right – I mean we normally use an abacus and then put tally marks on the cave wall.'

'Okay, point taken.' He produces another sheet of paper. 'On this side there's a list of winning racehorses and grey-hounds. On the back, I've added some First Division football scores. I wasn't sure you would have heard of Frank Bruno yet – he was a boxer?'

'Not sure – but then I'm not exactly a fight fan.'

'Well anyway, Frank's career really took off in '82. In his whole boxing career he only lost five pro fights out of for-ty-five. I've listed those five. Obviously, the rest are safe bets.'

She smiles with genuine admiration. 'You certainly did your homework last night.'

'Yeah, that's me – always the swot.'

By a quarter to eleven they're ready to leave – keen to get going whatever the outcome. 'Here we go,' Tom says as he shoulders his backpack and heads down the stairs in front of her.

His mother comes out of the kitchen and they stand awkwardly in the hallway. Arms folded she says, 'I hope you've both got your masks with you.'

'Of course.' Stopping short of producing the evidence, Beth simply smiles at her. 'Thank you for everything, Lana. I really don't know what I would have done if you hadn't let me stay here these last couple of nights.'

'It's been a pleasure.' She's surprised when Lana pulls her into a tight hug. 'Make sure you take care of yourself, young lady.'

'I will,' she tells her as they disengage.

Head down, Tom steps forward to stand in front of his mum; though she only comes up to his chest, he looks like a little boy who's been naughty. 'I'm sorry about earlier. You don't deserve to have such an ungrateful son.'

'Come here you,' Lana says. The two of them hug for much longer than might be expected for someone only driving a friend to the station and back. When they part, Lana sniffs, turns away to hide tears she quickly wipes away. Either Tom's told her, or she's guessed from his backpack he might be going for longer.

The dog circles around trying to get some attention and Tom bends down to stroke her head. 'See you later, old girl,' he says. Straightening up he says, 'Okay, I suppose we should get going.'

Lana touches his arm. 'Tom, remember what I said.' She

turns away; doesn't elaborate, doesn't stand in the doorway to wave them off.

In the car, he's unusually quiet, negotiating the narrow roads with barely a word to her.

Stomach churning, Beth's trying not to think too far ahead. It reminds her of when she was about to have a minor operation, her certainty that something would go wrong and she wouldn't wake up from the anaesthetic. On the way to the hospital, she'd controlled her rising panic by not allowing herself to think beyond the moment. Her fears were unfounded; she'd woke up minus four wisdom teeth with sore gums and no ill effects.

All the windows are open but not the sunroof because the sun's heat is constant and oppressive. To distract herself, Beth looks at the overblown hedgerows on either side of the sunken lane. Once they reach higher ground, she takes a long breath as she surveys another collage of undulating fields. They pass a herd of black and white cows and one of them lifts its head to watch them pass. Life must be so much easier when there's nothing to think about but which patch of grass to munch. Blissful for now in their ignorance, how many of them will be sent off to slaughter when the summer's over?

She's reminded of a Joni Mitchell song about not valuing things until they've gone for good. Tom would be able to press a few buttons and, like some magic trick, the tune in her head would be playing in the car. An everyday miracle he takes for granted. Concentrating on the road, he has a fixed, unreadable expression. She decides against disturbing his thoughts. Music might raise the spirits before battle but isn't going to help either of them face what may, or may not, be about to happen.

He flicks a glance in her direction but doesn't say anything; she wonders if he's having second thoughts. Both hands on the wheel, there's a sureness about his movements. In the short time they've known each other, he's been her only support, her confidant when there's been no one else to turn to. If he decides to bale out now, she'll have to face this journey – her fate – alone. Hidden by the seat, she crosses both sets of fingers.

They reach Cheltenham station with too much time to spare. There's no one else on their side of the platform. The departures sign tells them the train is due to leave on time.

For luck, she's wearing the same white blouse she wore when she caught the train before. Rachel's sandals are still pinching her feet. She turns to Tom. 'What about tickets?'

'Don't worry, I bought them last night – that's another thing you can do these days.' He holds up his device – his *mobile*. 'No cash needs to change hands – all I have to do is show this screen to the guard once we're on the train.'

'That's amazing,' she says. 'Do you think all this clever stuff you can do now makes people any happier than they were without it?'

'That's a very good question.' He gives her a long look. 'It ought to. Pandemic aside, I don't really think the sum of human happiness has increased that much as a result of the advances in technology.'

The station canopy offers some shelter from the midday sun. They sit down on a hard bench. There's a little ping and Tom checks his phone and smiles before he types a reply.

'That message,' she says, 'was it from your girlfriend – from Steph?'

A twitch of a smile. 'Steph's not my girlfriend – she's my ex. Just a friend these days. I suppose you'd call her my best friend.'

'It's none of my business, but why aren't you together if you're so close?'

'You're right,' he says. 'It is none of your business.'

Before she can respond, he puts a hand on her arm. 'Sorry, that was really rude of me.'

'No. I shouldn't have asked.'

'It's okay – just a bit of a sore spot, that's all. Truth is, we were living together until about six months ago when Steph decided she was more attracted to women – well, one woman in particular. The two of them were about to get married before the virus put paid to all that.'

'Wait,' she says, 'you're saying lesbian couples can now officially get married?'

'Yep – they can and they do. Gay men too, of course. Steph and I are meant to be just good mates these days; would you believe she even asked me to be her best man? I often wonder what would have happened if I hadn't foolishly introduced her to Kelly – her fiancée.' He gives a wry smile.

'Wow. Being best man at her wedding to someone else – are you alright with that idea?'

'No, not really.' Tom looks down at his hands. 'During lockdown, since I've been staying at Mum's and everything, I've been thinking I should tell Steph it might be best – for me anyway – if she was out of my life; at least for a while.

She keeps sending me all these funny little messages. They're amusing alright, but they only remind me that we're no longer a couple. To borrow a rather hackneyed phrase: I need to move on.'

'Have you told Steph about me – about all this?'

He shakes his head. 'Where would I start?' He picks up his phone and, without hitting the letters, pretends to type. 'Hi Steph – you'll never guess what happened today…' He stops. 'She'd think I'd gone completely bonkers.'

'Or you were high on acid.'

A young man in a green camouflage T-shirt is walking towards them. 'We should put our masks on now,' Tom says. 'We don't want to accidentally infect previous generations with this virus.' He pulls out the ladybird mask; it might look ridiculous but it fits a lot better than the paisley gentlemen's scarf.

'Shit, that would be terrible,' she says. 'In Star Trek, whenever they travel back in time, they're always careful not to change the course of history. Even small alterations can have unforeseen consequences. You can't go back and kill Hitler, for example, because you risk all sorts of other things happening that might turn out to be even worse in the long run.'

'I did some reading last night.' He moves closer to allow her to hear him through the material. 'Theoretical physicists seem to be in agreement that anything a time-traveller does in the past has to be consistent with the world they've come from; you can't change things so much you wouldn't exist as you currently are in the present.'

'That's really interesting,' she says. 'Let's hope they're right about that.'

Chapter Twenty-Four

Tom

A few more people have joined them on the platform. Two headlights shine out from the approaching train; one of them really bright, the other dull like a suppressed wink. As it gets closer, he recognises the distinctive yellow nose and flat windscreen. A plume of diesel smoke rises from behind the driver's cab. Unmistakeably, it's a 125.

'So far so good – it's the right sort of train,' he tells Beth. With her face half-covered, it's impossible to gauge her reaction.

The echoing station announcement is hard to decipher but it acts like a starter gun for the handful of waiting passengers and they begin to walk towards where the standard-class carriages are likely to come to a halt.

The two of them remain where they are as the engine drifts past. Tom can see the driver and then, finally, read the nameplate. He's tempted to cheer at the words: *Gustav Holst.*

With a double thumbs-up, he says, 'Let's go.' When he takes Beth's hand, she grips his back. Together they march along the side of the now stationary train until they reach the right compartment.

He has to swallow his impatience at having to wait two metres behind an elderly man struggling with a cat basket. Under normal circumstances he would offer to lend a hand. 'That must be old Schrodinger,' he says once the man is on the train.

Beth smiles. 'There's got to be at least a fifty percent chance it'll die in that box on a hot day like this.' Steph would never have got that reference.

Tom returns her smile. 'You ready?'

'As I'll ever be.'

He lets her climb aboard before him. 'Turn left,' he tells her once they're both safely inside. It's even hotter than it is outside. Whilst the train's been laid up, no one thought to fix the air-conditioning. There are only two other passengers in their carriage – the cat man and someone of indeterminant sex wearing a yellow smiley face mask that looks more ghoulish than friendly. Both are sitting by the window.

They walk down the corridor and the cat emits a series of destressed cries and hisses. As they pass by, both passengers turn their heads away to avoid sharing the same air. Doors are being slammed shut. A whistle blows.

At the end of the carriage, the door opens automatically to let them into the vestibule. The whole train shudders before it pulls away. Tom notices the various signs reminding customers to stick to the Covid rules along with flagging up the potential fine for not covering your face.

Scanning the walls, he spots the little pentangle scratched

into its otherwise smooth surface. Legs braced to steady himself, as the train picks up speed, he points at it. Beth is already nodding. 'We've been really lucky so far,' he says not quite believing it.

'Shhh.' She holds a warning finger up against her flowery mask. 'Don't go and jinx it – not now.'

Sweat is already running down his back. The breeze coming in through the top half of the door isn't enough to disperse the tang of disinfectant from the toilet cubicle. Seeing Beth fan her face, he checks to make sure the glass is pushed down as far as it will go.

Once he's satisfied himself there's no one else within earshot, he opens his backpack and pulls out the roll of notes. 'I think you should put this money into your handbag,' he tells her. 'Just in case the two of us get separated.'

She grabs his arm. 'Are you having second thoughts about coming with me? Tell me now; I don't want to find out at the last minute.'

They sway together. 'You're not getting rid of me that easily,' he says, smoothing back her hair where the mask strap has ruffled it. He leans into her ear to say, 'We're in this together, I promise – whatever happens.'

She reaches up to pull his head down towards hers. They're eye to eye; if their mouths weren't covered, he would kiss her. 'Then let's hedge our bets,' she says. 'Why don't we halve the money.'

Any observer would conclude this is simply a romantic moment. Shielded by her body, he divides the cash up and then slips half of it into her handbag. She won't have noticed he's given her the more valuable notes. When it's done and she's closed her bag, he says, 'Shall we go and find a seat?'

Her bare legs remain pressed up against his jeans. 'Why don't we stay here,' she says. 'Just in case…'

'In case what?' It's a struggle to collect himself. 'Nothing can happen until we've been through Upper Threshing, at the earliest.'

Her eyes have lost their humour. 'And what if they don't divert the train through the tunnel – what then?'

'What happened to not putting a jinx on things?'

'Tell me all the same.'

'Then in slightly under an hour and a half we'll reach the glorious Berkshire town of Reading.'

'Oh God.' She turns away. 'And I'll be stuck here for good.'

'Not necessarily.' To lighten the mood he adds, 'Besides, Reading's an okay sort of town. There are far worse places to end up – Swindon, for example.'

Unaware of the local rivalry, it's clear Beth doesn't get the joke. 'Listen, we can always try again another time,' he tells her.

She shakes her head. 'I don't think I could bear to go through all this again. Could you?' Yet another good question.

'Tickets please,' a masked guard sings out as he appears in the doorway. The beads of sweat on the man's forehead are ready to roll down into his surgical mask. Tom finds their tickets on his phone and holds the screen at arm's length until the man gives a nod of satisfaction.

'No need for you two to be standing up; there's plenty of seats to be had in any of the standard carriages.' He has a soft Welsh accent – the reassuring kind. 'And I'm afraid you can't stay here; we need to leave room for other people to get through to the toilets and so forth.'

'We just needed a bit of fresh air.' Tom gestures towards the outside door. 'I promise we won't be out here for much longer.'

'Fair do's. Can't say's I blame you, to be honest. I see you're booked through to Reading. Just so's you know, there won't be any announcements today due to a technical fault with the system.' He shakes his head. 'These old trains, eh.'

They move aside so he can pass at the required distance. The guard nods an acknowledgement. 'Oh, and by the way, I like the fancy face-coverings – your ladybirds after her flowers, are they?' Before either of them can answer, he disappears into the next carriage.

'We should probably go and sit down,' Tom tells her. 'If somebody complains that we're in the way, it could stop us being out here when it really matters.' He squeezes her shoulder. 'Nothing's going to happen for a while.'

'Yeah, okay.' The train lurches and Beth stumbles into him. 'I'm not bein' funny,' she says, 'but your ladybirds reckon my flowers are crackin', don't they?' She does a pretty good Welsh accent.

He leans down until their foreheads are touching, the bridge of his nose resting against hers. 'What do you think?'

They choose a seat just inside the carriage. Remembering his lost rucksack, Tom puts his backpack on the floor, wedging it between his legs. It's going nowhere without him. Bolt upright, Beth has her handbag clamped to her chest like a lifebelt.

'Try to relax for a bit,' he tells her though this applies equally to him. 'The door's just there behind us; we can nip back there in thirty seconds, tops.'

Beth's head flicks round every time there's a noise. Her nervousness is only adding to his. When he holds her hand, it feels clammy. 'This waiting,' she whispers leaning on his shoulder, 'I just want it to be over with one way or another.'

He tries distraction. 'That cat's gone quiet,' he says. 'D'you think it's half-dead or half alive?' She shakes her head; doesn't smile.

After the train's stopped at Gloucester, a tall, broad-shoul-dered man in a black mask walks into the carriage and sits down some distance away from them. His longish grey hair is surprisingly bushy. He looks familiar; not that anyone is recognisable with most of their face covered. Though the man occasionally looks up, the two of them studiously avoid making eye contact.

They reach Stroud and the cat man gets up to leave. He takes his time getting off; the animal's renewed cries becoming more and more desperate. It's obviously survived the journey. In his thought experiment, Schrodinger hadn't taken the cat's potential loud protests into account. Through the window, Tom watches the man struggle with the weight of the carrier as he leaves the platform.

A woman in a hijab peers into the carriage and, finding something not to her liking, goes off to sit elsewhere. The creepy smiley-face man might have done the trick.

They set off again. Leaving the outskirts of the town behind, the train rises up through the wooded landscape – familiar to him from his many walks in the area. 'They call this the Golden Valley,' he tells Beth though he doubts she's listening. 'Some people say it's all the trees – when the leaves change colour in the autumn, they make quite a picture.'

His legs are getting jittery; he leans on the knee that's touching hers to still its shaking before she feels it too. 'Other people say it's because of all the money the local mill owners made from the wool. That was back in the eighteenth century. Some of the mills are still standing today …' He can't go on.

'I feel physically sick,' she says.

'Me too.' He squeezes her hand – won't let go. 'We just have to keep it together for a bit longer.' Her head comes to rest against his; he feels the weight of it, the responsibility.

The journey seems interminable and yet, when he glances at his phone screen it's only been ten minutes since he last checked. Looking out at nothing and everything, his vision blurs into indistinct shades of green that are present one second and gone the next.

Steph had shown him how to practice mindfulness. Staring at the back of the empty seat in front, he concentrates on his breathing, tries to slow it down and allow his mind only to dwell in the here and now and not stray beyond.

Despite his efforts, misgivings creep in. Is he about to make the biggest mistake of all time?

He's never been much of a gambler, but if this plan works, he'll be set up for life. He lets himself imagine the opportunities that could lie ahead. Doors open when you have plenty of money; they'll stay firmly closed if he doesn't take this chance. And then there's Beth and the promise he's just made.

On the other hand, what if it all goes wrong and *he* is the one who gets marooned out of his own time? What then?

Tom turns his head to stare at his own reflection as it moves through the countryside. He shuts his eyes. They're racing towards something; neither of them knows what will happen if or when they reach that tunnel. The risk is huge for both of them. Is it too late to persuade her to get off this train with him at the next stop?

When he opens his eyes again, something is shining out like a homing beacon. Sticking up through the trees, he can see the distinctive weathercock on the top of the church spire. As they get closer, other landmarks confirm it. He turns to Beth. 'They've diverted us; we're coming into Upper Threshing. I guess this is the point of no return.'

Chapter Twenty-Five

Beth

Brakes squealing, the train judders to a stop. Shouldering his backpack, Tom stands up like he's about to depart. He looks down at her expectantly. They're still hand in hand but she lets go to slip the strap of her handbag over her arm before getting to her feet. The carriage's only other occupants turn to watch them leave.

Inside the vestibule, Tom waits for the inner door to close. 'Time to choose,' he says. 'Either we stay right here and risk whatever the tunnel brings, or we get off and take our chances together in the twenty-first century.'

There's no one on the platform waiting to board the train – nothing to buy her more time. Caressing her hand, he says, 'Whatever you decide, I'm along for the ride.'

She looks up into those deep brown of his eyes and then lets her gaze fall to the pentangle – a symbol of magic or evil. 'I'm staying right here,' she says.

He grabs her other hand. 'Then I am too. All for one and one for all.'

'There's only two of us.'

A hard smile. 'Same principle applies.' Hand in hand, they sway like country dancers as the train pulls away.

Over Tom's shoulder, she catches a glimpse of people sitting under striped umbrellas outside the pub – The Green Man. That had been them only a few days ago. A blue car negotiates the bridge spanning the track. Two fishermen sit some distance apart on the banks of the same river they'd walked beside. It's almost an anti-climax to see people going about their ordinary lives in the summer sunshine with no inkling of what's about to happen.

'How long do you think before…?'

'No idea. I wasn't exactly taking notes last time.'

They stagger as the train shifts beneath them. The points must have been changed to divert them onto another set of tracks. A few clunks and then the train begins to pick up speed. Though she's never made a parachute jump, this must be how it feels just before you bale out. A primal fear runs through her body, weakening her legs and throwing her off-balance.

Tom pulls her into a close embrace. She breathes in his now familiar smell. He says, 'I think the tunnel might be coming up.' His last words.

The darkness is sudden and complete.

Suspended.

In mid-air.

Drifting.

She might be floating or upside down.

Then sinking back; back into her body, back into Tom's arms wrapped around her.

Dropped into blinding light.

She's alive. Tom's alive. Through watering eyes, she can see the train is still rattling along. The whooshing in her ears begins to fade away; her heart is no longer beating out of her chest.

Able to breathe freely again, she swallows down nausea, focuses instead on what she can see outside. Leafless trees. Grey branches frosted. Empty fields in corduroy ridges topped with a sprinkling of snow. Sun low in a featureless sky. Lights on in the houses they pass.

'We're through it,' she says squeezing Tom tighter, her handbag wedged uncomfortably between them.

'And look,' he says, 'not a single dinosaur.'

She spots a dog and then the hunched over person walking it.

Tom says, 'It's not very post-apocalyptic out there.' She's shivering violently, no longer from fear but from the bitter cold. Ice-laden air is pouring in through the open half of the door. 'We made it!' His hug lifts her off her feet. 'And we're both still in one piece.' He pulls down his facemask and says, 'Bloody hell it's cold.'

When she pulls her own mask down, he plants a kiss on her lips. A real smacker. Then he does it again with more feeling. The train tilts and they stagger together like drunks holding each other up. She doesn't want to let go of his warmth, but he releases her to pull up the glass pane in the door. It makes little difference to the temperature.

All the virus notices have disappeared. She sees Tom check his device; 'No signal,' he tells her. 'No signal! I mean it's not even showing me the time. I'm pretty sure the mobile phone network doesn't exist yet.'

'And that's a good thing, right? What you wanted?'

'Yeah, of course,' he says. 'Don't know about you but I'm feeling a bit light-headed. Brain still feels a bit scrambled.'

Cursing her shorts and sandals, Beth pulls down her rolled up sleeves then crosses her arms in a futile attempt to warm herself up.

His smile is less than convincing now. He peers out of the window and says, 'We've obviously jumped a month or two. Apart from that, everything appears to be going to plan.'

Her initial relief waning, she says, 'But what if it's longer than that? What if this isn't my time, or yours?'

'Only one way to find out.' Tom makes a move towards the carriage and the door opens. A fug of heat laced with cigarette smoke steals into the vestibule together with the hum of conversations. It looks to be busy inside; passengers are packed in together – a dark sea of winter coats and jackets. The luggage racks are full. No face masks in sight.

Taking his arm, Beth pulls him back from the doorway. 'Safe to say we're not in 2020 anymore,' she whispers. 'We'd better hide these masks.'

'You're right.' He stuffs his in his back pocket. 'We need to do our best to blend in.' He looks down at her bare legs. 'Although that would seem a tad optimistic given how little we're wearing.'

'You're not kidding.'

'Head up, Beth; we need to just style this out.' It's not a phrase she's heard before, but she can guess the meaning.

Ignoring the paused conversations and curious stares, she leads Tom by the hand into the welcome warmth of the carriage and the first empty pair of seats she can find. He's forced to apologise for clipping a man's head with his backpack. Around them people continue to stare open-mouthed at their foolhardiness. It's such a relief to sit down.

The noise levels have risen again; attention has moved away from them. For a long while neither of them speaks. This morning they'd discussed all this in the abstract; now she's overwhelmed by the enormity of what's happened. It's hard to get her head around the fact that they're sitting side by side in an ordinary train carriage, having made the most momentous journey known to man. Or, more accurately, *unknown* to man, since they're unable to acknowledge what's happened except in low whispers to each other.

A few rows in front of her, someone is holding up a newspaper and Beth squints at it hoping to read the frontpage headline but it's a bit too far away. It will have the date on. She's tempted to get up and snatch it from them. In fact, she's about to stand up when the whole carriage goes out of focus. A second later everything's so sharp and loud it overwhelms her.

She nudges Tom. 'I felt a bit weird just then. Like I was stoned or something.'

'Well, for a start you must be freezing.' Tom opens his backpack and, after a bit of fumbling around, he extracts a grey jumper. 'Here, put this on.'

'But what about you?'

'Can't a man still be chivalrous in whatever century this is?'

Accepting his offer, she pulls it on. The wool smells of him. Wearing it makes her feel less conspicuous – a bit more normal.

He produces a creased T-shirt and pulls it on over the one he's wearing, smoothing down the creases as if that's all that's wrong with how it looks. 'What?' He grins. 'You never know, the double T-shirt look might catch on.'

'But you *do* know,' she reminds him. 'And I'm guessing it doesn't.'

'Can't tell what year we're in yet,' he says. 'Some people are smoking although they're looking a bit furtive about it. They didn't finally ban smoking on trains until I was in my teens; which would have been the early noughties.' Seeing her confused expression, he says, 'That's what they call the decade after the year 2000.'

This is important. She needs to concentrate. The nearest smoker is hiding his cigarette behind a cupped hand. 'I can't see any signs to say this a smoking carriage,' she tells him. 'They're looking guilty because they're not meant to be doing it in here.'

He nudges her. 'So, what about the date? Can you spot any clues from what they're wearing?'

'I'm not sure, I mean woolly hats are woolly hats, overcoats are overcoats – dark and generally a bit boring.'

'Yes, but fashion changes, styles change. It's often in the details. Seems to me there's some pretty big shoulders on some of these people – specially the women. Unless we've stumbled into a carriage full of female boxers, I'd say shoulder pads are involved.'

'Women boxing, eh?' Beth was still rubbing her arms to warm up. 'You know, you do have such daft ideas.'

'In 2020, lots of women box. They also play rugby and football, in fact they're involved in lots of previously male-dominated sports these days. Well, not in *these* days obviously. In *my* day.' He rubs at his forehead. 'Christ, I sound like some nostalgic old man.'

Though her top half is a bit warmer, her legs and feet are icy. Tom nudges her. 'See that man over there with the spiky hair – does he look to you like he's channelling Rod Stewart in his heyday?'

'Yeah – he does a bit. Shit, he caught me looking.' She chuckles. 'He's just given me a do-ya-think-I'm-sexy wink.'

'Wait, you're suggesting that wasn't aimed at me?'

She nudges him back. 'You know it's probably easier for you to spot the differences. I mean – aside from the two of us – everybody in this carriage looks fairly normal to me.'

'That has to be a good sign.'

'It even smells right. I may be unsuitably dressed, but it definitely feels like I'm back home again.' She sits further back in her seat. Though still shivering a little, she relaxes into the comfort of the worn fabric. 'Everything's just fine,' she tells him.

'Great,' he says. His smile slips as he turns away from her, less pleased about it than he ought to be.

Chapter Twenty-Six

Tom

Beyond all the steamed-up windows, the bare fields have given way to houses and some sort of industrial park. He recognises one or two familiar brand names but nothing that helps him to peg the date.

He studies Beth's profile. Her eyes are closed and she looks remarkably relaxed for someone who's just travelled back thirty-eight years through a time portal. Too relaxed. He's tempted to prod her to check she's alright.

They're running parallel to a road allowing him glimpses of the cars. He picks out a brown Mercedes – a classic W126 which he's pretty sure they made until the early nineties. A Ford Escort – the hatchback model. Red Fiesta – too quick. Big silver car; could be a Renault 25? When did they…?

Damn – his view's blocked by a brick wall.

He turns his attention back to Beth. Eyes open, she's looking at him in an odd sort of way. 'You kissed me,' she says. 'Just now. Twice in fact.'

'I did, didn't I.' He grins. 'You didn't appear to object.'

'Far from it,' she says, her face softening. 'Did you mean to do it, or was it more of a spur of the moment thing?'

'Both.'

'Mmm – so this kissing thing is a new development in our relationship.'

Tom rubs at his chin. The word – relationship – sets a few hares running. After a moment he says, 'You know, there's an old film my mum really likes – which probably won't have come out yet. Basic scenario – there's this bus that's been rigged with explosives and will blow up if the driver goes below a certain speed, killing all the people on the bus. This one man comes to their rescue. Spoiler alert – at the end of the film, once they've saved the day between them, the bus driver and the rescuing hero share a passionate kiss.'

'You're telling me two men actually snog in this film?'

'No – the bus driver is this really good-looking woman. Although, by the way, gay characters kissing in films is not a big deal in the twenty-first century. Anyway. There was a point – though I seem to have lost it.'

'Was it about people kissing?'

'Ah yes. So anyway, in this film, after they kiss, the Sandra Bullock character says something about how it's easy to get swept away in the heat of the moment, but you can't trust passion that's forged in a crisis because those feelings don't usually survive when things get boring and normal again. What I'm trying to say is – '

'What you're trying to say is you only kissed me because we're both on the equivalent of an out-of-control bus.'

He frowns. 'I wouldn't have put it quite like that.' He

searches for her hand. 'Look, I've made it pretty obvious how I feel about you –'

'You're right; it's only because we're on this crazy ride together. Once the music stops, that's it.'

'I didn't –'

Beth holds up her hand to silence him. 'It's okay, I get it.' She turns away.

Shit. That whole analogy had sounded way better in his head.

Neither of them speaks while the train continues to hurtle along – speeding them both towards an unknown future.

Tom can't sit still, needs to take control of the situation and that has to start with finding out exactly what year they're in. The person who was so conveniently holding up a newspaper earlier seems to have disappeared.

He touches Beth's arm. 'I'm just going to see if I can find out more.' She seems oddly untroubled. The pupils in her eyes appear to be a little larger than they ought to be. 'I think it might be better if you stay here,' he says. 'I mean, that's if you don't mind. I'd hate for us to lose each other.'

Beth shrugs. 'Yeah, okay.'

He stands up. 'Won't be long.'

She pats the backpack he puts on his empty seat to stake his territory. 'Don't worry, I'll guard it with my life.'

Not sure exactly what he's looking for, Tom walks the length of the carriage and then through into the next one. He can see no evidence of anyone using modern technology. People are mostly staring out of the window or chatting to the person next to them. The ones doing neither glower at him as he passes like he's a stranger walking into a Wild West saloon. If there was a piano player, they'd have stopped playing. Is it his double-T-shirt-and-no-jacket look, or the holes in the knees of his jeans (which this morning seemed quite eighties to him) or does something else about him bother them?

One minute he's standing halfway up the carriage, the next he's moved on several metres. He has no recollection of the steps he must have taken in between. Could be a symptom of some kind of time-travel jetlag. He takes hold of the grab handles on both sides to steady himself.

In his experience, trains are littered with discarded newspapers at this time of day. Not today. It might be something to do with having to pay for them.

At last, he walks past a woman bent over a crossword puzzle. Her newspaper's folded in half with the wrong bit facing him. 'Excuse me, madam.' She looks up at him through heavy-framed spectacles. Tom clears his throat. 'I was just wondering if I could take a brief peek at your newspaper; if you wouldn't mind. Only for a sec.'

She puts down her pen and, peering over the rim of her glasses, assesses him. Her expression suggests she's far from impressed with what she sees. Before she can outright refuse, Tom smiles and says, 'I don't want to read it; I only want to know today's date.'

'It's the eighth of January,' her male companion tells him. 'Now hop it.'

'I will,' Tom says, 'I just need to know what year this is.'

Nearby passengers have started muttering. With a mirthless laugh, the red-faced man opposite says, 'Goin' around botherin' decent people – you need to sort yourself out, son.' He waves his paperback at him like he's about to swat a wasp. 'Look at you – unshaved and dressed like it's ruddy summer and you don't even know what flamin' year it is.' He looks around for reinforcements and receives a few nods of agreement. 'If I was you, son, I would get meself off whatever it is yer on.'

'Oh, for goodness sake,' the woman says. 'It's 1983. And, in case you're wondering, it's Saturday. Now, if it's all the same with everyone here, I'd very much like to get back to my cross-word.' Her companion wordlessly wafts Tom away.

'Thank you for supplying that information.' Tom bows his head then glares at the red-faced man. 'I hope you enjoy the rest of your day.'

'Bloody nutter,' someone declares to his back.

On his way back, Tom chuckles, delighted that it's all gone more or less to plan. A few months here or there hardly matters. He runs his hand over the trimmed stubble he's quite proud of. When he checks, the men around him are either clean shaven or bearded – anything in between must be frowned upon.

Swaying with the rocking motion of the train, he's shaken when the lag thing happens for a second time and he finds himself back inside the right carriage with no recollection of the time in between.

At least Beth is still where he left her. Looking more alert now, she moves his backpack onto the floor as he approaches. 'Well?' she says. 'Don't leave me in suspense.'

Tom sits down heavily. Leaning across, he whispers, 'Turns out it's Saturday the eighth of January 1983. Afraid we've lost a few months.'

'But that's …' She counts it up on her fingers. 'Shit, that's almost five months after I left only two days ago.'

'Which also means quite a few of the events I suggested you bet on have already happened.' He shakes his head. 'We'll have to go through the list together – change our strategy a bit or it could seriously reduce our seed money.'

'And *that's* your main concern, is it?'

'No, obviously it's not my only–'

'I've lost five months of my life!' Clutching her head, Beth's voice goes up several more notches. 'Shit a brick – Rach must think I've done a runner. She's probably let my bloody room out. Fuck – they'll have given my part to some other actress.'

Heads turn their way. The woman in the seat behind says, 'Would you please mind your language, young lady.'

Beth turns around to spit back at her, 'I'll mind my language when you mind your own bloody business.'

'Calm down,' Tom tells her. 'I don't suppose things are as bad as all that.'

'We're talking about my whole life going down the pan. For you, this has only ever been about making money.' She shrugs him away. 'Why don't you piss off and leave me alone.'

'You can swear and shout all you like; it's water off a duck's back. You're not getting rid of me that easily,' he tells her. 'We're in this together, remember?'

'Disgusting behaviour.' The woman gets up and leaves the carriage.

After an intake of breath, Beth says, 'Lewi must think I bottled out – got stage fright or something. After I finally got a chance at a leading role…' She throws her hands up. 'That play was due to run for two months – it'll be over by now. Someone else will have played Lexi – not me.'

When he squeezes her hand, she snatches it away again. 'I'm sure there'll be other parts,' he says, 'better parts even. And don't forget...' He lowers his voice. 'You'll soon have plenty in the bank to tide you over between jobs. The financial pressure will be off.'

She glares at him. 'You know, for some people, money isn't everything.'

'But money can *buy* pretty much anything.' He doesn't believe that, so why did he say it? Why make himself sound like the type of person he hates?

Tom's glad an announcement drowns out her reply. He turns away from the disappointed expression on her face.

The train's slowing down. He's definitely not keeping a proper track of time because they're already coming into Reading station.

Chapter Twenty-Seven

Beth

An icy blast infiltrates the carriage as the doors open, chilling her feet and bare legs. few passengers get off, many more get on filling up the carriage to the point where people are left standing in the aisle. One or two overcoats are dusted with snow along the shoulder. Within seconds it melts.

The doors close and a few sharp whistles send the train on its way. Beth begins to warm up again. Her head's much clearer now, thank goodness. From memory she knows they'll reach London in about half an hour. She tries to think through the likely scenarios that might have played out in her absence.

Glancing sideways, Tom looks a bit vacant. He's staring at something or someone. Either that or he's dreaming up more money-making opportunities.

Out loud she says, 'Aunty Joan must have been worried sick when I didn't show up. When I didn't phone, she would have tried to get hold of me at the flat. Eventually she'd have spoken to Rach.'

Tom's attention flicks back on. 'Your flatmate won't have

had a clue where you were any more than she did. Or do I mean *does?*'

'Maybe they'd have waited a few more days to see if I showed up. Eventually one of them would have phoned the police. Shit – am I a Missing Person? They might think I've been abducted. Or even murdered.'

'On the other hand.' Tom does that thing with his hands like he's dampening down a fire. 'Remember lots and lots of people go missing all the time. Especially in London. I'm fairly sure they won't have put up any *have you seen this woman* posters. You'll be another sad statistic – one of many.'

'Except for Kyle.' Her hand flies to her mouth. 'Oh my God – Kyle my ex-boyfriend – he was really cut up when I dumped him. Came to the flat pissed up; he turned really nasty when I made it clear I wanted him to leave.'

'Sounds like a charmer.'

'Yeah, well, ordinarily, Kyle wouldn't hurt a fly. I suppose he couldn't handle rejection. Anyway, the point is, Rach might have put two and two together and made too much. What if the police suspect he's murdered me?'

'Ask me, it'll serve him right. I mean the man's obviously a total dick-head who didn't deserve you in the first place.'

'You're very quick to pass judgement given you've never even met the man.'

They're silent until Tom says, 'He might deserve it, but, even if they interviewed him, I doubt the police gave him the full third degree. I mean, murder's a pretty big leap to make with no evidence and no body. Seeing that you're such an arty type, they probably think you upped and ran away with the circus.'

She nudges him. 'I suppose in a way I did.' They share a smile and then she tells him, 'When we get into Paddington, I'm going straight to the nearest police station to give myself up.'

Tom laughs – a big loud laugh that echoes around the carriage. 'You're not a master criminal, Beth – you've done nothing wrong. They most probably assumed you'd gone off to sit in a field and chant stuff in order to discover the meaning of existence. Didn't people used to *drop out* fairly regularly in your day?'

'This *is* my day,' she tells him. 'And no – that was much more of a seventies thing.'

Sooner than Beth was expecting, she recognises the outskirts of London. Various landmarks suggest that unless they're held up for some reason, they'll be in Paddington in about ten minutes.

Every second they're drawing closer to her old life. Shouldn't she feel more excited to be coming home? Truth is, it won't be home – not like it was before, not without a roof over her head or a job to go to.

'I'm beginning to panic,' she says. 'What on earth am I going to say to the police?'

Tom shrugs. 'Well, if you want my advice, I wouldn't just walk into Paddington police station and say...' He goes for jazz hands: 'Hi folks, I'm back!'

'Okay, so seriously then, what would *you* do?'

Another shrug. 'I'd probably do nothing at all to begin with. I'd definitely phone my aunty – your aunty – from the station and put the poor woman out of her misery. Then I'd contact Rachel and explain that you're very much alive and would like your old room back if it's free. If it became absolutely necessary, I would go to the police and declare myself a non-missing person. A present person.'

He's right. 'Seeing's you have all answers,' she says, 'tell me – how am I going to explain where I've been all this time?'

'For a start, you're not obliged to explain yourself to the police. You're not dead or injured so it's really none of their business. As for your aunty and your friends, why don't you say – I don't know – that you've been suffering from some sort of amnesia for the last few months and you've just recovered your memory.'

She scoffs. 'Doesn't sound very plausible.'

'Okay it's a corny story – a narrative cliché.' He grins. 'But you're an actress – you should be able to convince them even if it's a rubbish scenario.'

'I suppose so.' She's played a man playing a woman, a knife wielding psychopath, even a talking camel. By comparison, amnesia can't be too much of a stretch.

'Of course, there's one other option.' He squeezes her hand. 'You could tell the truth.' A snort. 'Good luck with that. I'm guessing in these less-than-enlightened times, if you stick to that story, you might end up in an institution with some Nurse Ratched type shoving drugs down your throat day and night.'

He lets go of her hand, turns his face to the window and says, 'Don't look now but something's not right here.'

'What's the matter?' It shocks her that his whole demeanor has altered.

'I've always been suspicious of coincidences and this is a pretty big one. Too big.'

As subtly as possible, she surveys the carriage. Nothing appears to have altered except the passengers are gathering their stuff together ready to leave. Everything looks more or less the same as it did a few minutes ago.

'I said don't look. That's it – keep your eyes on me. There's a man a few rows up who keeps staring at us.'

'So what? Lots of people have been doing that.' She laughs away his concern. 'We're dressed for summer in the middle of winter; I'm wearing these stupid shorts that barely cover my arse.'

'There's a man in this carriage I recognise. I've only seen him once before but I remember him distinctly because he looks a lot like Liam Neeson.'

'Who?'

'You know, the famous actor.' When she shakes her head, he says, 'I suppose he might not be very famous yet.'

'Then how do you know it's not him? If he's not famous yet, he could easily be on this train going into London just like everybody else.'

In a tone usually reserved for children, he says, 'First of all, I don't think it's actually him – Neeson would be a lot younger than this man is in 1983. His hair wouldn't be grey.'

'So it's not him.'

'No; but the point is I've seen him before. He was on this very train going the other way just before I bumped into you; right before we went through the time-tunnel together for the first time.'

'Was he still on it after we passed through the tunnel?'

Tom shakes his head.

'Then it's just that – a coincidence. They do happen you know.'

'But how often do you see the very same people on a busy train into London?'

'Probably more often than you think.' She lets this sink in. 'I thought you were the logical one but now you're sounding a bit paranoid. You only remember the man because of who he looks like.'

'Okay, so supposing you're right, why does he keep staring at us?' His head flicks round then back again. 'He's still doing it. Most people avert their eyes if you catch them looking at you, but this guy doesn't even blink.'

She chuckles. 'Could be because we're both young and, let's be honest, not bad looking. Maybe he fancies one or both of us.'

'Maybe.' He smiles at last. 'Yeah – I'm sure you're right; I'm being paranoid. Could be a symptom of time-travel lag. That and saying stupid things you don't even mean.'

'Is that an apology for your crass comment earlier?'

'It could be.' His smile works like a charm all over again. 'So,' he says, 'you think I'm good looking then.'

'My actual words were you're *not bad* looking – there's a difference. I hate to break it to you but neither of us are flawless. If I ever make it into films, they'll have to shoot me from the left, otherwise my nose looks wonky.'

'But that only makes you interesting to look at.' His breath warms her neck. 'Before you take offence, I should add that there's nothing at all I'd change about the way you look.'

'Such flattery could easily turn a girl's head, Mr Brookes.'

The train pulls into Paddington. Around them the other passengers are out of their seats and crowding the narrow aisle. They pull on hats and scarves and various other layers she's envious of. Once the outer doors open, they all surge forward. Beth finds herself separated from Tom – forced towards the exit well ahead of him.

On the platform, the cold hits her like a slap in the face. Looking back for Tom, she can see he's stuck behind a woman who's trying to manoeuvre a pushchair as well as a wailing baby and a toddler clinging to her leg. When she looks again, he's done the decent thing and picked up the pushchair for her.

Beth's shivering so hard her teeth chatter. It's too cold to stand still. 'I'm just going to ring my aunty,' she shouts over her shoulder.

'Meet you by the steps down to the Underground,' he shouts back. She gives him a thumbs-up.

People are coming at her from all sides. Spotting a whole bank of telephones, she fumbles around in her bag until she finds her purse. There's no sign of Tom but she's not unduly worried.

Chapter Twenty-Eight

Tom

'*Such flattery could easily turn a girl's head, Mr Brookes,*' she'd said like a Jane Austen character – making light of the compliment he'd just paid her. Until that moment, he hadn't realised how much he'll miss her once they go their separate ways. She was smiling at him, her face glowing from the heat of the crowded carriage. When they held hands, it felt right – like finding that matching sock you've been looking for. Not the most romantic of analogies. Of course, he hadn't said that; he hadn't said anything.

In a mad moment, he'd wondered if they might be able to see each other from time to time – tunnel permitting. A crazy idea; the risks involved were off the scale. Conducting long distance relationships was difficult enough at the best of times; the hazards of this one beyond comprehension. And yet he was tempted to suggest they try.

Thinking this through, he'd looked up and caught a different person staring at him. Short mousy hair with a face that had a shrew-like quality. Like Neeson, this man didn't look away. Didn't blink either.

He'd said nothing to Beth – she was wound up enough, had enough to process without him introducing yet more evidence of his growing paranoia. Besides, thoughts of her had distracted him again.

His way is blocked by a woman struggling to unfold a pushchair while juggling a baby and a toddler. 'Here, let me help you,' he says.

'This is so kind of you,' the mother says while he wrestles with her pushchair. The thing seems to want to fold itself up again. There are too many catches and levers for a novice to figure out.

'Take the baby for a minute,' she says, passing him the infant so her hands are free to adjust the various catches that keep the pushchair stable. Such a rash thing to entrust her baby to a stranger. The baby – malodourous and a boy judging by the blue padded outfit – screams his outrage into Tom's left ear, which is still ringing when the woman relieves him of his burden.

'Thank you so much,' she says. It's hard to judge her age from her careworn face. The toddler begins to whine about being hungry. 'I really don't know how I'd have managed without your help,' she says. He hopes the woman has a partner waiting to take over when she gets home frazzled from this journey.

'My pleasure,' Tom tells her, though of course it was no such thing.

And now he's lost sight of Beth amongst the swell of people. It strikes him again how close the people are to each other; brushing past strangers, taking their fellow travellers' winter coughs and sneezes in their stride with no fear of infection.

Beth's phone call is bound to take ages. In no hurry, he watches the woman and her children turn right through the arch he remembers used to lead to the taxi rank; and now it does again.

As the platform clears around him, the man in front of him turns round. Dressed entirely in black, it's the shrew-faced man who'd been staring at him in the carriage. By stark contrast to his black clothing, a bright yellow loop is hanging out of his coat pocket.

Seeing Tom notice it, the man grins. 'Oops,' he says, pulling on the cord. 'Seems you've caught me out.' He holds the freed object up for Tom's inspection.

It's a smiley-face mask.

Tom can't process this development, can't square this bizarre circle. His heart thumps in his chest; his brain does another leap so that he can't tell how much time has passed.

Behind him, someone clears their throat. 'Tom.' He spins around to find the Neeson lookalike blocking his way. A tall broad-shouldered man with his legs splayed – he's a formidable obstacle. 'It's a pleasure to make your acquaintance at last.' He gives a truncated bow as if they've been introduced at some party. A thin smile. 'I can see you recognise me.'

'Who are you?' Tom shakes his head. 'And what the fuck is going on?' A creeping sensation runs up the back of his neck. That mask – these two men must have travelled through the portal with them. Fuck!

'My name's Ford. I'm afraid you've come to our attention, Mr Brookes. As a somewhat dispassionate observer, I give

225

you full marks for perseverance and ingenuity.' He gives a half-hearted clap. 'Of course, without our considerable assistance, neither of you would have made it to this point today.' He spreads his arms out wide. 'For you, this will only be a fleeting visit.'

Legs trembling, Tom takes a step towards him. 'Listen, Mr Ford – if that's your real name – I have no idea what you're talking about. As for my being here, or what my plans might or might not be, that's none of your business. Now, if you and your friend here will excuse–'

'You must understand, there are certain rules that cannot be broken. Your remaining here has been judged a risk; ergo, that risk must be eliminated.'

From the man's heavy breathing, he can tell Shrew-face is behind him. Aside from the three of them, the platform is strangely empty – devoid of witnesses. Where is the cleaning crew for the train; why aren't they doing their job?

'Are you threatening me, Mr Ford?' Tom demands.

This produces a smile of sorts. 'It's just Ford. And no, I'm not threatening you. That is not our way. Fortunately, a mistake that should never have occurred has now been rectified. Disregarding a few missing months, your travelling companion – the lovely Miss Sawyer – is back where she belongs. And now, my fellow Guardian and I are here to escort you to *your own* rightful time and place.'

Tom shuts his eyes hoping that when he opens them again the two men will have disappeared.

It doesn't work.

Shrew-face laughs. 'You can't get rid of us that easily.'

Two against one – the odds aren't with him. If he kicks up a fuss, maybe other people will come to see what the noise is about. Ford extends one arm towards the carriage like a compere introducing an act. 'Now, if you wouldn't mind stepping back aboard the train, Mr Brookes.'

'And if I refuse?'

'You will find that's not an option.'

'What about Beth? At least give me a chance to say good-bye to her otherwise the poor girl will spend her whole life wondering why I ran out on her with no word of explanation.'

Smiley-face scoffs. 'Not a chance.'

'Have a bloody heart.' Tom is close to tears. 'Please let me just say goodbye to her; after that I'll come with you willingly.'

Another scoff from behind, but Ford's narrowed his eyes like a man thinking over the suggestion. Sensing a small advantage, Tom says, 'It won't take more than a minute or two. What possible harm can it do?'

Catching an almost imperceptible flicker in Ford's right eye, Tom wonders if he's just received instructions. The man's lips open; his face unfreezes. 'You have five minutes, Mr Brookes,' he says. 'She's waiting for you.'

Brushing past Shrew-face, Tom breaks into a run, dodging around the many and various obstacles in his path. Entering the main concourse area, he slows for a moment until he picks Beth out at the top of the steps leading to the tube. She's scanning the crowd and it breaks his heart to think how long she might have stood like this if they hadn't granted him this chance.

She sees him at the last minute; he almost knocks her over.

He grabs her shoulders; between breaths he says, 'No time to explain. Trust me. We need to go right now.'

'Wait. What's happened?'

'It's our only chance.' He finds her hand, grips it; pulls on her arm in the direction of the steps. 'They'll stop us unless we go right now.'

'Okay.' She matches his step as he takes the stairs two at once. No time to buy a ticket, he leaps over the turnstile; she does the same but gets stuck. Tom pulls her over, sets her onto her feet.

'Oi! You two!' someone shouts.

They make the escalators, weave a path through the other people to reach the bottom. Breathing hard, he won't relinquish his hold as they race through the tunnels to one of the platforms where, thank God, a train is waiting. They push through the people standing inside before the doors close behind them.

Bent double and fighting for breath, Beth says, 'I hope you've got a good explanation for this.'

Chapter Twenty-Nine

Beth

At least all that running's warmed her up. The tube they're on is packed out and smells of damp clothing; it's strange to be back in a world where people don't especially mind being pressed up against each other.

Her heartrate is returning to normal. They grin at each other. 'I can't say that wasn't fun,' she says, 'but what the hell happened back there?' She searches his eyes. 'Who were we running from?'

'Main thing is we got away.' Tom glances around to be certain. To her, their fellow passengers look no more threatening than the usual cross-section of Londoners. 'Yep, we've lost them,' he declares. 'That's all that matters, for now.' Seeing her expression, he adds, 'The situation – our situation – let's just say that it's far more complicated than either of us guessed.'

'You're scaring me.'

'Everything's fine now.' He rubs her shoulder. 'I'll explain later, I promise.' His smile wins her over. The body heat rising from all the other passengers is making her forget how inadequate her outfit is for the weather outside.

Tom's looking pretty pleased with himself. She trusts him, trusts that they're not in any immediate danger though she has no idea where they're headed. There must be a tube map somewhere, but other people's heads are blocking her view.

The carriage lurches, pitching them closer together. They both grab the overhead rail while the train sways them one way and then the other. Head on one side, Tom's looking at her in a way she rather likes. On impulse, she throws her free arm around his neck, pulls his head towards her and kisses him.

He pulls away. 'Beth, there's no time –' She silences him with a deeper kiss; his reluctance melts away and he kisses her back with passion. Eyes shut, she concentrates on enjoying the moment.

A sharp American voice jolts her back to the present, 'You two needa get a room.'

Tom stops kissing her to turn to the speaker – a middle-aged man who looks embarrassed by his unexpected attention. '*That*, my friend, is an excellent idea.'

People are chuckling; someone slaps Tom on the back like he's some sort of hero. Lapping it up, he asks the general crowd, 'Where the hell's this damned train going to anyway?'

Amid the general laughter, someone shouts, 'Elephant and Castle, mate.'

'That's right at the end of the line,' a heavily made-up blonde woman tells them. 'You don't want to go all the way down there.' She smiles at Tom. 'Take the girl to the West End. Show her the sights before you do anything else.'

'What you talkin' about woman?' The man next to her

shakes his head. 'The bloody sales are on; a West End hotel room'll cost him an arm and a leg.'

'And I'm saying he should start as he means to go on,' the woman says. 'Show the girl she's worth it.'

Before the situation can get any more farcical, Beth tells her, 'Thanks all the same but *she* can decide things for herself.'

Brakes screaming, the train slows down. 'This is the Edgware Road, in case you're wondering,' the blonde woman says standing up. She looks at Beth. 'You don't want to end up here.' Tapping the side of her nose, 'Just remember, darlin' – start as you mean to go on.'

Once the doors open, Beth notices how Tom's attention turns from those leaving, to those people getting on. He's studying each of the newcomers. Reassured there's no immediate threat, into her ear he says, 'Oxford Street's only four stops on. It'll be packed with bargain hunters; I can't think of a better place to hide.'

'You haven't even told me who were meant to be hiding from,' she whispers. 'Give me a clue at least. Is there someone I should be looking out for?'

He nods. 'Remember the man on the train – the one I pointed out to you.'

'The one you'd seen before who looks like some famous actor I've never heard of?'

'Well, he's one of them. If we catch sight of him, we definitely need to run.'

'You said *one* of them.' She frowns. 'You actually think more than one person is after us?' All her previous certainty evaporating. 'Why on earth would some random actor and his mates want to chase the two of us around London?'

He's still scanning the passengers. She lets go of the rail to shake his shoulders. 'Tom, look at me, why would all these people be after us?'

The doors open. More freezing air rushes in. 'Scuse me,' a man in a brown coat knocks her arm as he exits the train. The sign on the platform tells her they're in Marylebone.

Tom's checking the people crowding on. It occurs to her that going through the tunnel might have scrambled his wits. She directs his chin, forcing him to look at her. 'Nothing you've said makes any sense.'

'Look around you,' he whispers. 'Do you think any of the people here would believe you if you told them the two of us had time-travelled here from the twenty-first century?'

'No, of course not, but–'

'But nothing.' He picks his backpack up from the floor, delves into it and pulls out the roll of banknotes. Then he opens her handbag and drops the money into it.

'Why did you do –'

'Because I want to show you it's not about the money or any of the rest of it. Right now, the two of us being here together on this tube train – don't you see it's nothing short of a miracle?' He lets his backpack drop to the floor. Leaning forward, he cups her face in his hands; his lips brush against hers. 'I don't know how you feel, Beth, but I'm not ready for that miracle to end.' Looking into her eyes, he waits.

She sweeps the hair away from his extraordinary eyes. 'You're right,' she tells him. 'It's taken a miracle to get the two of us here in the same place, I'm not going to argue with the forces of the cosmos.'

They get off at Oxford Circus and file up the steps behind everyone else to emerge into the street just as it's getting dark. The temperature is plummeting, but all the Christmas decorations lift her spirits. 'It looks so pretty,' she says.

Tom isn't distracted for a moment. 'We need to buy clothes,' he says. 'Half dressed like this, we stick out a mile.'

'What if we go back to my flat. I ran out of change earlier, so I didn't get a chance to phone Rach. Even if she's rented out my room, I'm pretty sure she won't have thrown all my stuff away. Although none of it will fit you, of course.'

'Not a good idea in any case,' he says. 'That's exactly what they'll be expecting us to do.'

'You seriously think this actor knows where I live?'

'Beth – he's not an actor. I don't know who he is. He calls himself Ford though I doubt that's his name. He referred to himself and the other man as "Guardians".'

'Guardians of what?'

'I'm not exactly sure. The point is they knew both our names. It was obvious they must have been watching us for some time. One or both of them came through the tunnel at the same time we did.'

Beth stands still. Surrounded by shoppers on a mission, they're an obstacle in everyone's way. 'This is totally crazy,' she says. The people all around them are going about their everyday lives while the two of them are apparently being pursued through time by people who look like actors and call themselves guardians.

'Beth, we need to keep moving.' Linking arms with her, he propels them both forward.

All the big department stores are lit up and plastered with adverts for the bargains to be had inside. Music is spilling out into the streets they walk along. Slade fades to John Lennon then Tony Bennett's version of Winter Wonderland. The shops are packed out.

'Let's take this a step at a time,' Tom says, 'First priority has to be to try to blend in.'

'Down here,' she says leading him off of the main drag into a narrow, darker side street. They come to the shop she had in mind. It sells surplus army and navy clothing, all of it piled up on tables outside or in wire baskets trimmed with threadbare tinsel. 'You want us to be inconspicuous,' she says. 'So, let's buy some camouflage gear.'

He grins. 'We're in Central London with hardly a tree in sight.'

Beth picks up a dark green coat that's about his size and so thick she can barely lift it. 'Yes, but this must be really warm; and it's only £6.99.' She turns to the exotic-looking vendor. 'Have you got this in my size?'

'Small, medium, large.' She can't place the man's accent. 'This one large.' He looks them up and down. Studying Tom, he says, 'He need medium.'

Beth points to herself. 'And for me?'

'Small too big.' The man searches through a hanging rack. 'This better,' he says extracting a padded coat that's more or less the colour of dung. The label has the price scratched out.

'Five pounds,' the man says, holding up five fingers for emphasis.

There's no way of knowing whether that's the regular price or he's exploiting her desperation. Beth gets out her purse. 'How much for the two? Cash.'

'Hold on a minute – don't I get a say in this?' Tom says. 'Shouldn't we at least try them on?' He turns to the man. 'You said I need a medium one?'

Understanding more than she suspected, the man hands Tom a different coat. 'Ten pounds for two,' he says. 'Bargain price.'

'Actually, this is really cosy.' Tom turns this way and that. 'How do I look?'

'Like a large shrub,' she says, handing over a tenner. The shit-coloured coat is a bit big for her, but shivering like she is, Beth's past caring.

She points to her bare legs. A smile creases the man's face and after a quick search he hands her a pair of combat trousers – the sort they wear in desert wars. She shakes her head. 'Have you got any jeans like his?' She pats Tom's leg.

The man goes into the shop and comes back with a shape-less pair of denims that look about her size. Now she's warmed up, she's more inclined to be fussy. 'Can I try these on?'

'Changing room.' He extends an arm towards the back of the premises. On the way through she notices a basket full of plimsols – the type she wore for PE at school. She picks out a pair that look around her size.

When she emerges, Tom gives her the double thumbs-up. 'I'm sure I look completely ridiculous,' she says, 'but at least I'm warm.'

'Not many women could pull off an outfit like that,' Tom tells her.

She giggles. 'Don't think I didn't notice your clever use of equivocations there.' She turns to the vendor. 'How much for these?'

When he holds up three fingers, she shakes her head. 'I'll give you two-fifty.'

'Turns out Edsel here is from Mindanao in the Philippines,' Tom says, 'It's such a beautiful island.' While Edsel nods with enthusiasm, he adds, 'I'd love to take you to the beaches in Samal someday; you wouldn't believe how perfect they are.'

Before they leave, the man hands her a pair of white gym socks. 'No price,' he says, 'for good customer.' Resting a hand on Tom's shoulder for balance, she pulls them on and it makes such a difference.

'Thanks, Edsel,' Tom slaps the man on the back like an old friend. Out of earshot he says, 'This time of year it will be around 27 where he comes from.'

'Not Fahrenheit?'

'No, Celsius – centigrade if you prefer. That's about eighty on the Fahrenheit scale. Nice and hot anyway. Goodness knows what that poor man must make of London in January.'

'Sounds like you've travelled a lot. Me, I've only ever been to Spain. Oh and a weekend school trip to France.'

'Yeah – I used to travel a lot. It was my thing.' He waves a hand at everything and nothing in particular. 'Not this year, obviously.' He smirks. In fact, in *this* year I'm not even a twinkle in my father's eye. Not that I have any idea who he might have been.'

'My dad died before I was two,' she tells him. 'Mum didn't seem to be able to get it together after that. If Aunty Joan hadn't stepped in when things got really bad, they would probably have put me in a children's home.'

'You haven't told me what your aunty said when you spoke to her.'

'At first she was relieved that I wasn't lying dead in a ditch somewhere. I tried the amnesia story, but clearly I'm a bad actress because she didn't believe a word of it. Then she implied the apple hadn't fallen far from the tree. Before I could persuade her I hadn't been off on some drug-fuelled bender, I ran out of change and we got cut off.'

'You should phone her a bit later,' Tom says. 'Once she's had a chance to calm down.' He puts his arm around her shoulder, and a few steps on she slips hers behind his back.

Side by side, they reach the end of the street and turn right into the main road. 'Tell me,' she says. 'If I was playing a role on stage, what would this outfit say about my character?'

'Mmm, let's see.' He stops to look her up and down. 'I'd think she was probably a keen amateur runner; certainly no fashion slave. And judging by that coat, I'd suspect she was completely colour-blind.'

Chapter Thirty

Tom

Having grown used to social distancing requirements, Tom's alarmed at having to dodge around so many oncoming pedestrians. He resents the way they casually press themselves against him at every turn. A surprising number of them openly cough or sneeze. They should use a bloody tissue, or better still stay home instead of spraying their flying snot droplets at everybody in range.

Central London is looking a lot scruffier than his recent memory of these same streets.

The old Routemaster buses are running almost nose-to-tail and getting snarled up with taxis and private cars at every traffic light.

He steers Beth away from the more overcrowded streets, away from all that coughing and spluttering. They pass a Midland Bank, its door firmly shut. A notice about their hours of business informs customers they're closed at weekends. Damn.

'You won't be able to open an account until Monday,' Beth says, as if he hadn't already figured that out.

A few streets further on there's a branch of Girobank – another brand destined to be swallowed up by various mergers and acquisitions. Yet another bullet they'll need to dodge.

They've been walking aimlessly and now he's not sure exactly where they are. 'I'm really hungry,' Beth says, 'can we get something to eat?' She stops at the entrance to a big fast-food place. 'We could get a burger in here.'

He's reminded of his own hunger. Despite some misgivings, he says, 'Okay – yeah, why not?'

Heavy rock music greets them along with a waitress wearing a sun-visor bearing the company logo. Tom looks around for the hand sanitiser, then worries that the fear of contagion is now engrained in his psyche. He'd read somewhere how the multi-millionaire and famous germaphobe Howard Hughes used to walk around in tissue boxes to protect his feet from potential infection.

The waitress leads them over to a table which, like the others, is bathed in the sort of restless lighting normally reserved for a nightclub. Beth takes off her coat and hangs it on the back of her chair. The light above them mutates towards shades of orange and red reminding him of a Tate Modern exhibition a girlfriend had once dragged him along to. He must have been about eighteen at the time. The Turbine Hall had been lit by an artificial sun that encouraged loads of people to lie out on the cold concrete floor like they were sunbathing. He'd been blown away by the effect. Odd to think that, if they were to go over there now, that same Turbine Hall would be part of an empty and redundant power station.

Slung across the back of his chair, Tom's coat is so long and bulky it trails on the floor like a half-sloughed skin. He looks around while Beth sits back and smiles; relaxing under the influence of that orange light. Her face becomes edged with purple and then slowly turns green. 'This is such a nice place,' she says. He's thinking the exact opposite. The music changes to a driving beat that's almost impossible to talk over. 'Simple Minds.' She points a finger at the ceiling as if the band are up there playing, then she leans forward to ask, 'D'you think we're safe here?'

Tom wants to reassure her but he's just as much at sea. He shrugs then shakes his head. 'No idea.' Their fellow diners are all chatting and joking; with no phones to keep checking, they seem more in the moment than their twenty-first century counterparts.

A different waiter arrives with menus. Eyes shaded by the company sun-visor, he's tall, black and athletic looking – the sort of bloke who could handle himself if he needed to. 'I'll be back,' he declares with no suggestion of irony because Arnie hasn't yet used that line. Even so, it's disconcerting.

'You promised to tell me everything.' Beth almost has to shout.

'There's not a lot more to tell.'

'I saw you get off the train,' she says into his ear. 'When I looked back, you were helping some woman with her push-chair.'

Thankfully, the music enters a quieter patch. 'Like I said, those two men from our carriage, they ambushed me on the platform while you were off phoning your aunty. Now I think about it, that can't have been a coincidence – the timing I mean. The station was really busy, but then suddenly it wasn't. Somehow, they made sure there were no witnesses. They called themselves Guardians like it was an official title. Though they didn't say exactly what they were guarding they suggested we'd broken the rules. Somehow – and this is the part I really can't figure out – they knew exactly who we were and where we'd come from. One of them said that you were now back where you belonged.'

'He used those exact words?' The damned music is building again.

'More or less,' he yells. It's impossible – he lets the track play out.

In the silence that follows it ending, he tells her, 'They said they wanted me to get on the train and go straight back to where they'd decided I ought to be.'

'Did they threaten you?'

'In a way, but not with violence; it was much more subtle.'

The next song has a slow tuneful intro which soothes him a little. Beth angles her head. 'But you didn't want to get on the train?'

'No, I didn't.' He looks into her eyes – a moment made cornier when the romantic lyrics kick in. He does his best to ignore the song. 'I asked them for a few minutes to say goodbye to you and they said okay, that I had five minutes.' He sits back. 'You know the rest.'

She opens her mouth to say something but stops when Arnie arrives with their cutlery.

'What can I get you folks?' He brandishes a notepad. After a quick glance at the menu, Tom orders a chicken club sandwich and a bottle of lager.

'And I'll have a larger and a cheeseburger. No chips,' she says without considering any alternatives.

'Oh, and can we have a jug of tap water please?' he asks.

The waiter frowns. 'We've got soda water – the mixer sort.'

'Forget it.' Tom waves him away with a grin that's meant to suggest he'd been joking.

Beth says, 'There's something else you haven't explained.'

'What's that?'

'Why were you so desperate to stay?'

He finds her hand and squeezes it. 'To be honest with you, I didn't know what I was going to do, or what I really wanted, until the moment I saw you standing there waiting for me.'

She waits a beat and then stretches and yawns in a way that looks less than genuine. 'I'm sorry if I'm boring you,' he says.

'Oh, I'm not bored – just sleepy. All that time-travelling business seems to be quite draining. In fact, after we've eaten, I'm pretty sure I'm going to need a long lie down.'

He can hear better when the vocals give way to the instrumental section. 'You want to lie down?' Tom says. 'Are we talking about a hotel room, for example?'

'Doesn't have to be anywhere fancy.' In a cockney accent she adds, 'Nothin' that's goin' to cost me an arm and a leg.' A throaty chuckle. 'To paraphrase an old joke, as long as it's got a bed, I'm sure the two of us will be able to cope with whatever might arise.'

He's still laughing when, across the room, he spots their waiter holding high a tray with two lager sized bottles on it. Tom clears his throat. 'Are you sure you're not too sleepy to eat?'

She shakes her head. 'I'm genuinely starving – in fact the smell of other people's food is driving me nuts. Besides, you know how it is – when you're ravenous, it's impossible to fully concentrate on anything else.'

Tom toys with her fingers. 'I wouldn't want to risk any lapse of concentration.'

'Here we go.' The waiter fills their table with bottles, glasses and a tray of unnecessary condiments. 'Your food shouldn't be much longer.'

Once he's disappeared, Tom leans in until their foreheads are touching. 'Did you notice that? The waiter was right over by the bar one second, and in the next he was over here serving us and now he's all the way over at that table there.'

'The man's efficient – so what?'

'The way he moves, it's too fast – unnaturally so.'

Beth frowns. 'You're worried by a waiter who's good at his job.' She pours one of the lagers into a glass. 'What I said about being tired – I was half-serious. Neither of us has eaten anything since breakfast. I suspect we'll both feel better once we've had something to eat.'

The opening bars of Eye of The Tiger fill the room with a driving beat. At any moment, Rocky Balboa might stride in shadow boxing. Although Tom says, 'I'm sure you're right,' he continues to study the way the waiter moves around. He'd once had a Saturday job in a restaurant and remembers how they'd allocate a section to each server. There'd been a regular pattern to it. The woman who showed them to their seats has just served the people to their right and now her pad is out and she's taking the order of the couple to their left. Why didn't *she* take their order?

'Something's not right here,' Tom says. 'I can feel it. That waiter – I'm sure he's watching us.'

'Only because you keep staring at the poor man.' She puts down her drink. 'Tom, listen to me. Let's suppose, for argument's sake, you're right. Ask yourself this – how could anyone possibly know we were going to come in here when we didn't even know ourselves until just before we stepped through the door? I mean, there are loads of other cafés we might have chosen instead of this particular one.'

He takes a moment to say, 'You're right – they couldn't know, could they. I'm being a bit of an idiot.'

She smiles at him. 'Let's sit back and enjoy our drinks, eh.'

He does as he's told; tries to give the impression of a person who's relaxed and not scanning the room for further signs they're under surveillance. While Beth is complaining about the blister on her toe, he watches the same waiter pick up an order from the pass and deliver it to a couple of women sitting some distance away. The next order to come out of the kitchen looks like it might be theirs. He drops of a bowl of chips off at another table and then comes over to them. There's nothing amiss with the way he moves.

'Sorry about the wait, folks,' he says looking at Beth, 'Cheeseburger for the lady. And here's your chicken club,' he says to Tom. 'Can I get you anything else, sir?'

'No – this looks great,' Beth's quick to tell him.

'You see,' she says once he's gone. 'He's perfectly normal. Everything's normal in here; there's nothing to worry about.'

'Like I said, you've convinced me.'

'Good.' Her skin turns a shade of purple with magenta highlights. 'This burger is absolutely huge,' she says. 'I'm definitely going to need a lie down afterwards.'

Chapter Thirty-One

Beth

Coming to consciousness, her eyes focus on the window where a thin light is showing around the edges of the curtains. It's hard to tell if it's morning already, or whether it's just that the streetlights are shining in. She's reminded of Juliet's lines:

> *Yon light is not daylight, I know it,*
> *It is some meteor that the sun exhales*
> *To be to thee this night a torchbearer.*

Tom's still asleep, one of his arms slung across her like an anchor. He shifts a little and she studies his profile – wants to trace a line with her finger down his forehead to his nose and on to those generous lips. In the half-light, his tanned skinned merges with his sleep-tousled hair. If she had a sketchpad to hand, she'd try to draw him, capture him exactly as he is right now.

A wave of affection runs through her. Their time together has been like nothing she's ever experienced or is likely to again in the course of her whole life; but reality is already sneaking up to whisper questions in her ear about their future beyond this moment.

"The Future" had been a bit like a package holiday to somewhere that hadn't lived up to the brochure. *Their* future held more promise. Although the two of them are more than star-crossed. For her and Tom to exist in this room at the same time required a leap into the cosmically impossible. Talk about cradle-snatching – she's snatched a man who won't be born for another ten years. If you snatch things that don't or ought not belong to you, in the end you usually have to give them back.

Tom mumbles something in his sleep and his forehead creases with concern. She wants to smooth out those wrinkles, assure him everything is okay and they're not in any danger. But that's not the case. The men who had tried to stop Tom had called themselves Guardians. A guardian's job must be to defend things against intruders. Tom had called the tunnel a time portal. Portal is another word for doorway. It seems likely these guardians are defending it against anyone who shouldn't have stumbled inside in the first place. Yesterday they'd escaped their clutches, but what about today? And the day after that? She didn't like their odds.

Beth shuts her eyes on the conundrum, on the seedy reality of the room they're in. For the moment, they're lying here together and the rest of the world can go to hell.

'Beth.' When she opens her eyes, he's smiling at her. Stroking the side of her face, he says, 'Last night was…'

She lays a finger across his lips. 'Shhh! Last night is still last night.' She runs her hand across his chest, aware only of his now familiar smell, the contours of his skin, his pulse beneath her fingers. He moves his hand to cup her breast and it feels like he's done it a hundred times before this. He plants a line of kisses down her neck and along her collarbone. When his head comes up she says, 'Don't stop.'

His breath hot on her skin, he says, 'I won't.'

When she wakes for the second time, the cool edge to the daylight is undeniable.

Her thoughts turn to her aunty. Tom had given her all his change from paying the restaurant bill so she could ring her again. And she would have done so last night if she hadn't been so distracted. 'You're far too impulsive, young lady,' Joan had said to her on the phone once she'd finished berating her. 'Too damned ready to run off after some silly dream exactly like your …' She'd stopped short of finishing that sentence but they both knew exactly where it was heading. It was a relief when they got cut off.

It might be better not to imagine what Aunty Joan would say if she could see her now; what cutting remarks she'd make about her lying here naked next to a man she only met a few days ago. Although, more accurately, it was nearly forty years from now. When she moves, Tom tightens his grip on her thigh. 'I need the loo,' she says extricating herself to his groans of protest.

The bathroom is unheated and musty. The pattern on the dayglow shower curtain hurts her eyes. When she flushes the toilet, there's a loud rush of water and a series of dull clangs guaranteed to wake anyone above or below. The washbasin is cracked in several places and a rusty streak runs from under the cold tap to the plughole.

Looking into the mirror above it, her face distorts from

thin to fat and back each time she moves her head sideways. She could be in a fairground. With her hair sticking up like bedstraw and her reddened cheeks still creased from the sheets, she looks thoroughly debauched – a barefaced floozy.

It's a surprise to see Tom's face appear behind hers. He slips both hands around her waist and pulls her to his naked body. Kissing the side of neck, he says, 'I've been thinking.'

'I should have warned you against that.' She stares into the sadness of her own expression. 'There is no solution.'

'Don't worry,' he says, 'it was nothing very deep. I was only thinking it might be fun to take a shower together.'

Her smile is shameless. Without further warning, he turns on the water, detaches the nozzle and points it at her. She screams, grabs it from him and aims it into his face. He blocks it with his hands and the water sprays back on her. Beth leans into the cubicle and turns it off.

'Shit, we've flooded the floor.' They both look down at the puddles around their feet. 'I can't believe you just did that.'

'*We* just did that,' he insists. 'We're equally culpable for this mess.'

'True,' she says, sobered to the core.

When she slips on the wet tiles, Tom grabs her forearm to steady her. 'Careful, you could fall.'

'It's too late,' she tells him. 'I already have.'

Emerging from the bathroom, she finds Tom already dressed and sitting on the end of the bed. It makes no sense that she's reluctant to drop her towel and stand naked in front of him like Manet's bather, picnicking with fully dressed men.

Her clothes were mostly on the chair but now they're not. Watching her search, Tom clears his throat, 'I have a small confession to make.'

'You're not wearing my underwear, are you?'

His laugh is long and loud. 'No, nothing like that. Your stuff's here on the bed; in fact, I'm sitting on some of it.'

'Why?'

'Because once we're both dressed, that's it – this night is over. You can't blame me wanting to string things out a bit longer.'

She pulls her underwear out from under him. 'And you thought that hiding my clothes was the right way to go about extending things.' She gives him a long look. 'Why don't we go and have breakfast together – it's included with the price of the room. Although I suspect it might be a bit like Fawlty Towers down there.' She chuckles. 'Whatever you do, don't mention the war.'

'Sorry,' he says, 'you've completely lost me.'

Chapter Thirty-Two

Tom

At the bottom of the stairs they're faced with the choice of two doors; one bears the label *Private* and the other *Breakfast Room*. Tom wishes the first one was an option.

A balding man in a checked suit looks up from his boiled egg. 'Morning.' They both return his greeting. The man's attention stays on them as they choose the table farthest away from him. Is he paranoid to think the man's interest is anything other than bored curiosity?

In places the flowery wallpaper has faded to the point the colours are almost indistinguishable. He can hear the traffic rumbling past outside. A forties-style sideboard stretches along the best part of one wall. Besides various items of crockery, it contains a selection of mini cereal boxes, a carton of orange juice and a glass percolator full of coffee. The coffee's bitter smell fills the room.

'You're meant to help yourself to cereal and all that,' the man tells them in a raised voice. 'Kathy does a good fry-up breakfast, that's if yer missus don't decide all that's off limits.' He taps his ample stomach with some pride.

Ignoring the coffee, Beth picks up the last box of Rice Krispies and pours herself a glass of the dayglow-coloured juice. Tom spots a small pack of Ricicles. 'I haven't seen these in years,' he tells her.

The two of them keep their heads down as they eat. It turns out Ricicles are sweeter and yet more tasteless than he remembers.

A woman, presumably Kathy, appears. She smooths down the front of her greasy apron as she waits to take their order. Beth only wants toast but she's cajoled into having two boiled eggs with it. Kathy beams with a feeder's pleasure when he decides on the full English – another delaying tactic.

Once the woman's gone, Beth puts down her spoon. 'We have to vacate the room by ten,' she says as if he wasn't already aware of that particular ticking clock. 'It's now a quarter past nine; we need to–'

'Yes, I know.' He exhales. 'It's not like I haven't been thinking about it.' He rubs a hand over his eyes several times before he finally tells her, 'I've come to a decision.'

'Wait.' She holds a hand up in his face. 'Do you only *think* you've made a decision, or have you definitely made it?'

'I think…' He smiles. 'I think I've definitely come to a decision.'

'Okay, good.' She glances behind her to make sure the man in the checked suit isn't looming over her shoulder. His paranoia must be catching. 'Because I think I've made one too.'

'You first.' He searches her eyes, hoping to detect a difference that might reveal her current frame of mind.

'No – it should be you.'

He shakes his head. 'I can't see why.'

She lowers her voice to a whisper. 'Because, like the Guardians said, I'm back here now – where I'm meant to be. Yesterday, you made a spur-of-the-moment choice to enter *my* world, which, after all, is one you don't belong in – not yet. Now that you've had a chance to sleep on it–'

'Although there wasn't that much sleeping involved –'

She doesn't laugh – doesn't even smile. 'Don't do that.'

'Do what?'

'I've noticed before, you have this tendency to play important things down. And now you're trying to trivialise or at least make light of what is a momentous decision for both of us.'

'I'm not trivialising anything.' He's stung by the idea that he's not taking this seriously.

The door at the end swings open and Kathy comes in bearing a laden tray. He clears some room on the table and then springs up to take the plates from her. 'Careful, they're really hot,' she tells him too late to save his hands; he tries not to wince from the resulting pain. Damn.

'Thanks,' Beth says.

'Yes, this looks really great.' He takes up his knife and fork more for the cooling effect of the metal than a desire to eat.

Surveying the table, Kathy beams with vicarious satisfaction. 'Well, bon appetite as them foreigners like to say.'

He winces at the woman's casual racism – something he'd have to get used to in these less enlightened times.

'That hurt, didn't it?' Beth says. Seeing his confusion, she adds, 'My plate is really hot.'

'I was hoping you hadn't noticed.' In his best nineteen

thirties voice he adds, 'A gentlemen needs to keep a stiff upper lip at all times.'

She touches his arm. 'That's another thing I've noticed – your manners are really good.'

He pulls a face. 'Damned by faint praise, eh.'

'The way someone treats other people reveals a lot about their character.'

'Or it shows they've been well brought up. My mum deserves more of the credit than I do.' He shouldn't have mentioned his mum; doesn't want to bring her into the equation.

It's too late.

'She's nice – your mum,' Beth says. 'A bit stern at times, but I got the impression she's quite a softy underneath. It must have been hard bringing you up on her own. If you were to disappear without a trace, I can't begin to imagine how Lana would feel.'

He shakes his head. 'So, you're saying you think I should go back because I–'

'You're right.' He sees no hint of regret when she squeezes his hand. 'I do think you should go back. Ten years from now there will be two versions of you alive on this planet at the same time. That's just crazy. As much as I love you, you can have too much of a good thing.'

'You just did the very thing you accused me of,' he says. 'You tried to joke your way out of a serious situation. And you're inconsistent: one minute you say you love me, the next that you want me to leave.'

'I have to tell you, Tom, it would blow my mind, I mean properly freak me out, if I knew there was another version of me walking around and actually living my old life and I could accidentally bump into them.'

It's impossible to argue with her. Tom shuts his eyes while she continues. 'I'm sure such a thing must violate some sort of unbreakable cosmic law. You told me yourself that what a time traveller does in the past, has to be consistent with the world they came from. If I was one of the Guardians of a time-portal, I would do anything, and I do mean *anything*, to stop something like that happening. We may have outrun them for now, but they'll never stop searching for you. However long it takes, they'll hunt you down and send you back where you belong.'

'But what if I've decided I don't belong back there anymore? What if I want—'

She lays a hand over his mouth. 'I told you I'd made a decision and it's that I don't want to lose you. In fact, I want to come with you. That's if it's okay with you.'

They emerge arm in arm under pale grey skies. The streets are emptier now; their steps ring out in unison. Yesterday's dusting of snow has melted. The area looks more rundown in daylight especially with empty boxes and packaging piled up in shop doorways awaiting collection.

'D'you have any idea where we are?' she asks.

He chuckles. 'Not a bloody clue. I'd normally just check my phone.'

'I usually have an A to Z in my handbag.' She snorts. 'When I left home, I was only catching the tube to Paddington; had no idea...' She goes quiet for a bit. 'I really ought to ring Rach and let her know I'm okay.'

She looks so downcast. 'You're taking a massive step,' he tells her. 'I have no idea if either of us will be able to leave here. The Guardians will be watching out for us. If we make it back this time, I'm not sure I'd be prepared to take the risk trying to get back here again.'

A rusty Ford Granada splashes through a puddle sending water over their shoes. 'Bastard!' Beth shouts after it. 'My feet are soaked.'

He looks down at her plimsols. 'Why don't we buy you some better shoes?'

'I know you said I shouldn't go back to the flat, but p'raps Rach could meet me somewhere. What I wouldn't give for my Doc Martens and some dry socks.'

'Cold feet.' He stops walking. 'Could be a sign that you need to think about all this for bit longer.'

She narrows her eyes on him. 'What are you trying to say?'

'As your aunty would tell you if she knew me – I'm not that much of a catch. My prospects leave a lot to be desired. I'm thrilled you want to come with me but just a bit worried you might regret throwing in your lot with such a loser.' It's impossible to say more over the street cleaning machine trundling past, hissing and spitting as its rotating brushes suck up all the cigarette butts but leave the empty bottles and lager cans to roll around by themselves.

'Maybe you're the one with cold feet,' she says once it's gone past. 'I'd understand if you don't want to be lumbered with me.'

'The one thing I'm certain of, is that I don't want to lose you.' He covers her cold hand with his. 'I'm only thinking of you and everything you're about to give up.'

They walk on until they reach a busy junction. Beth presses the button and they wait for the green man. 'Listen,' he says, 'you've got that list in your bag and we've still got some cash left between us; d'you think Rachel would be prepared to place a few accumulator bets for you?'

Beth is already frowning. Before she can protest, he says, 'If she put some of the winnings in your savings account, you'd have a decent nest egg sitting there for you when we get back.'

'I thought you said you'd forgotten about the money.'

'I had – but now I'm thinking the two of us can't carry on living in Stoatsfield with my mum; we'd both be bloody miserable. With some decent money behind us, we'd be able to afford our own place. Or we could go anywhere you like. Well, once the pandemic is over.'

'And what exactly am I supposed to say to Rachel? Oh, hi, Rach. I know I've been gone for five months with no explanation and, as it happens I'm off again for good; but, if you wouldn't mind, could you bet this money on these horses and then invest the winnings in these shares, and then just pop it all into my savings account for me if it's not too much trouble?'

'When you put it like that–'

'And we haven't even got to the bit where I explain that a sudden expert knowledge of horses, greyhounds and future investments is the indirect result of a bang on the head that left me with amnesia for five months until it all came back to me only yesterday.'

The green man is flashing at them. 'We should cross,' he says.

'Why's that?' She doesn't move. Meeting his eye, she says, 'After all, neither of us has any bloody idea where we're going.'

Chapter Thirty-Three

Beth

On the far side of a never-ending whirlpool of traffic, she spots the distinctive white structure of Marble Arch. After a nod in its direction, Tom says, 'Well, we both know exactly where we are now.'

He slips an arm around her waist and pulls her closer while they wait on the pavement for a break in the traffic. In front of them, buses, taxis, cars and lorries aggressively compete for space; horns honk like so many battle calls. She can taste their exhaust fumes.

'Where now?' she says as much to herself as to him.

'We obviously need to agree on the next step, *our* next step.'

Not wishing to brave the road crossings, they choose the underpass. In the tunnel entrance, a busker with a guitar assaults her ears with an off-key rendition of Streets of London. The hat in front of him contains only a handful of coppers. Having so recently found herself penniless, if she didn't need the change she had left, she would give it to him. When Tom throws a fifty pence piece into the hat, the man breaks off from singing to say, 'Thanks a lot, mate.'

The graffiti scrawled on the walls is of the ugly, offensive variety. She can smell urine mixed with the cloud of dope rising from a group of raucous students. Thinking of that other tunnel, she's pleased when they emerge into the daylight at Hyde Park Corner.

Without needing to discuss it, they head off into the park itself. She dodges around a large puddle by the gate. Her plimsols may have avoided another soaking but soon the moisture from the water-logged grass begins to seep in around the soles.

The receding traffic noise is replaced by someone bellowing into a megaphone. In front of them, twenty to thirty people are gathered around a middle-aged woman who's literally standing on a soapbox – although on closer inspection it looks more like a wooden vegetable crate. The surrounding crowd is made up of women of all ages. A couple of men stand around on the periphery looking bored. One of the onlookers has painted her face white and drawn a CND symbol across it. A raised placard declares: Women for Peace another: No Nukes – support the Greenham Peace Camp. They wave these around but fail to gain much attention from the people strolling on past.

'I've read about these women.' She nudges Tom. 'Do you know if their protest works? Do the nukes leave?'

'Yeah – I think so, in the end.' Tom looks distracted and anxious. 'We need to find somewhere quieter.'

The perimeter railing is obscured by hedging that finally becomes too high to see over. 'You know what,' she says, 'in these coats, if the two of us were to stand still, I bet no one would notice us.' He doesn't look amused. Instead he leads her along one of the carriage drives until they find an empty bench with its back to the traffic.

The wooden seat is cold and damp to the touch. 'Funny to think I was meant to meet my friend Davy here only the other day,' he says. 'That was the reason I was on that train in the first place. Mum didn't want me to go. If I'd taken her advice, the two of us would never have met.'

'And if I hadn't needed a pee when I did, I'd have stayed in my seat and never bumped into you.'

'Davy was going to tell me about some job. I was worried it sounded a bit dodgy.' He shakes his head. 'Anyway, all that is irrelevant right now.'

'Before I do anything else,' she says, 'I need to find a phone box and make those calls. That's Bayswater Road over there; bound to be loads of phone boxes along it. You never know, I might get lucky and find one that hasn't been vandalised.'

'Or pissed in.'

'As long as the phone's working, I'm prepared to hold my nose.'

A small child with a pink balloon on a string is walking towards them, trailing it through the air as she skips ahead of a woman with a pushchair.

'Have you worked out what you're going to say to them?' he asks.

'No – not exactly.'

Tom fails to pay the slightest attention to the woman even though, at first glance, Beth thinks she looks remarkably like the same woman he'd helped off the train. The woman turns to look the other way and now she's less sure it's the same person.

'D'you think you should rehearse it first?' The family pass right in front of them but Tom doesn't give any of them a second glance. The woman gives no indication of having noticed them either.

Relieved, Beth says, 'I'm hoping it'll come to me at the time.'

'Okay, then, once that's done, we have another choice to make. Either we head straight off to Paddington – which shouldn't take long. We're halfway to Lancaster Gate, from there it's no more than a ten-minute walk to the station.'

'Or?'

'Or we spend a few more days here. We buy you some proper shoes; then we find a couple of betting shops and put all the money we have left on a couple of accumulators with really long odds. Then we put those winnings into your savings account where it will gain a load of interest over the years. I doubt we'll make a massive fortune, but it might be enough to give us a start.'

'A start for what?'

'For a better life than we'll otherwise have.'

She stands up. 'Like I said, before I do anything else, I'm going to call Rach and then my aunty. I'll tell Aunty Joan I'm going off travelling again. No doubt she'll lecture me about rushing into things I might regret. Oh, and then she'll run through a few of my mother's disastrous escapades to illustrate her point.'

'And Rachel?'

'I'll probably say more or less the same thing to her. If I tell her I've fallen madly in love, she'll think it's dead romantic, go all gushy and wish me good luck.'

'I like the sound of *madly in love*.' He stands up to hug her.

'You know,' he says into her ear. 'I'd do it the other way around. Start with your aunty to get the lecture over with before all the gushy upbeat stuff. That's if I was in your shoes.'

'In my actual shoes, you'd definitely have freezing cold feet but at least not about the two of us. That I'm sure about.'

He holds her face in his hands; warm breath rising like smoke, he looks directly into her eyes, 'Do you want me to come with you? I'm happy to hold your hand either metaphorically or literally. I'm sure the two of us can squeeze into the phone box together.'

'Thanks for the offer,' she says, 'but –'

'Or I could stand outside and make sure no one mistakes it for the gents.'

'Really, I think I'd rather do this bit by myself.' She grins at him. 'Having an audience might affect the quality of my performance.'

His lips brush against hers and then he kisses her so tenderly it's hard to break away. 'I'll be waiting right here when you're finished,' he shouts after her.

Chapter Thirty-Four

Tom

It's hard to sit still.

Finally, he shoulders his backpack and begins to pace up and down in front of the bench like someone whose date has stood him up. Having attracted a few curious looks, he sits down again. It crosses his mind to go and look for Beth. She can't have gone far to find a phone. But then, what if she returns via another entrance and they miss each other?

It's too risky; much better to stay put like he promised he would.

His legs judder with a pent-up urge to move; to get on with whatever comes next. Instead, he looks at his hands and then out across the grass to where a cluster of swaying, bare limbed trees block his view towards the Serpentine. A squirrel runs down one of the trunks and scampers in loops across the grass in search of food.

Today, Hyde Parks isn't especially busy. In the summer it's always buzzing, whereas this time of year there are far fewer tourists. The bench he's on is next to one of the carriage rides and so a steady stream of people walk past him – rowdy groups of students, people intent on their daily exercise and solitary office workers, heads bent on a mission to get to the next meeting or snatch a quick bite to eat.

He doesn't know the time; his phone has no battery and, even if it did, none of its functions work in this time frame. Tom knows he's facing almost due south. The sun is barely visible – nothing more than a weak glimmer in the watery sky but it's more or less directly in front of him, which means it's got to be around midday give or take the odd hour. Not much of a surprise since they'd been wandering around for ages in no discernible direction.

He wonders how Beth's conversation with her aunty is going. The woman might still be pissed off with her disappearing off the face of the earth, but they clearly mean a lot to each other. She won't want to say goodbye to her on a bitter note. Then again, an affectionate note will only make their parting more heart-wrenching for Beth.

While he's thinking all this through, he's been idly watching an older woman in a fur coat and her small puffball of a dog. For some odd reason, the dog's wagging tail stops mid wag. The dog's elderly owner has also stopped dead.

Alarmed, Tom looks around for an explanation. The man on the next bench is holding a cup ready to drink but doesn't move. In front of him, two young women have paused mid conversation, their breath a static mist hanging in the air between them.

Heart thumping, Tom checks the other direction. A man carrying a briefcase is frozen mid-stride, as is the person behind him and the couple behind him. Even the steady hum from the traffic has stopped. He scans the entire park to find he's now inside a still photograph – a moment caught in time.

He jumps up from the bench, relieved to find he can move all his limbs, that his breath is still leaving his body in a visible white cloud. He checks his pulse to be sure it hasn't stopped. When he claps his hands, the sound is muted.

Across the grass the squirrel he'd been watching is poised with some morsel between its front paws like a taxidermist might have arranged it. Looking up from the squirrel, he notices none of trees are swaying.

A couple of pigeons are suspended mid-flight. Even in the countryside, he's never experienced such a deep and complete silence.

Between the frozen trees something moves.

It gets bigger. Squinting, he makes out the dark shape of a man walking in an unhurried fashion. The man is flanked from behind by two more figures; all three of them heading directly for him.

As they get closer, he recognises the leading man, had known in his heart it had to be him. Who else but that bastard Ford?

His first instinct is to run. Beth can't be far away – he just needs to find the right phone box. Over his shoulder he sees a movement. When he spins around, he's confronted by the shrew-faced man from the station. A smile sits uncomfortably on the man's face. He wants to wipe it off, smack him right in that smug mug.

Shrew-face's attention moves from him to a point over his

left shoulder. Very slowly, his legs shaking, Tom turns around. Improbably Ford has covered 300 metres inside a second.

The next second the two of them are face-to-face. The words, 'Hello, Tom,' enter his brain, though the man's lips didn't appear to move.

'What – so you're a fucking ventriloquist now.' He tries to control the quake in his voice. 'What the hell have you done to all these people?'

Ford surveys his handiwork. 'Just a little harmless demonstration. We want you to comprehend the full scale of what you're dealing with; what your ill-advised actions have potentially interfered with.'

'Okay, so you've got my attention; why don't you explain why you can't just leave me alone instead of interfering in my life and my personal choices? It's none of your bloody business.'

'Really, Tom,' He puts his head on one side. 'Twenty-eight and you sound exactly like some adolescent who's been caught smoking. I'm beginning to feel sorry for your mother.'

'You leave my mother out of this.'

Ford shakes his head. 'Look around you, Tom, can't you see the bigger picture yet?'

'Enlighten me.'

'In summary, a mistake occurred – one with far-reaching and potentially serious consequences. Our task is to rectify that situation. Did you really imagine you could outwit and outmanoeuvre us?' A tutting noise enters Tom's head. Ford then nods towards the two men behind him. Tom's astonished to recognise the waiter from the café along with the portly man who spoke to them at breakfast.

'As I previously explained in simple enough terms and not without considerable patience on my part, your displacement was the result of an error. It was, alas, a further mistake on my part, to grant you sufficient time to say your farewells to Miss Sawyer. An error I have no intention of repeating.'

'And what about Beth – where does she fit?'

'Frankly, she doesn't. The two of you should never have met. At this precise moment, your friend is in a phone booth in Bayswater Road. She isn't moving – won't even breathe again until we decide to relinquish control over her. We have no wish to continue this hiatus any longer than necessary. Once you have accompanied us to the station, your friend and all these people will once again continue with their everyday lives unaware that any of this ever occurred.'

Ford sighs like he's facing some miscreant pupil. 'To persuade you further, let me lay before you Miss Sawyer's current future. Armed with the list in her handbag – the one you so thoughtfully provided – she will shortly embark on the course of action you outlined and, as a consequence, will eventually become a wealthy woman. Money talks as the vulgarians say. Able to part-finance a troubled stage production, she will cast herself in one of the prominent roles and, as Elizabeth Trevino, go on to enjoy a highly successful career on screen as well as stage. This, Tom, is the future you risk robbing her of.'

Tom shuts his eyes. 'Are you sure?' He opens them to look directly into Ford's eyes. 'These things – people's lives – those things aren't predetermined.'

The man's shrug suggests they're arguing over the price of a coffee. 'When you get back to your own time, you'll be able to confirm what I've just told you using any search engine.'

'And what if she chooses to follow me back to 2020?'

'Alone, she won't be able to. It was direct physical contact with you, that sent her into the future. Without you, she will have no choice but to remain here.'

'You're saying I'm the only one who can time-travel; she can't do it by herself?' In place of an answer he gets a slight nod. 'So, what's special about me?'

Ford looks away as if avoiding his eye. 'We're wasting time here. You have a choice to make. If you truly care for Miss Sawyer, you'll want her to fulfil her ambitions – her dreams if you like. Suffice to say, any alternative path will not have the same desirable outcome. As the expression goes – *not by a long way.*'

That part of Ford's argument persuades him far more than the fact that it's four against one. In any case, what chance does he have against a group of people capable of pulling a stunt like this? That's if they *are* actually people and not some fucking weird superior lifeform.

The waiter clears his throat to speak. 'If you want to write her a goodbye note, we'll ensure she gets it.' It's hard to tell whether his lips moved or not. He extracts a pad and pen from his waistcoat pocket as if he's about to take a food order and holds it up for Tom to take.

They allow him to sit to compose the note. *They've caught me.* When he writes *you're better off without me* it's with some conviction. *Please don't try to follow me – I've been told it won't work* is accurate enough. He has to turn over the paper to add, *It's been wonderful knowing you. I'll never forget our time together. I happen to know you're destined for greater things. Tom xxx* He stops short of declaring his undying love – she doesn't need to be burdened with that. He ends by telling her she should always follow her dreams.

The waiter slips the note into his breast pocket. 'Swear to me you'll give that to her,' Tom demands.

'Of course.' A quiet chuckle escapes Ford's lips. 'She will receive it indirectly, but I assure you it *will* reach her.'

A dead man walking, he lets them escort him through all the static people towards Lancaster Gate where a black cab is the only vehicle with exhaust fumes coming out of its tailpipe.

The journey to Paddington is really quick since they're able to carve a path around the now stationary obstacles in their way. Surrounded by all four Guardians, Tom walks through the statue-like passengers in the station concourse. He has no choice but to climb aboard the train with them.

They're the only occupants in the First-Class compartment. The waiter steps off the train while, leaving nothing to chance, the other two take up positions at both exits. A satisfied expression on his face, Ford eases himself into the seat opposite Tom. 'You might as well make yourself comfortable, Mr Brookes. There's nothing to be done; your little adventure is over.'

Everything unfreezes as soon as the train glides away.

Tom has never paid the extra for a seat in First-Class; privilege certainly has a cleaner smell and more leg room. If asked for their tickets, they'll probably perform some sort of mind-trick on the guard; although he doubts anyone else will be allowed to enter this carriage.

Once they've cleared the outskirts of London, the train

rattles along through the wintery landscape. Sheep are still grazing on the sparse grass, birds are flying overhead or landing in flocks on ploughed fields. The rest of the world is blindly going about its normal business while he struggles to take in what's happened.

They reach Reading far sooner than he'd expected. The other three – he hesitates to call them men – say very little, although he gets the distinct impression they're communicating in some other way.

Breaking his silence, Tom leans forward in his seat, hoping to spot a giveaway twitch or some other type of tell on Ford's poker face. 'Back there, you didn't explain *why* I was able to travel back to the 1980s in the first place.'

'You're right, I didn't.' When he speaks, Ford's mouth moves as if he's on a transatlantic link and the sound is very slightly out of sync; not that you'd notice if you weren't studying his lips.

'Seems to me no other passengers travelled through the tunnel with me except for you lot,' Tom says. 'In the park, you told me Beth won't be able to go through by herself; that she wouldn't have done in the first place if she hadn't been holding onto me at the time. Ergo – as you might put it – there has to be something unusual about me. I must be rather special in some way.'

'I would strongly advise against pulling on that particular thread.' Ford affects boredom; he flicks at the material on his trouser leg as if brushing aside a few crumbs. 'All you need to know is that such a thing can't, and indeed won't, be allowed to happen again.'

Tom's about to probe further when Shrew-face walks over to announce out loud, 'Tunnel's coming up.'

Ford nods. 'Once we're safely through, we will leave you to your own devices, Mr Brookes. This train will take you on to Cheltenham Spa station where your mother's car is currently parked. To avoid a fine, you will need to put that face mask stowed in your backpack on. You will arrive back approximately two hours after you first drove into the car park. In fact, the parking ticket on your car will still be valid. There will be nothing amiss.'

'How very efficient of you.'

The sarcasm in his tone elicits no response. Ford continues, 'You will of course notice the rather dramatic change of season. It's also likely you will feel a little disorientated at first – a common side-effect which tends to be cumulative. I'd advise you not to drive until – how shall I put it? Until you feel able to fully *reconnect* with the reality of life in the twenty-first century.'

Tom snorts. 'I know plenty of people already struggling with that.'

'Nonetheless, I felt I should warn you.' In the most insincere of tones, Ford adds, 'It really would be most unfortunate if you had a car accident on your way home.'

Chapter Thirty-Five

Beth

It's difficult to juggle her handbag and purse as well as getting the right change ready to feed into the slot. She tries Aunty Joan's number again but there's no answer. It's easy to picture her phone ringing out in the hall, her aunty guessing it's her and deciding not to pick it up.

At least Rachel answers straight away. 'Hello?'

She waits for the coin to drop then says, 'Hi Rach, it's me.'

'Beth.' A long pause. 'Your aunty rang me yesterday. Tell me you're alright.'

'I'm alright. Fine in fact. Rach, I'm so sorry I didn't, I haven't –'

'Sorry? For fuck sake Beth, it's been months. I've been worrying myself sick, wondering where you might be and what awful thing might have… Your aunty said you'd been travelling abroad all this time. Morocco, she thought.'

'Yeah, um –' Someone raps on the misted-up glass; she points to the handset in her hand and then shoos them away. 'The Atlas Mountains,' she says. 'I would have phoned but they don't have, you know…'

'What the hell made you decide to take off after that use-less mother of yours? And without a word to anyone. How did you even get to Morocco when you left your bloody passport behind?'

'I hid in the back of a camper van.'

'You're saying you actually stowed away. Well, what a hoot that must have been. I bet you laughed yourself silly. D'you know I went to the police and reported you missing? They questioned Kyle. Then there were these two other girls who disappeared about the same time.' Emotion catches her throat. 'They warned me there could be a link. Jesus Beth… I just don't know what to say to you.'

Shit, the conversation isn't going the way she'd hoped. 'It wasn't planned,' she says. 'I didn't go looking for my mum – I'm not that stupid.'

'Don't tell me you were trying to find yourself 'cos I think I might puke.'

'It was nothing like that. I fell madly in love with a boy I met. Well, he's a man really. His name's Tom. I didn't intend to follow him – it wasn't a conscious thing. It just happened.' She's close to tears. 'I'm so sorry, Rach, the last thing I wanted was to upset you or Aunty Joan. You've been such a good friend–'

'Oh yeah – so good you couldn't even be bothered to leave me a note.'

'Please Rach, you have to believe me. It all just happened so fast; I got caught up in the moment.' She can't go on.

'So why phone me now?'

'Because I'm back in London.'

'Ah – I see where this is heading. The two have you split up and now you're back here with your tail between your legs hoping we'll swallow this whole, *I just got caught up in the moment,* bullshit. Don't tell me you want your old room back because it's gone. How was I supposed to pay the rent by myself? Did you even consider that?'

Her mind goes totally blank. She has a sense of being apart from everything; viewing herself from the outside. She leans against the cold glass trying to anchor herself in the moment; here, in a steamed-up phone box, looking down at the concrete floor with all the cigarette butts around her freezing feet.

'Rach, my feet are so cold; I've only got these soaking wet plimsols on and some thin jeans I bought because they were really cheap and I was wearing shorts.'

'Christ Beth.' The line goes quiet. 'Where are you now?'

'Bayswater Road – the Hyde Park side.'

'You know you're a bloody idiot, don't you?'

'I could really do with my Doc Martens and a jumper and my blue coat would be brilliant. My fingers are numb; if you can find a pair of gloves, that would be great.'

'Yeah okay. Why don't I meet you at the Lancaster Gate entrance in about an hour?'

'I can't wait to see you. I want you to know–' The phone goes dead.

Approaching the bench, Beth can see it's empty. Could Tom have nipped off to have a pee or something. She looks around hoping to spot him heading back towards her with a sheepish grin on his face.

She sits down to wait. Time passes and she gets impatient because there's still no sign of him. What the hell is he up to? It should only take her five minutes to walk to Lancaster Gate but all the same she doesn't want to be late for Rachel; at least she'll be able to say a proper goodbye to her friend this time.

Where is he? To her left, she recognises the same little girl walking along holding a pink balloon on a string. The same mousy-haired, weary looking woman is walking alongside her pushing a pushchair. Instead of walking on past, the family head straight towards her.

'Good morning,' the woman says sitting down next to her on the bench. 'Or should that be good afternoon?' She smiles. 'You know, I've rather lost track of the time. It's easily done.'

'Hi,' Beth says, checking to see if there's a real baby in the pushchair. There is. The little girl is running about a few yards away, trailing the balloon behind her.

'I believe I've seen you before,' Beth says.

'I'm not surprised. I've been walking around the park trying to get the baby off to sleep.'

'Yes, but you were also at Paddington Station yesterday, weren't you? My friend and I got separated after he helped you with your pushchair.'

The woman unwinds her scarf a little. 'You're very obser-vant.' Her tone has altered along with her expression; she seems suddenly much older – too old to be the mother of a young baby without a lot of medical intervention. The baby is still soundly asleep – quite possibly drugged. 'Your friend – the young man who so kindly helped me at the station – I'm afraid he won't be coming back. He's left you a note though. It was rather hastily written; not quite the scented love letter he might have composed if he'd had more time.'

Beth grabs her arm. 'What the hell have your lot done to him?'

'He's simply on his way back to where he belongs.' The woman shakes off her grip with some force. 'Let me make one thing crystal clear to you – there is absolutely no point in you attempting to follow him. Due to, what one might call an anomaly, Tom was able to make the leap and simply carried you through with him. By yourself, you won't be able to leave your own time however many attempts you make.'

'Look!' the girl shouts pointing to the squirrel in front of her. The woman returns a benign smile. Beth wonders who she's borrowed these poor children from. She hands her a scruffy piece of paper torn from a small pad. Reading Tom's scrawled message, it's obvious he must have written it under pressure. She reads it through again hoping to find clues to some sort of secret plan but there's nothing.

Beth shuts her eyes and tries hard not to break down in front of this bitch. When she opens them again, the woman is adjusting her scarf getting ready to leave. 'Wait a minute,' she says, 'you used the word anomaly just now; what did you mean?'

'I suppose it can do no harm if I tell you.' After a moment's hesitation, she says, 'Young Tom Brookes is not quite what he seems. He may not be aware of it but, biologically speaking – how shall I put this – he differs from what is usual. Whereas I'm afraid you're a rather more ordinary individual.' She stands up. 'And now you should go and meet your friend. With a little persuasion, she will allow you to sleep on the sofa and so, to all intents and purposes, you are back exactly where you belong.'

'Don't go!' She goes to grab the woman but is bounced back on her heels by something she can't even see. As if it hadn't happened, the woman walks off; the girl with the pink balloon trailing along behind her.

Chapter Thirty-Six

Tom

It's drizzling when Tom arrives in Cheltenham; the air is humid as a sauna. His T-shirt is sticking to his back. Too big to fit into his backpack, he carries the green coat over his arm. Beth is still wearing his jumper; *was* wearing his jumper. However sentimentally attached to it, she won't have worn it for decades.

The drizzle turns into proper rain. He welcomes the cooling effect as he walks across the car park. The key is still where he'd left it on the top of the left front tyre. Tom stuffs the coat and his backpack into the boot before he gets in, turns on the ignition and then the wipers. They begin to smear the summer's accumulated dust across the screen, obscuring his view. Faster than they need to be, they scrape at the glass until he turns them off to watch the world dissolve in front of him.

Taking off his mask, he tries not to think of Beth and then can't think of anything else. He makes himself confront the fact that a much older version of her has now replaced the girl he just left behind. Almost sixty – she'll look like one of his mother's friends. He grieves for *his Beth* – the one he's fallen in love with.

On that awful train journey, every mile he'd travelled away from her had increased the physical pain in his chest. Now It feels like someone is pressing down on his ribcage. If he's about to have a heart attack, he can do nothing about it.

Without thinking, he plugs his dead phone into the solar charger his mum keeps in the car and, after a bit of sulking, it comes to life. The time display confirms he's only been gone two hours; two hours but another lifetime.

When he comes to, he's not sure why he is sitting in his mum's car. Then it hits him again; Beth hits him again. His phone's working and so he starts to search for the name Elizabeth Trevino. Why did she choose that particular name? Halfway through typing it in he stops. Ford had given him the edited highlights but no one's life is all success. What if bad things have happened to her? What if she's been ill? Worse still – what if she's dead? He can't face knowing a thing like that.

Abandoning the search, he drops his chin and stares at the dangling keyring. His mother's. A silver phoenix, wings spread as if rising out of flames. He'd never given it a second glance before. Is that really an apt talisman for a person when they're driving? For some reason, the little bird continues to bother him.

A hand raps on the side window; a face is looking in at him. Tom wipes his eyes with the heels of his hands before he lets the window down.

The face retreats to a safer distance. 'You alright there,

mate?' The speaker is a middle-aged black man in dust covered jeans carrying a hard hat.

'I'm fine.'

'Only, I saw your engine was running and you just sittin' there starin' into space and lookin' miserable. To be honest with you, I even had a quick shufty around the back to make sure there was no hosepipe attached.'

Tom shakes his head. 'Thank you for asking, but I'm fine. Honestly.' To prevent further conversation, he puts the car in gear and drives away.

Pulling up outside the cottage, he's shocked to realise he can't recall the journey he's just made. His mum opens the door; he notices how she swaps a worried look for a smile.

'Hi, Tom,' she says, as he stumbles from the car. She looks up into his face before wrapping both arms around him, forcing him into a tight hug he's in no mood for. Releasing him, she says, 'You didn't go with her in the end then.'

He holds both hands up to demonstrate something though he's not sure what.

'Come and have a cup of tea,' she says.

'Ah yes, a cuppa – the universal panacea. Bound to sort me out in a trice.'

'I can see you're upset,' she says. 'Come on in out of this rain.'

'I'm finding this rain a bloody relief.' He twirls around, does a little dance then throws his head back and lets the water fall into his open mouth.

He's not sure how he got to be crouching on his haunches.

His mum is there – her hands under his arm, pulling him up, guiding him inside the house. For once she doesn't tell him to take his shoes off before leading him into the kitchen.

With her guidance he's sitting down. The dog leans against his leg. Next thing the kettle's whistling. A mug of tea is in front of him, as if by sleight of hand.

She comes to sit not in her usual chair but in the one beside him. Her hands feel rough from the garden as she holds his. 'Don't say anything,' he tells her. 'I don't want to talk about it, if that's okay with you.' She runs a hand through his hair, strokes it back from his eyes to see his full face, though he would rather she didn't.

He's lying down. Opening his eyes, Tom discovers he's in his own bed. The window's open; he can hear a robin singing to defend its territory. Like he'd been totally pissed, he has no memory of getting into bed or taking off his shoes and trousers. He's embarrassed to realise that his mum had had to put him to bed like a child – a drunken child. She will have assumed he'd been boozing. He groans at the prospect of the lecture about drunk driving that's about to come his way.

Sitting up, his head feels woozy. At first, it's hard to focus and then the room comes into sharp relief, though he wishes it hadn't. And he's ravenously hungry. Before a shower, he needs food.

The radio's on when he walks into the kitchen. What a surprise – it's Classic effing M. Poppy greets him with her usual enthusiasm. His mum is sitting at the table eating muesli with blueberries. He walks over to the fridge. Eggs, tomatoes, a half packet of bacon – a promising start. 'I thought I might have a fry-up,' he says. 'Can I tempt you with something less healthy?'

It surprises him when she says, 'Why not? Wouldn't it be boring if we were virtuous all of the time?'

'It's only a fried breakfast, Mum, not a coke-fuelled orgy.' Roused by the smell of cooking bacon, Poppy comes to sit next to the Aga in silent begging mode. Along with everything else, he throws a few leftover potatoes into the pan.

Aside from the music, they eat in silence. Tom wolfs down the food then wipes his plate with a piece of bread. When his mum's not looking, he slips the dog a few pieces of bacon rind. He waits for the lecture to come, but his mum continues to eat while occasionally waving a raised finger in time to Elgar's Variations.

After a shower he feels a bit better – physically at least. It smells like his mum is making some sort of chutney. True to her word, she stirs the pan and continues to bite her tongue; he can only imagine the inner struggle involved.

'I used up all the eggs,' he tells her. 'Just going to pop down to the shop to get some more.' He makes the fatal mistake of asking if she needs anything else and then is forced to wait while she writes down a whole list of things.

At the front door he says, 'I'm not taking the dog. I had to practically carry her back the last time.' Last time Beth had been with him. He wills away the rawness of the emotion this produces.

The air is fresher for the rain. There are drying puddles on the pavement. A bent over man is heading his way, his mask worn like a chin hammock. He recognises Mr Curtis. Seeing Tom, the old man looks terrified – like the grim reaper's heading straight for him. 'Morning, Mr Curtis,' Tom says stepping out into the road to give him plenty of space. His greeting isn't returned as the old man scurries by.

The shop is empty of customers. Kirsty, the nosy one, is alone behind the counter. He's often wondered what keeps her working here when she has to be long past retirement age. He fills a basket with the stuff from the list and then goes to the checkout.

Kirsty's a bit deaf; he raises his voice so she can hear him. 'No Marion today then?'

''Fraid not. She's under the doctor at the moment.' Tom's mask hides his amusement at her turn of phrase. 'Done her back in doin' the garden. I keep tellin' her: Mar you should leave the heavy digging for your Desmond when he gets home. Does she listen? Does she buggery.'

As soon as she scans each item, he puts them into his mum's shopping bag. 'Your young lady friend not with you today then?' She's taking her time, hoping to prolong the conversation.

'Sadly, she's gone back home.' Tom swallows hard and counts the few items left to be scanned before he can leave.

''Spect you must be missing her company, eh?' He doesn't answer, doesn't want to encourage her. 'Not much happenin' round here for you young people, is there?'

This doesn't seem to require a response. Only two more items to go, thank God.

'That Elsie Kirby is still goin' on about your mum and how

she saw some famous Irish actor sneaking out of your house the other morning.'

'Yeah – I remember you told me about that before.'

'Elsie couldn't remember his name and, a course, we all guessed wrong didn't we. Turns out, it's only Liam Neeson she reckons she saw. The woman's convinced he's your mum's fancy man. Liam bloody Neeson of all people! We had to chuckle. Eh, you should tell Lana – she's bound to have a bloody good laugh about it.'

Tom rams the last few items into the bag and waves his card at the machine. He manages to mutter, 'Sorry, Kirsty, got to dash.' Once he's clear of her curious eyes, he breaks into a run.

Chapter Thirty-Seven

Beth

Her old bedroom is now occupied by a girl called Linda. Eighteen, petite and chirpy, she works in a record shop near Shepherd's Bush Green. Everything about the girl is scaled down and cute; when she sits on the sofa, her tiny feet don't reach the floor. She has a line of teddies on her bed. They're a family, apparently. Linda likes to say ickle instead of little, and, thanks to her, they can't watch any films that feature guns or explosions. Disliking the girl would be like disliking a child. Even so, Beth can't stand her.

It's odd living back in the flat and yet sleeping on the sofa – a temporary arrangement that suits no one. A week or two at most they'd agreed, until she can find somewhere else. They insist she pays a third of the rent and her bedding and clothes have to be out of sight during the day. Beth's not in a position to argue.

It's after dark and raining hard. She's almost home when Kyle steps from the shadows to block her way, his face made ghostly by the streetlight. His opening line is, 'Did you know the police questioned me twice?' Rain dripping into his eyes, he adds, 'The second time I was in there for four bloody hours.'

'I'm very sorry that happened to you, Kyle.'

'Is that all you've got to say?' He comes closer, pulls his lips together like he might be preparing to spit at her.

She backs away. The rain is bouncing off the pavement, its ferocity chasing everyone indoors. It's hard to imagine how she once found this man attractive. 'I'm sorry you got dragged into it,' she says. 'That should never have happened. It wasn't my intention—'

'What were your intentions, Beth? Did you think about the consequences before you ran off after this bloke?'

Rachel must have told him. She could kill her. 'It wasn't like that,' she says.

'Oh really? What was it like?' He jabs a finger a few inches short of her face. 'You know, Beth, I never would have believed you'd be stupid enough to follow some random bloke halfway across the planet. And don't tell me there wasn't time to write a note or make one bloody phone call because that's total bollocks.' His hair is plastered to his head but he's clearly beyond caring. 'And where is he now, Beth, eh? He's only buggered off and left you, hasn't he?'

'That's enough,' she says. 'My life, whatever I choose to do or not do – it's none of your damned business.'

Before she can sidestep him, he grabs her arm. 'The police suspected me of terrible things. The people at work weren't much better. I thought they were going to arrest me at one point – all thanks to you.' He tightens the grip on her arm to the point where it hurts.

'That must have been awful. Look, Kyle, I've said I'm sorry for what happened to you. I phoned the police two days ago. You're totally off the hook and that has to be the end of it. Now will you please let go of me, or–'

'Or what, Beth?' His smirk is pure gloating. 'This conversation ends when *I* decide.'

She brings her knee up hard between his legs. Bending double, he lets out a deep groan, both hands flying to protect his balls from any further assault.

'Or that,' she says walking away.

Opening her eyes, Beth feels sick; she makes it to the bathroom just in time. It's the fourth day in a row; it doesn't take a genius to work out why. She tries not to think about what this will mean but can't help it. Tom had told her that whatever he did in his past had to be consistent with how things are in his future. Giving birth to a baby nearly a decade before its father is due to be born must violate the rules a bit.

After splashing her face with water, Beth stares at her reflection, turns her head sideways and back again trying to decide if she looks any different. She wonders if people will be able to tell; whether some difference will give it away.

When she comes back from the bathroom, Rachel is yanking the sitting room curtains apart. Against the light, her mane of blonde hair makes her head seem twice its size. Though it's bitter cold outside, she opens the window, leaves it that way, like she's trying to get rid of a bad smell. It's obvious she has something to say.

The girl's pale eyes turn on Beth. 'You've been back here

almost five weeks now.' She takes a breath. 'It's time you stopped brooding over this Tom bloke because he's not coming back. You need to sort yourself out – start thinking about the future, not the past.'

'That's all I have been thinking about,' she tells her. It's the truth. On the coffee table her handbag is lying open. Beth snatches it up; at first glance she can't see anything missing. 'You've been going through my stuff, haven't you?' She holds the evidence under Rach's nose.

'Okay, I admit I may have done.' Rach raises both hands. She looks a little shame-faced but not nearly as much as she ought to. 'But only because I'm really worried about you. Linda is too. I don't know where you've been going off to or what you've been doing, but there's a massive roll of tenners in there.' Her cheeks flush. 'You haven't got a job, but you're walking around with loads of cash on you. Please tell me you didn't get it how I think you did.'

The bitter air is making Beth shiver. 'What is it you think I've been doing?' She stares at her friend. 'Go on – I mean you're on a roll here, Rach; say what you've been wanting to say.'

'I can't.' Rachel looks away. 'I thought I knew you, but since you've been back you've changed. And I know you're hiding something.' She clears her throat. 'The thing is, Linda and me, we think it's high time you got a place of your own. You can obviously afford it and, well, we don't want any trouble here.'

'You mean you want your sitting room back.'

'Okay, that too. But it wouldn't be so bad if we didn't think…'

Beth goes right up to her. 'Go on, Rach – it was on the tip of your tongue just then, wasn't it? Spit it out.'

Without blinking, Rachel says, 'We think you're either dealing in drugs or …'

'Or what?'

'Or you're on the game.'

Beth laughs in her face. 'You're seriously telling me the two of you think I must either be a prostitute or a pusher. I mean, don't hold back – why not go the whole bloody hog and accuse me of both? Are you worried I might put a card in the window advertising my services? Roll up, roll up, get a shag and a spliff right here, folks.'

Rachel remains straight-faced. 'It's not bloody funny, Beth.'

'I beg to differ – I think it's absolutely bloody hilarious.'

'Are you saying you're not doing anything illegal?'

Beth rolls her eyes. 'You're asking me to prove a negative.'

'No, Beth, I'm not. I'm asking you to come clean about how you're making all this money. If there's nothing shady about it, why have you been acting so weird lately?'

Beth sits down on the sofa. 'I promise you I'm doing nothing illegal.'

Rach sits down beside her. In a softer voice she says, 'Then what the hell is going on?'

'Promise you'll hear me out.'

'Cross my heart and hope to die.' Smiling at last, Rach's finger draws a cross in the air above her chest.

'Tom was different. No – hear me out. He was really different. Like nobody else I'm ever likely to meet. I don't know how to put this, so I'll just have to come straight out with it. He knew what was going to happen before it happened.'

Rachel narrows her eyes. 'Wait – are you seriously telling me your ex-boyfriend was some sort of clairvoyant?'

Beth nods. 'Before he left, he wrote down a few lists for me.' She steals herself for Rachel's reaction. 'Of winning horses and greyhounds – all that sort of thing. He also told me which company shares to invest in. Don't ask me how but he knew which ones were going to be winners – he just did. He told me if I put money on them, I couldn't lose.'

Rachel opens her mouth to speak. 'Wait.' Beth holds up a hand. 'Let me finish. I've been using his list to place bets and it's worked every time. The only problem is that the bookies hate it if punters start to win too often. They get suspicious and refuse to take any more of their bets. I've had to keep going to different ones where they don't know me, which means I'm walking halfway across London every day.'

Rach's looking very sceptical. 'I know you don't believe me.' Beth opens her handbag, takes out the money and waves it in her face. 'But here's my proof.'

'Are you telling me you made all that money by gambling?'

'This is just what I've made in the last few days. I've been putting most of it into my savings account – for the future. It's been a bit knackering, but I've already won more money than I'm likely to make in a year.'

'Shit a brick.' Rach clamps a hand to her mouth. After a minute she takes it away again. 'Tell me you're kidding.'

'I swear it's all true. Honest. I've been putting on multiple bets so the winnings from one race get carried over to the next and then the next. I usually stop at three or they get too suspicious and won't pay out.'

'Christ, Beth, I just don't know what to think.'

The room's so cold they're both shivering. Beth goes over to shut the window. When she turns around, Rachel is grinning like she used to. 'So, are you going to let me take a look at this magic list of yours? I mean I'm still not sure I believe you but, as my mum always says, the proof of the pudding's in the eating.' She chuckles. 'I think p'raps I should come with you next time you're off to the betting shop. Wherever he gets his tips from, if it's been working that well, I wouldn't mind giving it a go myself.'

Chapter Thirty-Eight

Tom

Out of breath, Tom barges into the kitchen and slams the groceries down on the table. He looks around, ready to have it out with his mother but she's not there. He checks the snug but that's empty too. He picks up the familiar photo of her taken when she'd been pregnant with him. Her smile is so loving; he's often wondered if it was taken by his biological father.

His mum's not in any of the other downstairs rooms. He calls up the stairs, but she doesn't answer. The back door's propped open; as he walks out onto the garden, Poppy comes padding across to greet him.

'Everything's looking a lot perkier for that drop of rain,' she says, deadheading a rose. She's wearing a floppy straw hat – the kind more suited to a donkey. 'You weren't long.' *Snip.* 'Did you manage to get everything?' *Snip.*

'More than I expected.'

'Oh.' The head of another rose falls to the ground. She looks up at him with only mild curiosity.

'Did you know you're the subject of village gossip?' It's hard to gauge her reaction. 'Mrs Kirby from over the road has been telling everybody who'll listen about a man she saw leaving here the other morning. A man she's convinced is a famous Irish actor.'

'Really?' Her chuckle is so obviously forced. 'How ridiculous. I suppose they're all running short of things to talk about besides this ruddy pandemic.'

'Except I believe her.' He stares at his mother.

She lays down her secateurs, then stares straight back at him. 'You honestly think I'm messing about with some famous actor?'

'No, I don't think that.' It's hard to control his anger, to choose his words with care. 'But I do think you know someone who looks a lot like Liam Neeson.'

'This is absurd.' Shaded by the brim of her hat, her pupils have widened. 'It's a job for me to put a name to any actors. Unlike you, I'm not much of a film fan, as you know.'

'Are you honestly trying to tell me you've never heard of Liam Neeson?'

'Well, of course I've *heard* of the man, but I'm not sure I would recognise him if I passed him in the street.'

'You're lying.' He forces his voice down to a normal level. 'Film stars aside, I think you know precisely who I'm talking about. Come to think about it, I caught sight of him when he was leaving the other morning. I saw him get into a Range Rover. That was him, wasn't it? When I asked you who he was, you fobbed me off, told me he was some builder who'd come to look at the porch.'

She swipes up the secateurs and snips off another head. 'That man *was* a builder–'

'Oh, come off it, Mum. You know exactly who I mean. Tall, grey-haired and bloody sinister looking. Calls himself Ford. Besides being the double of Neeson, his other distinguishing feature is, that if you look very, very carefully, you can see his lips don't quite move at the right speed when he's talking.'

'Tom, I really don't know–'

'Stop treating me like an idiot. You've been lying to me all my life; it's time you told me the truth.'

'What on earth makes you think I haven't been?'

'I learnt something about myself recently and now a lot more things have started to make sense.' He paces in front of her. 'I must have been eight or nine at the time. D'you remember my teacher, Mrs Lavery, told you I was gifted?' He snorts. 'Her way of explaining why I was such an oddity. Not just nerdy, but wired differently from the other kids.'

'Then *you* must remember I refused to entertain all that *gifted* nonsense. I made sure you stayed where you were in an ordinary class in an ordinary school; that you were treated just like everyone else.' He can see she's close to tears. 'You had friends, Tom. And the main thing – the most important thing was – you blended in.'

'*Blended in?*' He looks up into the cloudless sky then rubs at his chin, failing to calm himself. 'You know, Mum, whether they admit it or not, most parents want their kids to excel in some way – they want them to rise above what's ordinary. But whenever I won anything, you were never very pleased about it, were you?'

'I didn't want all that nonsense to go to your head.'

'I remember you taking the piss until I cleared all my trophies off the shelf and hid them in the wardrobe.'

'I'm sure I did no such thing.'

'You called it my *ego altar*. You were never pleased that I was good at so many things.' Looking her straight in the eye, he says, 'Tell me, Mum – why didn't you want me to stand out?' Her lips remain closed. 'It's because I'm different, isn't it? I can do things I shouldn't be able to do. Don't look at me like that, I know you understand exactly what I'm talking about.'

Her face gives nothing away. 'D'you want me to spell it out?' He tries the good-cop approach. 'I'm giving you a chance to come clean, Mum. I'm sure you'll feel better if you finally get it off your chest. Just tell me the truth.'

She shakes her head for some time before she says, 'Your father. What can I say?' Each word is an effort. 'He wasn't. He isn't quite like everyone else.' She shuts her eyes, won't even look at him. 'He is an amazing man but, sadly, he's not tethered to this time in the same way that we are.'

'Wait.' Having asked for the unvarnished truth, he's not prepared for the worst. 'Tell me this isn't my Luke Skywalker moment? That fucking reptile Ford isn't my father, is he?'

She laughs – a proper laugh that has her almost bending double. 'God forbid; not him. I do have some taste, you know.'

When Poppy starts to bark, he remembers the fuss the dog made the morning Ford was in the house. Animals can sense these things. That must have been why she'd been shut out in the garden.

The dog's barking now. He squints into the sun, hoping Ford hasn't materialised in the middle of their back garden. To his relief, Poppy's barking at next-door's cat. Sitting on the top of the fence, the cat's twitching tail is like an angler's bait.

Above the racket he says, 'So I have a father.'

'Well it wasn't divine conception.' Having said it, she actually blushes. 'You know, I think I'd feel more comfortable if we have this conversation sitting down.'

Conceding this at least, Tom follows her over to the shade of the apple tree. When they sit down, Poppy decides to ignore the cat and comes over to nudge him, hoping to be stroked. He's far too wired to oblige. 'You've always refused to talk about my father,' Tom says.

'I thought it would only confuse you.'

'I assumed I must be the product of a one-night stand. I mean I've never laid eyes on the man. Wasn't he even a little bit interested in getting to know his own son?'

'But you did see him – quite a bit in fact; when you were younger at least.'

Tom finds he already knows what she's going to say. 'It's Uncle Matt, isn't it? He's actually my father.'

A flicker of a smile. 'We always wondered if you'd guessed.' She squeezes his arm. 'We tried so hard to make it work. Your father came to see us as often as he could – at least to begin with. But it only got harder every time he had to leave again. In the end, it was too much – too painful for us both.'

'So why did he have to keep buggering off?' Uncle Matt's visits are amongst his favourite childhood memories. 'Don't tell me he had another family somewhere.'

'Nothing like that. It became too risky – for you especially.' The dog rests her head on her knee the way she does when someone's upset. Almost in a whisper, his mum says, 'Your father is a Guardian.'

'You're telling me he's one of them – one of those evil bastards who forced me onto the train. Is that why Ford came to see you the other day?'

'Oh, Tom, it's all so complicated.' A heavy sigh. 'I really have no idea how to begin to explain.'

'Why don't you start with why Ford was here in our house.'

'He came because he wanted to discuss *the situation* – as he put it. They were horrified when you jumped into another time. Until then, they'd left us alone. The two of us were no threat; they didn't think you'd inherit any of your father's abilities. The Guardians hate to be taken by surprise. I won't say that they panicked exactly – they never do. It seems they held the train at Paddington so you could travel back here. When Beth came through with you, that represented yet another failure on their part. Don't ask me how they knew you were both staying here, but Ford was sent to take stock of the situation. They wanted my help to ensure Beth got back to her own time.'

Tom stands up. 'You were the one informing on us – telling them about our every move.'

'You think I would spy on my own son? I'd never do a thing like that, for heaven's sake.' He's pleased to hear it. She gives him a strained smile then pats the bench beside her. 'Please sit down.'

He does as he's told though he chooses to be a little further away from her.

She says, 'It was what they were hoping, but I refused to be party to it. I knew they'd be watching you both like hawks. It was obvious to me you were planning something, but I hoped you wouldn't be tempted to go back with Beth. I prayed you wouldn't be daft enough to go up against them and their rules because you can't beat them, Tom. You might get lucky and win a few rounds, but they have such power; in the end, nothing and no one gets past them.'

He stares at the ground, at a line of ants transporting prizes twice their size all the way back to their hidden nest. 'How come you and Uncle... my father got together in the first place?'

'Those were very different times.'

He frowns. 'I don't think so – aside from technology, not that much has changed since the early nineties.'

She leans forward to take his hand. 'That's the thing,' she says. 'You weren't conceived in the nineties. My passport might say I was born in 1959 but that's a complete fabrication. I was born in 1923.' She grins. 'Technically speaking, I'll be a hundred in three years. Which, I suppose, helps explain my arthritis.'

He's rendered speechless. Afraid to interrupt, he waits for her to carry on. A fond smile on her face, she says. 'I met your father in January 1944. Wartime obviously. During what they now call the Baby Blitz – although it didn't feel so insignificant for those of us on the ground, I can tell you. My digs in Pimlico got bombed out. Matt – well, he was literally my saviour. We started courting. Later on, when I fell pregnant, he told me the truth about himself; though to begin with I thought he was just making it up. He was frantic with worry. Single mothers in those days certainly didn't have an easy time of it. Matthew managed to persuade me he wasn't entirely off his rocker. With his help, I escaped, and arrived here in 1992

– a few months before you were born. I chose this village for all the reasons you dislike it – it's out of the way and life here wasn't so very different to the world I'd left behind. Except it was far safer, of course.'

'You're telling me I was actually conceived in 1944. Bloody hell – that makes me about 76, give or take. I don't know how to begin processing this.' Tom rakes his hair back from his eyes. 'What a complete and utter head-fuck!'

'Language, Tom,' she says, once again his mother.

Chapter Thirty-Nine

Beth

Not confined to the mornings, her nausea often lasts most of the day. She finds it hard to keep anything but water down. It's almost impossible to go anywhere or do anything except close her eyes and wait for it to pass.

The doctor she'd visited hadn't been very helpful. Ancient looking, with a seen-it-all attitude, he dismissed her symptoms with a wave of his hand. 'For most expectant mothers morning sickness can be regarded as a good sign. It tends to indicate the pregnancy is well-established.' He sounded like he was reciting from one of the pamphlets the nurse had given her. That was it. Turning his back, he told her, 'You can get dressed now, Miss Sawyer.'

Pleased to have that part of the consultation over, Beth was putting on her coat when he added, 'Of course, for someone in your situation, by which I mean being of a relatively young age, single and with only a temporary address, there is the option of a termination.'

Though she tried to interrupt him, he talked over her. 'The

procedure is permitted before twenty-eight weeks if the pregnancy is injurious to the patience's physical or *mental* health.' The stress on mental was impossible to miss. Taking off his glasses he'd given her a long look to make it clear he'd already decided she met the criteria.

'But I actually want to have this baby,' she told him.

'I see.' She felt herself being judged and found wanting as a potential mother. 'These are early days, Miss Sawyer,' he said. 'We still have time in hand, should you change your mind.' He'd worn disposable gloves to give her the briefest of examinations and yet afterwards had washed his hands like she might be carrying something he was frightened of catching.

It doesn't help that she's sleeping on the sofa. She's too nauseous to go flat hunting. Since they found out about her condition, Rachel and Linda fuss over her when they get back from work. They're fond of telling her she needs to keep up her strength or that she's eating for two. She'd be happy to eat for one and keep it down.

At least she has a healthy balance in the bank. The bulk of her winnings are still sitting in her savings account. Tom had listed the companies she should buy shares in, but she doesn't know how to go about such things. If she was feeling better, she'd make an appointment to see someone at the bank for advice.

With her not up to the long treks to unfamiliar parts of London, Rachel had been putting on some accumulator bets for her, promising to pay the winnings into her account. She'd had misgivings about handing over Tom's list but with a dwindling number left to bet on, there'd been no alternative. Her latest bank statements had revealed the sums deposited were a lot smaller than she'd anticipated. Rachel had explained about the problems she'd had placing the bets. Beth didn't entirely believe her. The new clothes the girl's been buying suggests she'd made a lot money for herself as well.

Beth wakes to find she's slept much later than usual. The others have already gone to work. Nibbling on a digestive, she sips at a weak tea. Finding herself still hungry, she takes a chance and boils two eggs and then toasts a couple of slices of bread. For once, it all stays down.

The weak April sunshine is illuminating the kitchen walls like an invitation. By mid-morning she feels confident enough to venture outside with the vague idea of finding somewhere to sit and read the paperback she stuffs into her handbag.

Her denim jacket is difficult to do up over her expanded stomach. Not that it matters; the air is so warm she soon undoes it again. It's good to be striding along, great to feel her leg muscles working again.

Venturing on past Shepherd's Bush Green, she finds herself facing the noise and commotion of the roundabout. Not wanting to turn back yet, she carries on walking in the general direction of Holland Park. At each crossing, the green man blinks at her.

Everywhere trees are blossoming in front gardens and squares; their fallen petals decorating the pavements like confetti. Though the air is laced with traffic fumes, from time to time she catches the sweet scent of all those blossoms. Flowerpots and window-boxes are sprouting garish tulips and gently nodding daffodils.

From Holland Park she heads towards Notting Hill passing all the grand terraced houses now sub-divided into more modest flats, their front paths cluttered by dustbins. Approaching Queensway, she begins to make out the green haze of trees up ahead. Hyde Park – she hasn't been back since it happened; isn't too sure she can face it now and yet her feet keep carrying her in that direction.

Along the Bayswater Road, she checks each phone box, hoping to identify the exact one she used to call Rach that day, as if knowing this would make a scrap of difference. She's since concluded that even if Tom had gone with her to make that call, the two of them could never have outrun the Guardians.

Feeling hungry again, she knows she really ought to turn back and yet instead she skirts the park and heads into the warren of streets leading to Paddington Station. At each set of lights, she looks for the green man like a sign of whether she ought to cross or turn back; each and every time the light turns green at her approach.

She recognises Praed Street and, further along on the opposite side, the bus stop she would normally get off at. She has her handbag with her and in her purse there's more than enough money to buy a ticket to Cheltenham. If she turns up on her Aunty Joan's doorstep, will she still refuse to speak to her?

The station is much quieter than at rush hour. Checking the arrivals board, she sees there's a train to Cheltenham departing in eight minutes. The ticket office is empty. Within a couple of minutes, she's in possession of an open return ticket to Cheltenham Spa.

She hadn't left a note at the flat. How will Rachel and Linda react when they find she's not there? They'll probably be delighted. In any case, she can call them from her aunty's house or, if need be, from the phone box around the corner.

Approaching the waiting train, Beth is shaken to see the words *Gustav Holst* on the engine. She clutches her stomach though she's not in any pain. 'Are you alright, madam?' a man in railway uniform asks. She catches his glance down at her hand as if he's looking for a ring.

'I'm fine,' she tells him. 'Blooming, in fact.'

Beth has misgivings and yet she walks along the platform heading towards the cheaper carriages. The train is half empty. Climbing on board, she glances around the hoping she won't recognise any of the passengers. It's okay – they're all strangers; there's no one reassembling Ford or any of his loathsome spies. She chooses a seat next to the window. When she checks again, no one is taking any interest in her.

The whistle is shrill and long. A minute later the train glides away so smoothly she's surprised to see they're moving. Finding it impossible to sit still, Beth dares someone to block her path as she stands up and heads for the vestibule. No one does. Why on earth would they?

The carriage door opens as she approaches. As London begins to retreat, she searches for the tiny pentangle etched into the paintwork – a sign left for others. To some it's an emblem connected to magic or sorcery. In medieval times it symbolised the five virtues. How does she know that? She must have read it somewhere. In any case, the little mark is still there and so she traces the unbroken line with her finger then draws the same sign in the air. Not that it will do her any good.

In the park, that awful woman told her Tom was extraordinary in some way and that was why he'd been able to go through the time tunnel. She hadn't explained how or why he was so exceptional though it sounded like it was something he'd been born with.

The woman had assured her there was nothing special about her. No point in her entertaining any hope that alone she'd be able to travel forward to Tom's time. So why is she even standing here?

She should go back to the carriage. Better to lose herself in her book than all these idle hopes.

Except she knows she won't be able to do that. She's used to putting on bets. What were the odds all the pedestrian lights would turn green in her favour? What were the odds a train would be about to leave for Cheltenham? What were the odds it was the Gustav Holst when it could easily have been a different train waiting at the platform?

Put together, it's quite an accumulator. It might be unlikely she'll win but something inside had guided her here today. There's no way she's going to give up now.

Chapter Forty

Tom

He's been exercising with a vengeance hoping it will help to get him through the draining despondence he feels. Today's hike takes him up the vertiginous side of an escarpment. High wispy clouds help to shield him from the full heat of the sun. Reaching the summit, he looks out over a vast field of ripening sea-green barley, fascinated by the way it ripples and sways with the breeze.

A couple of fields on, he sits down in the scant shade of a windblown hawthorn and takes a drink from his water flask. Wiping his mouth with the back of his hand, he notices that there's not a person or building in sight. Around him he hears only the sawing song of crickets and a number of chattering long-tailed tits fliting between different bushes. On the edge of the field the protruding ears of a hare give it away. He follows its run until it disappears into the hedgerow. As he'd hoped, the beauty of it all eases his mind a little. There's a moment of something close to enchantment when a red-admiral butterfly lands on his shirt sleeve, mistaking him for a flower. The next second it's gone again.

Tom doesn't linger long. Following the field margin, the baked hard path takes him past the site of a former World War Two aerodrome. It's hard to get his head around the fact that his mother was a young woman in wartime. Though he'd questioned her closely, she couldn't explain how Uncle Matt – he's not ready to call him his father – was able to come and go. 'He didn't tell me. He said I should never ask.' It made her sound like some meek little woman. Her act didn't fool him for a second; there was definitely more to find out.

The path runs parallel to a block wall about half a metre high – all that remains of one of the old hangars. With so much half-buried rubble, the grass is sparse – barely enough to sustain the herd of shorthorn cattle grazing it. Stretches of the old concrete runways are visible here and there. His boots trample over patches of wild camomile releasing their soporific perfume. Most of the cows are resting in the shadow cast by a half-ruined building that was once part of a barrack block.

Looking around, he can picture how the airfield looked back then. He knows it was used mostly by the RAF and very briefly by the USAAF; at its peak around 650 men and women were stationed right here.

When he closes his eyes, the images in his mind's eye become so vivid Tom wonders if he's about to step back into that time. Ant-like figures dressed in blue are streaming in and out of various camouflage green buildings. High in the control tower, the silhouettes of two people peer through binoculars. Next to one of the two runways, half a dozen Spitfires are preparing for take-off. The engine of the lead plane coughs into noisy life, propellors turn slowly then become a blur. He can smell the spilt petrol and feel the stiff breeze the aircraft is about to take off into. At the pilot's signal, the two mechanics remove the chocks and she taxis into position.

Before she takes off, Tom opens his eyes expecting to see the Spitfire rise up into the clear summer sky. For a moment she's right there; the next she dissolves into air. He's surprised to see the same group of nutbrown cows leisurely chewing the cud. Aside from the cattle, the airfield is empty, the tin-roofed ruin of the barracks home only to a dusty tractor and a pile of silage bales.

And yet the other time was so close, so tangible. On his travels he'd once or twice experienced the same sensation. He remembers being drawn to Lai Khe – the site of old US base camps in Vietnam; visiting the Victoria Memorial in Kolkata, the Latin Bridge in Sarajevo and being able to picture the past so clearly his whole scalp had prickled with it. The Guardians had admitted he had special abilities. Is it possible he can create his own time portal?

These thoughts are interrupted by a vibration in his back pocket. The caller ID says *Home*. It's unusual for his mum to ring him when she knows he's out walking. 'Hi, Mum,' he says. 'What's up?'

'Tom.' Her voice sounds strained, shaken even. 'I think you'd better get back here as soon as you can.'

'Why – what's happened? Are you alright?' Mind racing, he calculates it's going to take him at least an hour; perhaps ten minutes less if he really hurries. 'I'll be as quick as I can but if you're feeling ill, if it's an emergency, you need to phone an ambulance right now.'

'There's no need. I'm perfectly fit and healthy.' She doesn't sound it.

'Is it Poppy then?'

'No – she's okay. We both are.' The next thing she says turns into a crackle.

'Sorry, Mum, the reception's crap here; can you say that again?' He walks forward hoping to get more than one and a half bars.

'I said, there's no need to panic; it's not a matter of life and death. Although in a way… hard to explain … to see for yourself.'

'Mum you're not making any sense. Why – '

'Just come home as quickly as you can.'

'Okay, I'm on my way,' he says, sounding like a detective called to a murder scene.

Out of breath and covered in scratches, he's not sure what he was expecting when he rushes through the house calling her name. His mum is sitting in her usual place at the kitchen table. Once his eyes have adjusted, he notices someone is sitting opposite her cradling a cup of tea. When the person looks up, he has to grab the doorframe for support.

'Beth.'

'Hi, Tom.' She says it casually though the look in her eyes is uncertain. He runs a hand over his eyes to check he's awake. She looks exactly the same – discernibly no older than the last time he saw her. Her hair is possibly a little shorter – her skin paler than it was. A denim jacket is slung over the back of her chair. She's wearing a black and gold Duran Duran T-shirt. Can he be imagining such details?

When she stands up, he can see she's lost weight but put on a bit around her waist. Fearful she might dematerialise at any second, he rushes over to hug her; doesn't dare let go again. She's warm and soft to the touch. Her hair smells exactly the way he remembers.

'Tom, I can't breathe,' she says. He pulls back to study her face, checks the tiny constellation of freckles is still there across her nose. They're a bit faded but exactly where they should be. Holding her hands at arm's length, he shakes his head. 'How on earth…?'

Her smile reaches his heart. When her eyes fall, his gaze follows. The penny drops when she lets go and her hands go to the bulge of her stomach like she's defending it. 'The Guardians were quite right,' she says, 'I would never have been able to get here if I'd been by myself.'

Her grin is achingly familiar. 'They can't have been watching me; hadn't bargained on me having help. But I did.' At his stupefied reaction, she giggles. 'It seems he, or she, is going to be just as exceptional as their father.'

Later, sitting out in the garden after supper, his mum says, 'I'm so glad you're here, Beth but the two of you will need to be careful. If you stay here for too long, they might track you down.'

'We'll leave when we're ready,' Tom tells her. 'I can't speak for Beth, but I'm damned if I'm going into hiding.'

'Me neither,' Beth says. 'They can go fuck themselves.'

'Brave words.' His mum's about to give her opinion but thinks better of it. Instead she says, 'I think I'll go inside, it's getting a bit chilly out here.'

The night air is hanging on to some of the day's warmth. He fetches Beth a throw and they sit in the gathering darkness watching for each new star to appear. He wants to name each one out loud but thinks better of it.

'You haven't asked about the money,' she says. 'All the bets I put on.'

'I hadn't thought of it 'til now.' He squeezes her hand. 'I'm just glad that by some miracle you're sitting here with me.'

'Probably just as well,' she says. 'It's possible there's a bit of money in my savings account, though I'm not sure how I can go about claiming it when I should be an old woman by now.'

He sees her point. Above them he can pick out the Summer Triangle – the giant shape formed by Deneb, Vega and Altair the three brightest stars from the constellations of Cygnus, Lyra and Aquila. Vega is the brightest of all. A good name for a boy or a girl.

Beth gives a heavy sigh. 'I've had really awful morning sickness and Rachel took advantage of it. Of course, I was bloody daft enough to hand over your lists. You know, I bet she's made a fortune since.'

'If she's made that much money, we'll probably be able to track her down – find out where she lives.'

'What good would that do?'

'Think about it. She has no idea what happened to you

once you left. If you were to turn up now on her doorstep completely unchanged after nearly forty years, it's quite likely she'll take you for a vengeful ghost come back to haunt her.'

Beth says, 'You know, I wouldn't be averse to a bit of haunting.' Her face becomes sober. 'Thou canst not say I did it; never shakes thy gory locks at me.'

'Was that meant to be a Scottish accent?'

She chuckles. 'Yeah – you're right, it was a bit crap, but it's not like I'm ever likely to be cast as Macbeth.'

'Ah, but that's where you're wrong. In the twenty-first century women have successfully been cast as Macbeth and Hamlet – you name it.'

'Noo? Yer aff yer flamin' heid.'

He covers his ears. 'Enough, please. It's late; why don't we go to bed?'

She leans forward; her hand sweeps the hair away from his eyes. 'That's the best suggestion you've made all evening.'

The story continues…

'Play For Time' - the sequel to 'Running Behind Time' – was published in 2022.

About the Author

Before becoming a writer, Jan Turk Petrie taught English in inner city London schools. She now lives in the Cotswolds area of southern England. Jan has an M.A. in Creative Writing (University of Gloucestershire) and, as well as her seven published novels, she has written numerous, prize-winning short stories

As a writer, Jan is always keen to challenge herself. Her first published novels – the three volumes that make up **The Eldísvík Trilogy** – are Nordic noir thrillers set fifty years in the future in a Scandinavian city where the rule of law comes under threat from criminal cartels controlling the forbidden zones surrounding it.

By contrast, her fourth novel – **'Too Many Heroes'** – is a period romantic thriller set in the early 1950s. A story of an illicit love affair that angers the mobsters controlling London's East End at that time.

Jan's fifth novel: **'Towards the Vanishing Point'** is also set primarily in the 1950s and depicts an enduring friendship between two women that is put to the test when one of them falls under the spell of a sinister charmer.

'**The Truth in a Lie**' is her first novel with a contemporary setting. It is the story of a successful writer who has a complex and often difficult relationship with her mother and her own daughter as well as with the men in her life.

'**Running Behind Time**' is Jan's first time-slip novel. Written during the unprecedented events of 2020 with all the new social norms arising from the pandemic, she was inspired to imagine the contrast with life back in the early 1980s.

'**Still Life with a Vengeance**' – a contemporary literary novel. When Eve's rock star husband is accused of rape, he endures trial by media. He claims to be innocent, but should she believe him?

Play for Time – is the highly anticipated sequel to **Running Behind Time.** Beginning in August 2020, the novel continues the story of Tom and Beth.

Jan is a big fan of Margaret Atwood, Kate Atkinson, Philip Roth, Kurt Vonnegut and Jennifer Egan – authors who are always prepared to take risks in their writing.

Dear reader.

I really hope you've enjoyed 'Running Behind Time.' Thank you so much for buying or borrowing a copy. If you would like to help more readers discover the book, please consider leaving a review on Amazon, Goodreads, Bookbub, or anywhere else readers are likely to visit. It doesn't need to be a long review – a sentence or two would be fine. Many thanks in advance to anyone who takes the time to do so.

If you would like to find out more about this book, or are interested in discovering more about my other published novels, please visit my website: https://janturkpetrie.com

If you would like to follow me on Twitter, my handle is: @ TurkPetrie

Twitter profile: https://twitter.com/TurkPetrie

My Facebook author page: https://www.facebook.com/jan-turkpetrie

Contact Pintail Press via the website: https://pintailpress.com

Acknowledgements

This, my seventh novel, was certainly not without its challenges. I would like to begin by thanking John Petrie, my lovely husband, for reading and commenting on the various drafts of 'Running Behind Time.' His feedback was, as always, absolutely invaluable and his unfailing support and encouragement during this difficult year helped me to finish the book. I have to say I found writing it a pleasurable escape into a world I could control.

I would also like to thank my wonderful daughters Laila and Natalie for their unwavering love and support. Thanks also go to my wider family and in particular my mum, Pearl Turk, for her constant encouragement and those highly prized 'Pearls of Wisdom'.

As always, the feedback from my fellow *Catchword* writers in Cirencester proved invaluable to this project. Comments from members of the highly talented *Wild Women Writers* and the feedback from Stroud's *Little George Writers Group* was also extremely helpful.

Special thank you to Debbie Young and everyone in the Alliance of Independent Authors (Alli) group in Cheltenham for their impressive knowledge of indie publishing and their sound collective advice.

Lastly, I'm once again grateful to my editor and proofreader, Johnny Hudspith, and to my cover designer, Jane Dixon Smith, for their consistently excellent work.

Printed in Great Britain
by Amazon

13005133R00192